ALSO IN THE EMMY LAKE CHRONICLES

Dear Miss Lake

– *A Novel* –

AJ PEARCE

SCRIBNER

New York   Amsterdam/Antwerp   London
Toronto   Sydney/Melbourne   New Delhi

An Imprint of Simon & Schuster, LLC
1230 Avenue of the Americas
New York, NY 10020

In memory of my grandparents

We have heard a good deal about the end of the march being the most tiring, the last days of the battle most trying, and so on, but it is true. It helps when you realise that. And people who lose homes, health—or their nearest ones—at this stage of the war have our deepest sympathy of all. The sacrifice is no less worthwhile, but I feel that if possible, it may be just a little harder to bear. My warmest good wishes to you all.

—The Editor, *Woman's Own* magazine, 20 April 1945

Don't think, because I speak lightly, "She doesn't know what nervous fears are: She doesn't know the agony they can be, or she wouldn't joke about them." She does, I assure you, and do you know why she jokes about them? Because sometimes she's frightened, too.

—Greta Lamb, *Woman's Own* magazine, 19 May 1944

Hampshire, England

July 1944

CHAPTER 1

Bunty Has a Surprise

Guy Collins was a man of some talents, but until now he had kept motorcycle mechanics under his hat. As the sun shone down on a beautiful July morning, I walked up to the entrance of Dower Cottage to see both Guy and his brother flat on their backs marvelling at the workings of what, by the sound of it, was a terrifically fascinating valve.

"I say, well done," said Charles from underneath the Sunbeam Model 8. "That's definitely looking better."

Major Charles Mayhew, who also happened to be my husband, was on forty-eight hours' leave from his base just under an hour away. With Italy beaten and put firmly in its place, four months ago and to my absolute joy, he had been sent back to Britain, where he had been promoted and sent to work on something operational and, as ever, enormously secret. The fact that he was currently lying on the ground and covered in oil did not for a moment detract from the thrill of having him home. After over two and a half years of marriage, we were finally in the same country, and most important of all, he was safe.

"Hello, darling," I said, bending to retrieve a piece of rag and a spanner. "Has the old deathtrap been playing you up again?"

Charles looked up, smiled broadly, and leapt to his feet, greeting me with an enthusiastic kiss. "She's a trouper," he said, patting the cracked leather seat as if the motorcycle was a trusty old horse that had carried its owner though the Somme. "Guy has just worked a small miracle. I say, you look smashing." He kissed me again.

Guy, who was also now on his feet, wiped his forehead with the back of his hand, leaving a large black smudge. He had rolled his sleeves up and was up to his forearms in grease. "It should get you back to the base," he said, as he surveyed his handiwork. "Better test it out first though."

Before Charles could reply, I moved in.

"It's nearly lunch," I said, firmly. "I'm under strict instruction to bring you both up to the high field to meet the others. The children are mad keen to see you, and Bunty has laid on the most terrific spread. I'm to take you there straight away." I paused and looked at them. "You might want to clean up a bit first."

At the promise of food there was no argument from the men as they followed me into Mrs. Tavistock's cottage. Bunty's granny was always a generous hostess, and never more so than now. For the last fortnight, London had been under constant attack from Hitler's new flying bombs as he tried yet again to break British morale. Throughout the city, sirens rang out day and night with air-raid alerts. Under today's cloudless sky in the Hampshire countryside, it was quite possible to pretend that it wasn't having an effect, but that was far from the truth. There had been two direct hits where Bunty and I lived in London, and while our home in Braybon Street had been extraordinarily lucky, a desperate number of our neighbours had not.

The morning after the second bomb, our friends from the fire station, Roy and Fred, had come round, the colour drained from their faces.

"There's at least fifteen dead," said Roy, quietly, "and well over a hundred more injured."

"They won't put that in the papers," said Fred. "These new rockets are vicious blighters. I don't want to scare you, but if you can get the kids out of the city, we both think that would be a very good idea."

The children's mother, Thelma, had been one of our dearest friends. Almost exactly a year ago, she had been killed by the Luftwaffe and at her request we had become George, Margaret, and Stan's temporary guardians until their dad came home from the front. With the end of the war now in sight, nothing was more important than keeping the children safe. Roy and Fred were usually two of the biggest jokers we knew, but when they were serious, you listened.

"Don't wait for the end of term," said Roy. "Put them on the first bloody train you can find."

We didn't have to be told twice. Bombing raids might have been part of wartime life, but seeing the devastation they caused never became any easier. Now, with the arrival of the doodlebugs, and as it was so close to the summer holidays, a decision was swiftly made. A phone call later, and Bunty and the children were on their way to her granny's, two hours from London and with masses of room for everyone.

I had stayed on in Pimlico, working with Guy and the rest of the team at *Woman's Friend* magazine where we were doing everything we could to support our readers after nearly five long years of war.

It was a job that very much needed to be done. Everyone was exhausted. For Britain's women it wasn't just from the physical demands of war work, but the keeping things going—looking after the children, dealing with shortages of everything, or trying to turn carrots and potatoes into a new, interesting meal for the thousandth time. And when you added grief and loss and loneliness on top, not to mention the current bombardment from the V-1s, that was a very big weight to bear.

Today, I was grateful to be able to escape to the countryside and picnic with my friends. Guy and I had arrived the previous evening, relieved to deliver our precious cargo of Stan's two guinea pigs. Now, with the brothers having used a ration-defying amount of carbolic soap to combat the motorcycle oil, we headed off to the top field. It was only a ten-minute walk, and as we strolled along the narrow lane I breathed in deeply, savouring the fresh air. Tall spikes of purple and pink foxgloves lined our route as they poked up between the white umbrellas of wild carrot, while clouds of fluffy meadowsweet swayed in the ditches. There wasn't a florist in all of London that could come close.

"How is Harold coping without Bunty?" asked Charles as we walked, arm in arm. "Is he pining away now that she's moved down here?"

I laughed. Harold and Bunty had been seeing each other for some time and it was screamingly obvious to everyone that they were perfect for each other. Both, however, had been through difficult times during the war, and perhaps this was holding them back. Bunty always played things down and Harold seemed stricken with fear at the very thought of asking her to make things more official.

Having recently forced Charles to corner him and ask very severely what his intentions were, it transpired that Harold was absolutely convinced that he wasn't good enough for Bunty. Consequently, he couldn't bear the thought of what he was sure would be the crushing blow of rejection should he suggest anything permanent between the two. For his part, Charles had been equally hopeless and not thought to tell him to buck up and get on with it.

"You'll see for yourself in a minute," I said. "Although if you'd jolly well pushed him in the right direction, Harold would probably have proposed by now. Guy, couldn't *you* have a word?"

Guy stuck his hands in his pockets and shrugged. "You can't go around bullying people into this sort of thing," he said, sounding vague and looking over a hedge.

"It's not bullying," I replied. "It's Bunty. Honestly, you're both as bad as each other."

Charles and Guy exchanged synchronised raised eyebrows. I took my arm out of Charles' and marched on, telling them that I would obviously have to speak to Harold myself.

"That's torn it," said Charles.

"Poor chap," said Guy.

I picked up speed and put some distance between us. Then, as I climbed over the stile into the top field, I looked back over my shoulder. Nothing galvanised people more than a competition and I had always been a very good sprinter at school.

"LAST ONE THERE HAS TO TELL HAROLD," I shouted. Then I jumped into the field and began to run for it as fast as I could.

"That's cheating," yelled Charles. "Come on, Guy."

I didn't stop.

Within seconds Charles was at my heels, his older brother swearing in protest while bringing up the rear with admirable speed for a man of his years.

A few minutes later, the three of us collapsed in a heap on the ground, as an entirely unsurprised Bunty and Harold looked on.

"We had a race," I gasped, unnecessarily.

Charles lay back on the grass, breathing heavily. "Guy lost."

"I'm fifty-one," panted Guy. "I don't even run for the bus."

"Is there a prize?" asked Harold.

"NO," said Guy and Charles at the same time.

"More a forfeit at some point," I smiled. "Where are the children?"

"In the river, hunting for sticklebacks," said Bunty. "They were famished so I let them eat. They'll be thrilled now you're here, Charles."

I craned my neck and could see the three of them standing in the shallows, studiously looking for fish.

Bunty opened the lid of a large wicker hamper. "Shall we tuck in? The bread smells delicious."

No one needed more encouragement than that. Mrs. Tavistock's cook was an excellent baker and as the shop-bought national loaf was always slightly stale, this was a treat indeed. Bunty carved off big chunks and loaded them onto plates with slices of cheddar from the farm, tomatoes still on the vine, and fat blobs of sticky, home-made chutney. Then, and just as you thought life couldn't get any better, Harold went over to

the river and returned with bottles of cider that had been keeping cool
in a bucket, together with three over-excited children.

"MAJOR CHARLES," cried Margaret, as Charles stood up to
greet them. "Look what we've caught." She swung a jam jar at him.

"You didn't happen to come on the motorcycle, did you, sir?" asked
George, shaking hands in his role as senior member of the team.

"Have you seen the guinea pigs?" asked Stanley, making his pri-
orities clear. "They came on the train."

"I'm waiting for you to show me after lunch," said Charles. "How's
the country life suiting you all?"

The children plonked themselves on the ground as Bunty produced a large punnet of strawberries.

"It's very nice so far, thank you," said Stan, politely. "Even though
I'm not allowed to drive the tractor."

"Stan, you have to be twelve," said Margaret.

Her brother looked justifiably downcast. "That's ages away," he
sighed.

Harold, who was sitting next to him, gave the little boy a surrep-
titious nudge with his foot. "You just need to grow a bit taller," he
whispered. "Then we'll see."

Stan's face lit up as Bunty rolled her eyes.

"Harold," I said. "Prison is no joke and you'll be no good to anyone if you're locked up."

Harold laughed. "I'd better have another bottle of cider while I
still can then," he said.

"How about you all help me test drive the bike?" suggested
Charles. "Guy's just fixed it as it's been on the wonk."

At this the children were spoilt for choice in terms of who was the
most impressive grown-up, and as I listened to the chatter, sitting in
the sun, full of lunch, and surrounded by the people I loved, it was
almost possible to imagine everything was normal and at peace. I
would have given all the money in the world to stay suspended just
like this.

"Penny for them?" asked Charles.

"I was just thinking how wonderful it would be to stay exactly like this, forever," I answered. "I'm rather jealous of the children getting to live here for the summer. I don't really want to go back to London tomorrow. Sorry, Guy, I know that's a terrible attitude."

Our Editor in Chief, who was reading a slightly crumpled newspaper, stretched his arms and sighed. "I feel much the same," he said. As he spoke, two RAF transport planes came into sight, droning their way across the sky. "Never mind," he added, more heartily. "Job to do. Very lucky to get to visit."

"It would be nice though, wouldn't it?" said Bunty, keenly. "I do feel rather *I'm all right Jack* that work gave me a leave of absence."

"You're hardly a shirker," I replied. "And you are helping your granny with the estate as well as being in charge of this lot." I pulled a face at the children, who laughed.

"I suppose so," said Bunts. "But would you, though?" she added, chewing on a piece of grass. "Stay, if you could?"

"Of course," I said, without hesitation. "Lolling about with everyone for the summer. I'd move in tomorrow."

"Steady up, Miss Lake," said Guy, leaning back and turning his face to the sun. "You've a problem page to run."

Bunty was not put off.

"But Emmy could do that anywhere," she said.

"I can't really," I replied. "Can you imagine? '*Sorry everyone, could you forward my post as I've decided to stay in the country? PS: please send my sunshades as the sun's hurting my eyes.*' I'd hardly get top marks for that sort of managerial approach."

Now Bunty sat up. "What if you didn't have to?" she asked. "What if everyone else could come too?"

Bunty had stopped playing with the piece of grass. Charles shifted to look at her. Guy lowered his head and stared at her over the top of his glasses.

"Harold?" she said, giving him a meaningful look.

"Well, now," said Harold. "Speaking as *Woman's Friend*'s Business Director, we've had what could be a Very Interesting Idea."

For a moment, no one said anything. A bee hummed by, setting its sights on an open chutney pot. Bunty reached for the lid, disappointing the bee by screwing it onto the jar.

"We think you could *all* move in," she said. "The whole magazine. All the staff and everything you need from the office. The filing cabinets, the typewriters, everything through to pens and pencils. Bring everything here."

"We've been working it out," said Harold, now sitting up very straight. "Bunty and the children are staying with Mrs. Tavistock in Dower Cottage, so we've been looking at Rose House. Now that the US Army has left, it's just standing there doing nothing. You could fit half of Fleet Street in the drawing room. Why don't you all come for the summer or longer, if Hitler keeps chucking his buzz bombs about? For all that he's trying to wallop us, we know Victory isn't far off. Stay here for the last few months of the war where everyone can feel slightly safer."

Bunty nodded, her eyes shining with enthusiasm. "People could bring their spouses if they wanted, or families could visit at weekends, or of course they could go home if they preferred. But once they were here . . ." She looked around. "Who wouldn't want to stay?"

Bunty had hit the nail on the head. Rose House was at the very heart of Mrs. Tavistock's estate. An elegant and substantial home, it had been occupied by American officers for two years until overnight they had disappeared to take part in the Normandy landings. I pictured the *Woman's Friend* team sitting on the terrace in the evenings or eating their lunch on the lawn, for once not having to worry quite so much about air raids or rocket attacks, or the possibility of being bombed out. I wasn't naive enough to think that rural life was a utopia, but on a day like today a move for the summer sounded ideal.

"But isn't Rose House still under requisition?" asked Guy. He leaned forward and looked seriously from Bunty to Harold. "There would be all sorts of permissions."

Bunty looked smug. "I've been investigating that," she said. "I think we've got a good chance."

"The upside of Bunty working for the bigwigs at the War Office," added Harold, proudly.

"Granny's very keen," said Bunts. "She rather likes life in the cottage but worries about the house standing empty. She knows we'll look after it."

"It's a good point," said Charles. "Some of the requisitioned estates have been wrecked."

"Please say yes," said Margaret, wistfully.

"Don't dash our hopes, now," added George. Stan nodded and let out a long sigh. It was like watching an audition for the workhouse scene in *Oliver Twist*.

"Have you three been rehearsing this?" I asked.

"Nice work, Laurence Olivier," said Harold, patting Stan on the leg.

"What do you think?" I asked Guy.

"Well, *Good Housekeeping* have been over in Wales for most of the war," said Guy, thoughtfully. "They moved everything, lock, stock, and barrel. If they can do it . . ."

I thought of my colleagues—my friends. They were all endlessly hardworking, as tough as you like, no matter what Adolf threw at them. It could be like a working holiday for everyone.

"I think it's the most enormously generous offer. Thank you, Bunty, and of course, your grandmother. We need to ask the team. And obviously Monica would need to be on board," Guy continued.

That was an understatement. Monica Edwards had been at the very centre of *Woman's Friend* since we had taken over ownership at the end of the previous year. Now she was both our Publisher and quite irreplaceable Fashion and Beauty Editor.

"Do we think people would mind living together?" I wondered.

"Darling, you're not about to ask them to share a bunk room," said Charles, sensibly. "Rose House is the size of a decent hotel."

"We have given it some thought," admitted Bunty. "Everyone would have their own room, and there are lots of spaces so no one would be on top of each other. It's a shame we couldn't have done it before."

"It would have been a terrible squash with all the Americans," said Harold.

"That sounds rather fun," I said, cheerfully.

"Good job I've been posted back," said Charles, calmly throwing a crust of bread in my direction.

"Not a moment too soon," agreed Harold.

"Speaking of which," said Guy, looking at his wristwatch rather pointedly. "All these plans sound super. But, um . . ."

"Yes," said Charles. "Lots to do."

There was an odd silence.

"Is that a hint that you've had enough lunch?" grinned Bunty. "I'll start packing up then, shall I?"

"I'll give you a hand," I said.

"Harold," murmured Guy through his teeth, sounding like a ventriloquist.

Charles stifled a laugh and clapped him on the shoulder. Guy made a slight face. Then they stared at Harold.

"No time like the present," said Charles, almost under his breath.

Now I was baffled. Bunty appeared much the same. Harold looked flushed.

"Ah," he said, in a voice that came out very small for a very large man. He cleared his throat. "Yes. Right then. Gosh."

Guy gave him the kindest smile.

Bunts, who had been about to stack plates, stopped what she was doing.

"Is everything all right?" she asked, sounding concerned.

Harold nodded. He took a deep breath, then put his hand into his pocket and took something out.

"Bunty," he said. "Darling, I have something I would very much like to ask you."

Nobody said a word.

Harold moved from where he was sitting next to Bunty and now knelt down on one knee. He took another large breath and then spoke in the clearest of tones.

"Miss Marigold Tavistock," he said. "Will you marry me?"

CHAPTER 2

Operation Summer in the Country

Of course Bunty said yes.

Then pandemonium broke out. Shrieks, cheers, kisses, and the double celebration of the best news in the world together with three men congratulating themselves on pulling off the surprise of the year.

"I even ran up a bloody hill, so we didn't give it away," said Guy.

Harold had been plotting it for weeks.

Immediately, plans for a country wedding began, and rather than being sidelined, the idea of moving the *Woman's Friend* office to Hampshire for the summer became part of the excitement.

The next day we all leapt into action. Bunty scored an early win, taking advantage of going to church for Sunday service to cross off "Snaffle date w Vicar" as Harold had put it, while with Mrs. Tavistock's permission, I riffled through her Edwardian wardrobes to find candidates that might be transformed into a wedding frock for my best friend. Charles and the children undertook a reconnaissance mission to ascertain what condition the US Army had left Rose House in, and George, who had recently achieved an A in his Technical Drawing exam, began work on an impressive floor plan to make sure everyone could fit in. That left Guy on telephone duty, starting with all-important calls to first Monica, and then Mrs. Mahoney, as we all knew that nothing would ever get done unless our Head of Production was on board.

None of us took it as read that the *Woman's Friend* team would agree to the move. Upping sticks for the summer was all very well, but we worked with people of all ages and familial situations. I just hoped they would want to come.

The fact was everyone at *Woman's Friend* had been working flat out for years. It didn't matter what was asked of them, or what was going on in their own lives, they always rose to the challenge. Working for a women's magazine might not have been the same as being in uniform or doing the night shifts in the factories, but we knew we had the ability to make a difference, and we took that very seriously indeed.

Our job at *Woman's Friend* was to help keep up morale, to share information, offer advice, and perhaps as much as anything, show women that they had our friendship and respect. We received hundreds of letters, week in and week out, asking for help. The flow of problems never, ever let up. They may have been from strangers, but we did everything in our power to respond. You could put us on the moon and the team would continue to work their socks off.

Now, Bunty and her granny's offer gave us the rarest chance to give the *Woman's Friend* team something special. For the first time we really could offer them safety. Far from guaranteed of course, but as it was clear that Hitler was targeting his new bombs at London, moving to the country was a chance to keep people dear to our hearts safe.

On Monday morning Guy, Harold, and I sat on the train home as it made its slow way into Waterloo station, looking out of the windows at the bomb damage that had spared neither suburbs nor city. Gaps in terraces where people's homes had stood, boarded-up buildings, large patches of land with nothing but heaps of rubble: by the time we got off the bus in Pimlico and walked the final part of the journey home, the opportunity to move everyone to the country felt almost too good to be true.

Monica, who had told Guy she was entirely on board for the move, had come into the office early to discuss details before the rest of the staff arrived.

"Do you think they'll say yes?" I asked. "It's either all of us or not at all. And I'm not sure everyone likes the idea of evacuation or communal living."

"I very much hope so, and we all get on very well," said Monica, brushing an invisible speck of dust from her jacket. "I don't know anyone who hasn't had to bunk in with someone they've absolutely loathed at some point. Guy, do you remember my aunt who stayed with me during the Blitz?"

Guy grimaced. "Dreadful," he said.

"Quite," said Monica. "She spent the entire time reminding me of the shame I had brought on the family due to getting a divorce. I put up with it until she called a lovely friend of mine a filthy coward because he wasn't in uniform." She grimaced.

"He took it well, all things considered," said Guy. "'I do appreciate your concerns, madam, but sadly I have just the one lung.'"

Monica laughed. "And then you said, 'Jonathan, didn't you lose the other one just before they awarded you the Victoria Cross?' Emmy, my aunt was gone the next day. So, don't worry about our team. I'm sure they've all put up with far worse. Now, Harold, please tell me everything about your proposal. I'm so thrilled for you both."

We had decided that when the *Woman's Friend* team had all arrived, fully expecting a run-of-the-mill Monday editorial meeting, the first thing would be to break the news about the engagement, which we knew would get everyone's spirits up.

As the staff began to appear, Harold sidled up to my desk.

"I'm going to hide upstairs until everyone's in," he said. "It's been bad enough keeping the secret this long. It's not good for a chap's nerves."

"You were in the Bomb Squad," I said. "You don't have nerves."

"I do about this sort of thing," he answered. Then he shouted, "GOOD MORNING, MRS. MAHONEY," as if she was half a mile away rather than three feet.

"Good morning, Captain Thomas," she answered in a normal voice. "How was your weekend?"

"Dull as ditch water, thank you," said Harold, managing to moderate himself but beaming at her like a loon.

"Is the captain all right?" whispered Mrs. Shaw to me as she took off her coat.

"Oh yes," I said.

"He doesn't seem it. No offence meant."

"None taken," I answered. "Morning, Hester. I like your hat."

"Good morning, Emmy," said Hester. "Thank you very much. Did you have a lovely time at Bunty's?"

"Bit dull," I said, smiling at Harold.

"I'm getting Guy," he answered and hurried out of the room.

This did nothing to dispel Mrs. Shaw's suspicions, and certainly didn't help the whole Run of the Mill plan, but thankfully everyone had now arrived and when a few minutes later Guy led Monica and Harold back down, I had herded us all into the same room.

"Morning all," said Guy. "I trust you had pleasant weekends. Shall we start the editorial meeting now? A little earlier than usual, but there's lots to do."

Mrs. Shaw gave me an I Told You Something Is Up look as we all scuttled to find our places.

"Captain Thomas. You have something to say," said Guy as the meeting began.

Harold's ears went pink.

"I'm getting married," he said, simply.

"Hurrah!" cried Monica, bursting into applause which was taken up by the entire team.

"Congratulations, Captain," said Mr. Newton to his boss.

"How wonderful," said Hester, who at eighteen was a keen romantic.

"And about time too, if you don't mind me saying, Captain
Thomas," said Mrs. Shaw. "You were lucky Miss Tavistock didn't
give up waiting and move on to somebody else."

"Thank you, Mrs. Shaw," said Guy firmly, before Mrs. Shaw ac-
cidentally took the wind out of everyone's sails. "I think we can all
agree it is very nice news."

Then Harold had to give another word-for-word account of the
proposal.

"It's just like the films," said Hester, putting her hand to her heart.

This set off Mrs. Harewood, who let out a gasp of emotion, stood
up, and then sat down again.

"For he's a jolly good fellow," began Mr. Newton, and everyone
joined in. Harold looked pleased as anything.

I wished that Bunty could have been here. Everyone was so very
delighted for them both. They all knew what a rotten deal of things
she and Harold had had. If anyone deserved to find happiness it was
them. With Harold almost overwhelmed by the attention and good
wishes, I sat quietly, listening and watching so that I could remember
everything in as much detail as possible to pass on to her. This was a
special, if perhaps bittersweet, day. I was all too aware that our office
was in the very room where three years ago I had tried to make sense of
the news that Bunty's fiancé, Bill, had been killed. The thought of her
ever being happy again had seemed beyond imagination at the time.

With everyone on a high, Guy rode in on the congratulatory wave
and introduced the idea of a move to the country.

"So," he said when he had outlined the plan, "what do you
think?" He was sitting at the end of the office where the sun came
through the window to bathe him in an incongruously angelic light.
"Of course you may want to give it some thought. It's not exactly
a holiday, but a change might be something of a rest, especially in
the light of Hitler's current attacks. It should be far quieter in the

countryside." He paused and looked around the table at his staff. "Goodness knows you all deserve a break. Now, does anyone have any questions?"

For a moment there was a silence. Then Hester's hand shot up, making her look as if she were asking to sit at the front of the bus on a school trip.

"Hester," said Guy. "Don't worry, there's no need for hands."

"Yes, please, Mr. Collins," she said, ignoring the directive. "I'd be ever so pleased to come, if that's all right. And I can help as much as you need."

It was entirely what I had expected from our much-loved assistant. Since joining the magazine straight from school, Hester had become one of the hardest workers of us all, and always as keen as mustard to join in, whatever the suggestion.

"Excellent," said Guy, as I gently put my hand on Hest's arm which was still sky high. "Thank you very much. Ladies?" He turned to the group of women who worked with me on "Yours Cheerfully," the magazine's problem page.

"And so, we would all live there?" asked Mrs. Shaw, narrowing her eyes at Guy as if he might be setting an elaborate trap. "In a big country house?"

I could tell that Mrs. Shaw was already picturing herself as the temporary chatelaine of Hampshire's answer to the Palace of Versailles. Rose House was big by most people's standards, but to avoid disappointment I did hope she wasn't expecting to find courtesans and chevaliers lurking about.

"In a sizeable property, yes," said Guy, admirably keeping a straight face.

"Living *together*?" said Miss Peters, which made things sound concerningly biblical.

"That's right," said Guy.

"Goodness," said Mr. Newton, who was given to worries. "I don't know."

"All very much above board," I interrupted before our Advertising Manager ran for the hills. "We've worked out everyone's rooms, so you won't have to share or anything."

Mr. Newton looked aghast at the thought.

"We do realise you will need to consult with Mrs. Newton about the move," said Harold, sensitively. "Spouses will of course be extremely welcome."

It was nicely done by Harold. If anything was going to clinch things, involving Mrs. Newton was it.

Mrs. Shaw tutted. "Of course, my Ernest is dead," she said, sounding slightly put out.

"Yes," I said, quietly.

"And now he's missed out," continued Mrs. Shaw, as if he had only himself to blame. "That's wearing a damp vest for you."

It was hard to know quite how to respond.

"A cautionary tale," murmured Guy, respectfully.

"I'll say," said Mrs. Shaw. She sighed but then appeared to perk up. "Anyway, there we are. Comes to us all. Mr. Collins, I would be very pleased to attend, thank you very much. Especially if there aren't many stairs to my room, what with my knees, as you know. But either way, I won't mind."

Guy answered that this was splendid news, and as the idea of a summer adventure began to sink in, within a few minutes more, almost everyone had said they should very much like to join in. The only person who felt that she couldn't was Mrs. Harewood, who lived next door and worked for us part time. As she also ran a very selective boarding house, where Harold currently lived, it would be impossible for her to leave town. It was a rotten shame and would also leave us a part-time man down, but even this wasn't without an upside as Mrs. Harewood very pluckily volunteered to watch over the house while we were away.

Questions and suggestions began to flow. Hester volunteered to be ration books monitor while Mrs. Mahoney went straight to her desk to get onto the printers. Mr. Newton planned to rush home at lunchtime to speak with his wife, and Miss Peters was sure she knew someone who could lend us a van to help transport everything we needed from the office.

It was the most excited I had seen them in an age. As the hubbub died down for just a moment, an all too recognisable sound came through the window. The mournful wail of the siren signalling the start of another raid.

The move to Rose House could not have come at a more welcome time.

CHAPTER 3

A Team Settles In

Within a fortnight we were ready to go. From Bunty getting dispensation for use of Rose House while still under requisition through to Mrs. Mahoney negotiating processes with the typesetters and printers, preparations for the move swiftly fell into place.

On a bright and cheery Sunday morning, the team arrived in Hampshire eager to explore and settle in. Guy, Monica, Hester, and I had made up an advance party the day before, arriving in a packed van to join Bunty and Harold, who had already been hard at work setting up rooms and rearranging furniture. Producing a weekly magazine did not allow for the luxury of the entire company taking time off, and we worked late into the night so that it would appear home from home, or rather office from office, when the rest of the team arrived.

Bunty and I went down to the railway station to give everyone a decent welcome and help with the luggage. While we had been lucky to get hold of enough petrol for the van, we now turned to the sort of horsepower that came with four legs. As a result, and thanks to a couple of very kind neighbours who had known Bunty for years, the *Woman's Friend* editorial team were greeted by two horses and carts with more than enough room for all the suitcases and personal packages as well as anyone who fancied a ride. Almost everyone climbed up, with Mr. Brand our much-loved Art Director and his wife, who were both over seventy, springing onboard and saying it reminded them of their wedding day just after the old Queen's last Jubilee.

Bunts and I walked alongside, pointing out local landmarks, which meant the church and the pub, and enjoying seeing our friends on what looked like a works summer excursion. After a little over a mile, the horses turned past Dower Cottage and up the long drive, plodding between the sturdy old oaks lining the route and then past the paddocks and small lake. As we approached Rose House, our group's chatter ebbed away as they craned their necks to get their first view. The two-hundred-year-old Georgian manor did not let them down. It had always been an impressive sight, and it still was, even with what had been a flawless front lawn now turned into rows of vegetables that would soon need to be dug up.

"Gordon Bennet," said Mrs. Shaw. "Look at that!"

"Oh, Larry," said Mrs. Newton, squeezing her husband's arm.

"It's beautiful," whispered Miss Peters.

"It's absolutely freezing in the winter," said Bunty, cheerfully. She was always one to play down the fact that her granny was well-to-do. "And I hope you're not worried about bats. But we've tried to sort things out, so you'll be comfy. Thankfully the Americans were very well behaved and have left everything in pretty good shape, other than marking out some sort of funny sports pitch in the garden and painting a great big picture of Betty Grable in a halter neck in one of the sheds." She laughed. "It's rather good, actually. Here we are."

With Monica and Hester joining the party, we quickly unloaded both people and luggage, and with heartfelt thank-you's to Bunty's neighbours we led the team into their temporary new home.

"Let me show you around," Bunty said, as we stood in the newly spotless reception hall. "Or would you like a cup of tea?"

No one wanted tea. Everyone wanted to explore. If I said it myself, we had done a fine job. What had been the drawing room and library were now transformed into a bigger and more splendid version of the Pimlico office. In the drawing room, our trusty old typewriters were set up in a line along a vast dining room table, while boxes holding each person's stationery and files had been neatly stacked by each chair. Hester had even carefully put place names written in immaculate script, which gave the air of a high-level meeting where attendance was strictly by invitation only. The library had been given to the Art and Production Departments, allowing Mrs. Mahoney a luxurious amount of room for weeks of the magazine's flat plans and almost an entire studio space for Mr. Brand's artwork and illustrations. Best of all, every seat faced towards the rooms' enormous sash windows, through which the summer light streamed. Should anyone care to look up from their work, they would have a perfect view of the garden where currently several sheep were making the most of the grass.

It was such a contrast to the dear old battered London we had left behind.

"Well, I never," said Mr. Newton.

"Will it do, do you think?" I asked.

For once, even Mrs. Shaw was lost for words.

"The bedrooms aren't nearly as grand," said Bunty, self-consciously. Hester, who had seen the accommodation, looked doubtful about that.

"I don't think I'd mind if I was to sleep in a tent," said Mrs. Shaw, recovering herself and speaking for us all.

"You'd probably end up sharing with the sheep," smiled Bunty. "Anyway, it's still the weekend so we really should show you your rooms. Hester, may I hand over to you?"

At this Hester took up the reins as our very happy group followed her out to the reception hall, and having collected their luggage, up the polished oak staircase that led to their bedrooms. With the promise of a light lunch of summer soup and peach cake for pudding, to be followed by a celebratory Sunday dinner later on, no one had the slightest doubt that the move to the country had been a most splendid idea.

———

The next morning, it was still hard not to feel slightly giddy at the novelty of it all. Even though I had known Bunty since we were five, visits to Rose House had always been exciting affairs involving madly running around, cadging biscuits off Cook, or sliding down banisters when Mrs. Tavistock wasn't looking. It was easily as good as the best children's novels, even though the reality for Bunty was that the only reason she lived there was because her parents were both dead. As Bunty once said, getting to lark around in your granny's duck pond and being slightly spoilt by her could only make up for that sort of thing to a certain extent. If you happened to be invited for the summer however, as well as being lucky enough to still have the full complement of family, the place was an almost ludicrous delight.

Sunday evening had gone well, as everyone enjoyed the unusual experience of eating together, not to mention the fact that someone else had prepared the meal. With a dozen mouths to feed and the challenge of pooling coupon resources and kitty, looking after us all was too much for Mrs. Tavistock's own cook at the cottage. Instead, we were all chipping in so that Mrs. Whiteley from the village could come on board as cook at Rose House.

To start things off with a bang, Harold stood up and invited everyone to the forthcoming wedding, which went down terribly well, especially when he began with, "My fiancée and I." Bottles of beer were unearthed, which added to the festive air, and all too soon it was bedtime when everyone became awfully polite and started saying, "No, please, after you," to each other as if we'd all only just met.

Hester and I had assigned bedrooms on a combination of age and whether people were with their spouses, which meant Mr. and Mrs. Brand quite rightly hit the jackpot for the best one and Mrs. Shaw's knees didn't have to cope with going up to the top floor, so that went down very well. There was only one potentially tricky moment when Miss Peters saw she was on the same bathroom rota as Harold, and confided in me that her dressing gown wasn't quite up to pre-war scratch. Luckily, any awkwardness was averted once I assured her that he had probably experienced far worse working with UXBs and also having been blown up now couldn't see much out of one of his eyes.

"There's always an upside," said Harold, when I gave him the gen after breakfast. "Hadn't realised that would be one of them. Good-oh." Then he thought for a moment. "Perhaps I should stay in my room until you give me the nod that the Miss Peters coast is clear?"

It sounded a bit much having to wait around for Miss Peters to finish her ablutions every morning in order to spare everyone's blushes.

"Captain Thomas," I said, sternly. "You're about to marry my best friend. I'm afraid you're going to have to get used to coping with ladies' dressing gowns. It's a prerequisite for the job."

Harold looked down at me from his considerable height. Despite being absolutely walloped by a German high explosive, he could still cut a dash. Now, he gave me an amused smile.

"Don't worry, Emmeline," he said, dropping his voice, "I'm pretty sure there'll be no complaints."

"Cripes," I said, pulling a mock-horrified face.

Harold gave a roar of laughter and walked off to the library with a spring in his step.

"What are you two scheming?" asked Bunty, who had just arrived from Dower Cottage.

"That Harold fellow is simply awful," I said, sitting down at my new desk as Bunts nodded, happily. "But I can't talk, work to do."

"Likewise," said Bunts. "Where do you want me to start?"

As if coming up with a summer retreat wasn't already enough, in the absence of Mrs. Harewood, Bunty had volunteered to help out with the readers' letters and the problem page. This was a big relief. Keeping up with correspondence from our readers had become an almost impossible task. With sales of the magazine going from strength to strength, the number of letters arriving continued to grow by the day. As the person whose name was on the "Yours Cheerfully" page, and the one who wrote the advice, while I read as many as I possibly could, I needed a team of ladies to sort through them, decide which could be answered with an informative booklet, and hardest of all, pass to me those people who were the most desperate for help.

If anyone thought working on a women's problem page wasn't a serious job, or even had a patronising snigger behind the back of their hands (and I had met many who did exactly that), they should spend a day reading our post. People's problems did not stop during a war. They just got a lot worse.

With Bunty newly on board, she and I, along with Mrs. Shaw, Miss Peters, and Hester, drew our chairs around the end of the dining table and worked out who would do what for the week. Our holiday postboys, who happened to be George, Margaret, and Stan, were already at work going through the mailbags that we had brought with us from London. With redirected letters due to arrive at any minute, we were already running behind. The three of them stood studiously at the other end of the room, slicing the tops of envelopes with letter openers, but under strict instructions not to remove or look at anything inside.

I turned to Hester first. Officially, her job was Personal Assistant to Guy, Monica, and me, but whenever she could, she would type up compliment slips on my behalf and send out booklets from the *Woman's Friend* Information Library. It meant she could help but not have to be exposed to some of the more delicate or graphic concerns.

"Hest, could you make a start on the new *Becoming a Woman* queries please? We've just done a reprint so there's a backlog. Mrs. Shaw, can you and I start with dictating some replies, and then as you're typing them, Miss Peters, can you take over, and then Bunty, the same, please? The usual relay."

The women nodded. Bunty had made notes in rapid shorthand.

"It'll be quite a change from the War Office," I said. "Very few problems from anyone in the Cabinet for a start."

"Let's hope so," said Bunty, smiling. She turned to the others. "I do hope you'll tell me if you see me doing anything wrong. I'm good at typing but I don't know a thing about all this."

It was a smart move. The combination of being the heir to a large house and coming straight from working in Whitehall could easily have made Bunty look grand. Now, she made it clear she was the new girl. It went down well.

"Not at all," said Mrs. Shaw. "Look at how fast you are. Mr. Churchill himself couldn't keep up."

Bunts said she hadn't actually worked for the Prime Minister, but it was a detail roundly ignored.

I opened a much-used buff folder which held some of the most pressing queries to be tackled as well as a list of regularly answered topics.

"Here are the problems we get the most," I said, for Bunty's benefit. "The list is getting longer. Affairs—some of them are utterly heartbreaking. Pregnancies with the wrong person—gosh, there are more and more all the time. Financial worries, especially from war widows. I'm afraid there's been quite an increase in those since the invasion in France. Wives and families of prisoners of war—we're still getting so many letters about trying to get information about the men, especially in the Far East. We've just printed a new leaflet on that. Relatives—so many people are living together now and having problems, particularly with mothers it would seem, being unreasonable, sometimes even cruel. No offence meant, Mrs. Shaw."

"None taken," she said. "Me and my Brian are very close."

"Of course," I replied. "So, yes, Bunts, parents being awful about who their daughters fall in love with. That happens a lot. You'd think

trying to be happy is a crime. Then, of course, husbands losing interest, men at work taking advantage, readers trying to avoid having
more children, others who desperately want to have children, and
then some who can't cope with the ones that they have." I paused for
a moment and then surprised myself by sighing heavily. "It's quite a
list, isn't it?"

No one replied. Our job was to help, not to dwell. But as I sat
listing the saddest of situations, not needing to look at any notes
because there had been so many and there would always, *always* be
more, I felt somehow remiss. It was as if I had been purely reeling off
an inventory of misery, without the emotion any single one of these
problems, or more to the point, the person who had written to us,
deserved.

"The rotten thing, Bunts," I said to my friend, "is that even if just
for this summer, you'll read hundreds, probably thousands of letters,
all of which merit our help. I don't know if Mrs. Shaw and Miss Peters would agree, but I think things are getting worse. Everything is
just . . ." I paused again.

"Hard," said Miss Peters.

"Very," agreed Mrs. Shaw. She turned to Bunty. "I know I can be
blunt," she said, "and I do call a spade a spade. But it doesn't mean
I don't care. I've done this job for two years now and I think Miss
Lake is right. It is getting worse. Women have either been kept apart
from the people they should be with or forced together with ones
they shouldn't. Everything's upside down. The war has gone on for
so long."

Mrs. Shaw and Miss Peters exchanged looks. The younger woman
nodded.

"We just have to find a way to help them through," Miss Peters said, quietly. "Until we've won. Then perhaps things won't be so
muddled."

For a moment the four of us sat in silence. We hardly ever talked
like this. Perhaps it was the move to Rose House.

The sun shone through the drawing-room windows as prettily as it had the previous day, and the view of the sheep munching contentedly looked as if it had been there for all time. We were tremendously lucky. Our short-term home was idyllic. More than ever, our job had to be to try our hardest to help people whose lives had become anything but.

"I know not all the problems we're sent are awful, but I always think it's very brave to write to a stranger when things are at their worst," I said, looking down at my file, which held some heartbreaking stories. "Especially if you're alone."

Now Bunty spoke up. "That's the whole point of what you're all doing though, isn't it?" she said. "People aren't alone. Not completely. You may be strangers, but you're here and you're listening. The readers know that, otherwise they wouldn't bother to write."

I glanced over at the children who were emptying two huge sacks that had just arrived. Letters flooded out onto the burr walnut dining table.

"You're right, of course," I said. "For the price of a stamp, we're here. And if I ever sound as if I am just reading out problems from a list, please remind me of that. We might be helpless in terms of putting an end to this war, but as Miss Peter says, whatever time and effort it takes, I promise that we will do everything we possibly can to get our readers through to the end."

CHAPTER 4

The Man from the Ministry

Perhaps it was the novelty of a new office or that a change really was as good as a rest, but the *Woman's Friend* team settled in seamlessly, and within a couple of weeks, it was as if we had been at Rose House, and more surprisingly, living together for years. We quickly learned each other's more personal routines and what might have kindly been called foibles.

It was soon noted that in the absence of walking to work, Mr. Newton enjoyed a morning constitutional which took him on a brisk two miler before two slices of toast and a large tea, while Mrs. Mahoney admitted to enjoying the first weekday lie ins she'd ever had in her life. Hester and I were both good in the mornings and took it in turns to set out a cold breakfast so people could help themselves. Rations were scrupulously adhered to and while it was easiest in most cases to pool resources, in terms of breakfast, each person had their own pat of butter on a plate in the pantry with their name on it. As Mrs. Whiteley said, we might be living in the country, but cows didn't grow on trees. It was a confusing point, but one we all took on board.

Many of us were keen letter writers even if we had spent most of the day doing just that for work, so after dinner people would go off to their rooms or onto the terrace, or sit in a comfy chair and write inside. Mr. Brand volunteered to show Marg and Stan how to draw cartoon animals just like Walt Disney, and when Hester discovered a not entirely out of tune upright piano, to her astonishment and slightly bashful delight, within hours Guy had taught her how to play "Chopsticks" as a duet.

Small social groupings also emerged, as the wives, Mrs. Newton and Mrs. Brand, became chums and by the middle of the first week had roped in Miss Peters and Mrs. Shaw and started a knitting circle. If they could make the numbers up to six, they'd be able to get coupon-free wool to make comforts for the Royal Navy, so the next evening Monica, Hester, and Bunty joined in. To everyone's surprise Mrs. Tavistock came too, which gave the whole thing an almost royal seal of approval and meant that Mrs. Shaw could now live in the happy knowledge she had once shared a balaclava pattern with someone who had been photographed for *The Tatler*.

Within days all the women had enrolled, including the worst knitter in the world, which was me.

"Perhaps you could make pompoms?" suggested Bunty over lunch. She had seen my woollen efforts before. "That's mostly winding a lot."

"Ah yes," grinned Harold, holding a jug of water in mid-air. "Pompoms. Just what you need on a battleship in the middle of winter."

"Not for the navy, you nitwit," said Bunty, with affection. "As decoration. Perhaps they could be for the wedding?"

It was a kind, if unconventional, idea. Everyone stopped eating at the thought.

"It was never going to be normal, was it?" sighed Harold. "Not with you two."

"Don't worry, old chap," said Guy, calmly. "Charles says it's easiest if you just give in and let them be strange."

Bunty and I looked across the lunch things and raised our glasses to each other.

"Let's face it," she said, "Emmy and I have already had twenty years together. Harold, darling, you're just going to have to fit in."

"Charles said that as well," I said, laughing as Harold appeared unperturbed at the thought. "He says once he'd got the hang of that, it was all very straightforward."

Mrs. Brand smiled from the other end of the table. "Does that ring a bell, Bernard?" she asked her husband.

Mr. Brand smiled back. They had been married for over forty years and he still looked at her as if they had only just met.

"Five sisters," he said, in his gentle voice. "I knew if I could convince them, I was in with a chance of winning your hand."

"I'm so very glad you did," said Mrs. Brand. "And I think wedding pompoms could be lovely."

"So do I," said Hester. "White ones, like little snowballs. Although it's the wrong season."

"I could just come along to the meetings and take notes while you're all knitting and talking about the wedding plans," I suggested. "There's still tons to organise."

"That's a super idea," said Bunty. "All in favour?"

The women of the table said, "Aye."

And so, the *Woman's Friend* Knitting Circle officially became Bunty and Harold's Wedding HQ.

The pompoms were never mentioned again.

———

A fortnight after the move, Guy and I had been scheduled to have a meeting at the Ministry of Information in London, but it had been re-arranged to take place at Rose House. We had already found that rather than clients and business contacts expecting us to travel to their offices in the city, word had spread that a train ride to Hampshire wasn't too much trouble when there was a very nice pub at the end of it.

Today, it was the turn of Mr. Langley, who had admitted he was more than delighted to leave the hallowed corridors of the Ministry's Senate House and head out of town. A good friend of Guy's, Richard Langley was one of the many journalists to have offered his services to the Government's press relations team. Both Guy and Monica had known him for some years, and Monica, who was perhaps missing the London press's social scene more than she would let on, had suggested he stay overnight in the pub, and as he was a keen cricketer, join them on Saturday when a match was taking place on the green.

"Ahh," sighed Guy, as we awaited Mr. Langley's arrival in what had once been Bunty's grandfather's study. "Friday afternoon meetings. They're the best sort."

"If only we could get our hands on some gin," said Monica.

"Drinking in the office would be good old Fleet Street giving Hitler one in the eye," agreed Guy, happily.

"Did either of you ever do any proper work before war was declared?" I asked.

"No point overdoing it," said Guy, running his hand through his hair as if he were sitting on the deck of a yacht.

They had both already worked a sixty-hour week.

"Is there anything we want to put on the agenda?" asked Monica, moving into business mode. "What do you have, Emmy?"

"We're getting lots of letters from readers wanting to switch jobs, either into other parts of the war effort or postings overseas," I said. "And masses of questions about what's going to happen when the war ends. Mainly, how quickly will the men come home? Also, what will happen to the ones who are prisoners of war? We're getting letters about more or less *everything* to do with demobilisation, masses of concerns about wages, pensions, housing, employment for women. You name it. Where do you want me to start?"

Guy nodded but was frowning. "Hmm. Langley's a press man," he said. "He's not the Government's oracle."

"He's as close as we can get," I said. "How many times have we told the readers to just keep going until Victory? Well, we jolly nearly *are* at Victory and they want to know what's coming next."

"I agree with you both," said Monica, diplomatically. "Let's see what we can prioritise."

For the next ten minutes we weighed up the issues we felt mattered the most to our readers with where we thought our visitor might be able to help. Then there was a knock on the door and Hester appeared.

"Mr. Langley for you all," she announced, showing in a tall, sandy-haired man in the standard Ministry livery of a smart dark suit. He was carrying a briefcase and bowler hat. Hest disappeared to collect tea from Mrs. Whiteley as cordial greetings were exchanged.

"Very nice to see you, Miss Lake," said Mr. Langley. "What a lovely place to have an office."

"It's very good of you to come all this way," I answered.

"Mr. Langley was bribed with beer and cricket," said Guy, as he and Langley shook hands warmly. "How are things? Please tell us that the news of headway in Europe is real and not being conjured up by your propaganda chums for national morale."

I knew Guy was kidding, but the three of us looked at Mr. Langley just in case he was about to give away all the Ministry's secrets.

"Nothing to do with us. It's entirely our boys in uniform being as brave as ever," he confirmed. "We just write press releases and ask people to grow their own beans."

"Ah, come now, Richard," said Monica. "You did your brave stint in the last war. We're all doing what we can. Oh good," she broke off as Hester returned. "Thank you, Hester. Miss Wilson will be taking the minutes so shall we get the business part of things going? We're always keen to let the staff close the shop early at the end of the week."

"Of course," said Langley. He opened his briefcase and took out some papers. "First, I would like to thank you for the work *Wom-*

an's Friend has been doing. It is much appreciated by all the departments."

This was nice. The Ministry's people weren't known for dishing out compliments.

"Particularly your articles in your 'Women's War Work' section, Miss Lake," he continued. "For what it's worth, I happen to think you are one of the best young journalists in your field."

"Thank you," I said, warming to Guy and Monica's friend. "It's very much a team effort."

"True," Mr. Langley agreed, "but you're the one writing so persuasively. Your pieces on women ship builders and WAAF photographers were excellent. Exactly the kind of inspiring publicity we need. I hope you're happy to do more?" He took a folder out of his case and handed it to me. "We'd like you to go to an RAF Transport Station next week to interview the nursing orderlies. They're the girls bringing the wounded home from France so it's quite some job."

"I would be delighted," I answered. "And if you'd ever like us to interview the ones in the field hospitals over there, please just say the word."

I knew I was onto a duffer on this point. Women journalists weren't allowed on the front lines, or at least British women journalists weren't. The American press agencies were different.

"Sorry," said Langley. "You know that such an assignment would have to be covered by Mr. Collins."

"Oh, the joy of double standards," said Monica, unimpressed. "Women can stand in blood all day long trying to save lives, but they can't possibly file a report. Let us try to patch up the hell men put each other through, but don't let us write about it." She shook her head.

Mr. Langley shifted in his seat.

"I know, Richard," said Monica, relenting just a little for her friend. "You don't make the rules."

"Well, Langley," said Guy, "I certainly wouldn't go if Miss Lake couldn't. That's not how we work here. Although to be honest I've seen enough of this sort of thing in my time to be quite happy never to see another field hospital again."

The atmosphere in the room had cooled, which was my fault. I knew the rules and really shouldn't have suggested it.

"Mr. Langley, I apologise," I said. "It will be privilege enough to interview the women who bring our boys home."

Mr. Langley nodded in acknowledgement. "We would be grateful," he said.

Then I grabbed the bull by the horns.

"Journalism aside, our readers are very interested in opportunities to work overseas, and since D-Day there has been more interest in nursing than ever. Women really do want to help."

"I quite understand," he answered. Then he hesitated and grimaced slightly. "I wish I could give you an encouraging response, but the thing is, we need them to stay in the jobs they already have. Well-meant though it is, if your readers aren't trained nurses or in the services already, they aren't going to get approval to switch. What we do need your help with is domestic workers. Hospitals, nursing homes, children's homes . . . they're all crying out for staff. Cooks, cleaners, housemaids, you name it." He bravely attempted to lighten his tone. "If any of you know anyone who might be interested . . ."

"If I don't get a Fashion Assistant soon, I'll be tempted," smiled Monica, taking the invitation to get back onto friendly ground. "Although I'm not sure about Guy. He's hopelessly messy."

Mr. Langley laughed and said, "So, I've heard. Look, I know domestic work won't seem as glamorous to your readers as the idea of flying out to Gibraltar with the Wrens or what have you. But the fact is, if we don't have enough domestic workers the fancier-sounding jobs can't be done effectively, and we need your help."

"Of course," I answered. "Could you get someone to send a list of contacts in the areas you need promoting to Miss Wilson?" I glanced over to Hester who nodded as she continued to write. She had become a dab hand at calling complete strangers and convincing them to be interviewed for a national magazine. "Don't worry, Mr. Langley, our readers will come through. They always do."

"I don't doubt it for a moment," said Langley. He looked round at each of us. "I know we ask a lot, but it won't be for much longer, and you must always let me know if I can be of help. I mean that."

I had met many Ministry men and women over the years, and Richard Langley struck me as one of the good ones. Decent, I thought.

"Thank you," said Guy. "That's very good of you. Now, let's crack on with the rest of our lists. It's half past three and I hope I am not the only one who is thinking of calling it a day at four o'clock and encouraging my staff to repair to The White Horse?"

"Seconded," said Monica. "And then we can stop with the whole Mr. Langley, Miss Lake business as it will be the weekend, and Richard you can get rid of the Ministry's bowler and become human like the rest of us. No offence meant."

"None taken," said Mr. Langley. "We've known each other far too long."

"Dear man," said Monica fondly, which was hardly appropriate while we were still in an official meeting, and I hadn't even managed a "Richard" yet. "Emmy, are you coming too?"

"Can Charles and I join you later?" I asked. "That's my husband," I added. "He's coming down for the evening and we're taking the children to the pictures. *Chip Off the Old Block* with Donald O'Connor."

"I saw it on Monday," said Richard Langley. "It's a hoot."

"See," said Guy. "Human. Sort of."

Richard raised an eyebrow and checked his watch.

"Sadly, not until four," he smiled. "Until then I must remain relentlessly demanding and unreasonable about modern women." He opened another folder from his case. "Now. Diphtheria inoculations. We're going to need a very big push."

CHAPTER 5

Do You Think He Might Borrow a Spit?

Richard was right. *Chip Off the Old Block* was a scream, and when Charles and I joined the others at The White Horse, any sign of disagreements over women reporters had been forgotten by all concerned. As Monica had said, he didn't make the rules. The Man from the Ministry was a good sort.

While Richard had left us with a long list of items the Ministry needed us to promote, which added to an already mountainous workload, really the focus of excitement for the entire house was that there was a wedding to arrange.

A date had been set for the end of August, and it was absolutely no surprise that the suggestion of a very small service followed by a low-key wartime tea went out of the window as soon as the *Woman's Friend* team became involved. As Mr. Newton said, it was the perfect opportunity for us to say thank you, both to Bunty and to her granny.

It wasn't just because Mrs. Tavistock had entrusted us with her ancestral home. Always a dignified, if not imposing, figure with the straight-backed bearing of a dowager aunt, since joining the knitting circle, the grande dame of Rose House had become a team member of the first order. She had arrived with her own basket, generously sharing the contents with anyone who had left vital supplies in London, joining in with the chat, and showing an interest in every person in the group. As Miss Peters put it, it was like having our very own Queen Mary, only far less frightening. Bunty said it had done her granny the power of good. As far as Mrs. Tavistock was concerned, nothing would be too much trouble if it meant the much-loved couple had the best day of their lives.

Everyone was given a job. Monica and I concentrated on the wedding party's frocks, while Hester took on accessories and accommodation for guests. The Letters Ladies joined forces to work on plans for flowers, and everyone consulted their coupons to see what they could spare. Guy phoned Mrs. Croft our cookery expert, and within a day she had sent a package of handwritten seasonal recipes that were near miraculous in their use of ingredients that could be found in the Rose House kitchen garden. In the middle of it all Bunty sent out invitations and consulted with Margaret who, as perhaps the most enthusiastic Chief Bridesmaid any of us had ever met, had Executive Approval over everything.

Thankfully, Marg was a benign ruler, despite making the rash decision to accept my brother Jack's offer of providing transport to and from the church for the bride. I blamed myself, as having just returned from the RAF Transport Station for the Ministry's article, I was finishing my edits one evening when Jack called. The piece needed to go to the Government's censor in next day's first post, so when Marg said Jack was on the phone, I said I would call him back.

Moments later, everything "had been agreed."

Marg explained that there was to be a very nice car, Jack would be chauffeur, and then something about his squadron leader "not minding really."

"He hasn't told him, has he?" said Bunty, cheerfully. The three of us had grown up together, and Jack was almost as much her little brother as he was mine.

"I shouldn't think so," I said. "At least he's not planning on 'borrowing' a Spit."

"Do you think he might?" whispered Marg, who already had the beginnings of a crush.

"Oh dear," said Bunts, crossing her eyes at me. "Another one bites the dust."

"She's not the first, and won't be the last," I said, giving Margaret a hug. "Now then, who wants to hear about my trip today? They let me look inside a Dakota. I've never been in one before. It was huge."

Marg looked at me.

"I bet that was interesting," she said, kindly. "It's just not the same as a Spitfire though, is it?"

———

The evening before the wedding everything was nearly in place. The church had been decorated, the bridal party's posies were in buckets of water in the cool of the dairy room, and the amount of activity in the kitchen suggested we were expecting a visit from Henry the Eighth and his entire Tudor court.

"Just how long has your granny been saving sugar?" asked Harold, dipping his finger into some jelly which was now ready to be built into a trifle.

"When did you two first meet?" I said, looking into the bowl. "Because I think it was around about then."

"Coming through," bellowed Mrs. Shaw, making us all jump. "Custard waits for no man, not even you, Captain Harold. Mind your back, please."

"Custard," said Harold, longingly.

"No fingers," snapped Mrs. Shaw, beginning to pour it onto the jelly. "You'll burn yourself and spoil Miss Tavistock's day."

It was clear where her loyalties lay.

"Mrs. Whiteley may have a spare syrup biscuit if you're lucky," I said, seeing Harold's face fall. "And then can you come and help in the garden? Mr. Newton's up a ladder with some bunting but he looks awfully wobbly."

"He's just fallen off," said Stan, who was watching from the window.

"What?" I replied. "Why didn't you say?"

"It's all right, he's in the hydrangeas."

"Stanley."

"Now Guy and Mrs. Newton are trying to pull him out."

It was like listening to the radio commentary when the Grand National was on.

"And now Mrs. Newton has fallen over."

"All right, Stan, thank you," I said, heading for the door. "Harold, come on."

Harold, his syrup biscuit, and I rushed out and round to the side garden where we found Guy, now being helped by Monica, successfully righting the Newtons. They seemed none the worse for wear.

"It's my fault," said Mrs. Newton. "I was supposed to be holding the ladder. I've had an early sherry," she added, confidentially.

"I think your husband is very adventurous," replied Monica. "I can hardly go up a step without putting money on a tumble."

We all found that hard to believe.

"Perhaps we don't need bunting to go all the way around the house?" said Harold, trying to help. "After all, the party will be on the main lawn."

"If a job's worth doing, Captain Thomas," answered Mr. Newton, brushing down his waistcoat. "Someone might wish to use the lavatory and come this way by mistake. We can't have them thinking we're below par backstage."

Mr. Newton had thought it through with some logic, which undermined the impression of a carefree bohemian that was now being given by the white flower stuck in his hair.

"Perhaps you could hold the ladder, Larry," said his wife. "That's the job that takes the real strength. Then someone else could go up."

Within seconds, Mr. Newton was out of the flower bed and picking up the ladder as if it were merely a twig.

"Bless him," whispered Mrs. Newton to me. "That's the ticket," she called. Mr. Newton gave a broad smile back.

With everything back on an even keel, Harold and I left them to it and walked through the kitchen garden to the other side of the house where the reception was to be held after the service. With fine late-summer weather forecast for overnight, the trestle tables were already set up, along with several dozen wooden chairs that were standing in stacks beside them. Flanked by Hester and Margaret, Mr. Brand was on his hands and knees, paintbrushes in hand, making large flowing strokes on a panel of hardboard. As we got closer it became apparent that he had created several of them, all covered with the most beautiful loosely formed flowers in a sophisticated palate of pastels, softly muted rather than sickly sweet. Designed to form artistic arbours around the seating areas, they were modern but romantic, and immediately felt entirely appropriate to the setting and special occasion.

"Oh, Mr. Brand," I said. "They're beautiful. Has Bunty seen them?"

"Not yet," said Mr. Brand. "The girls have told her to stay clear until they've dried and I can hide them away. I'm doing them out here so I'm inspired by the garden. I do hope they'll be a nice surprise."

"They're perfect," I answered. "She'll love them, won't she, Harold?"

Harold nodded, seeming almost overcome. "Everyone's being so kind," he said.

I put my arm through his. "You really have no idea how much you mean to us all, do you?" I smiled. "Everyone's just so happy for you both."

Harold was now lost for words, so we stood together quietly watching as Mr. Brand worked.

A few moments later, the silence was broken by Mrs. Mahoney calling my name, and we turned round to see her walking along the terrace with Charles, who was unzipping his leather jacket. Having waved a hello, he offered Mrs. Mahoney his arm, escorting her down the steps and onto the lawn to join us.

"Hello, Miss Lake," he said, wrapping his arms around me. "You look lovely." Then he looked over my shoulder. "Hold on, how rude of me. Who's this lady? Have we met?"

Marg leapt up, beaming. "It's me," she said, as Charles let go of me so she could give him a big hug. "It's my hair. Hester's done it. We've been practising for tomorrow. Do I look grown up?"

"Very much so," said Charles, authoritatively. "We shall have to lock you in the bathroom, or they'll make you join up. Hello, Harold, how are you feeling? Nerves setting in yet?" They shook hands. "I say, Mr. Brand, that's extraordinary. No, please don't get up. It's very nice to see you, sir."

As Charles said his hellos, Hester stood quietly to one side. She had always rather admired him and was apt to go a little shy.

"Good evening, Hester," said Charles. "How lovely to see you. Emmy tells me you've been working your socks off on the wedding."

"Hello, Major Mayhew. Thank you. It's very exciting," said Hest, looking thrilled.

"You've worked wonders on old Marg," said Charles. "Well done."

"Jack's coming tomorrow," said Marg, dancing around. "Emmy says he might bring a Spitfire."

"He's supplying the wedding car," I clarified. "Don't ask where he's getting it."

Charles snorted with laughter. "Dash those RAF boys. They always make the rest of us seem so dull. If all else fails, Harold can borrow the motorcycle and Bunty can go pillion."

"Not on your nelly," interrupted Mrs. Mahoney. "I nearly had a seizure when I saw you roaring up the drive. Now you're home safe we need you to behave."

"You mustn't worry, Mrs. Mahoney," said Charles, giving her a big smile.

"But I do worry," said Mrs. Mahoney, fondly. "All this daredevil business."

"Do *not* mention what you've been doing this week," I said, reading my husband's mind.

"Jumping out of aeroplanes," said Charles. "They let us desk boys have a go."

Mrs. Mahoney looked as if she was going to faint.

"I'd love to have a crack at that," said Harold.

"Harold Thomas, you'll do no such thing." Bunty and the others had appeared.

"DON'T LOOK," shrieked Margaret. "IT'S A SURPRISE."

I hurled myself at Bunts only marginally less hysterically.

"Shut your eyes and face the other way," I ordered. "That's it." I turned her round just in time to see Stanley come skipping around the side of the house.

"Have you heard?" he was shouting. "They've just said on the radio."

"Heard what?" someone asked.

"It's Paris," said Stan. "The Germans have surrendered and Paris has been liberated!"

It was the most wonderful news we'd all been hoping for. Everyone broke into a huge cheer.

"This," said Harold, "is going to be a *very* good weekend."

CHAPTER 6

Will You, Marigold?

It was the afternoon of the wedding, and Jack had arrived at Dower Cottage to take the bride to the church.

"Bunts, old girl," he was saying. "I know Harold's a smashing chap and a war hero and all that, but if things have secretly gone on the wonk and you're having second thoughts, just say the word and I'll step in. Swift as a whippet, I'm your man."

Margaret gasped as my brother looked at Bunty with the face of a man entirely confident that he hadn't a chance.

"Thanks, love," said Bunty, equally robust. "That's awfully good of you. It's just I do still like Harold very much." She glanced over at the antique clock on the living room mantelpiece. "And what with the church being booked for three o'clock . . ."

"It would be a shame to change your mind now," I finished for her.

"Quite," agreed Bunty, smiling widely. "But thanks for offering." She turned to Marg, who was agog. "Don't worry Marg, he's joshing. Harold's quite safe."

"It's always good to have a backup though," said Jack, sagely. "Handy hint."

Marg giggled. This was conclusive evidence that Jack was not only tall and clearly miles better than any of the idiotic boys at school, but now also thrilling and mad.

"Had my chance," he explained. "Muffed it."

Now Bunty laughed out loud. "You've never had a chance," she said. "I'm practically your sister." She gave him a big hug. "Thank you for being here," she said. "It wouldn't be the same without you. And thanks for the car too, even if it does mean you'll get court-martialled."

"Well worth it," said a man's voice. "It's a beauty. May I come in?"

Guy was standing in the doorway. Normally vaguely ruffled in a non-conformist sort of a way, today he was immaculate in a perfectly cut blue three-piece suit, his hair swept back out of his eyes.

"Gosh, you look nice," said Bunty.

"I hope it will do," said Guy. He walked into the room and went over to her, where he paused for a moment. "Bunty," he said, softly, "you're exquisite."

"Oh, Guy, you'll make me cry," said Bunty, giving him a kiss. "Thank you."

It was already too late for me. Jack and I exchanged looks and he surreptitiously handed me a hankie from his pocket. He was dewy-eyed himself.

Guy was right. Bunty was beautiful. I had managed to make her wedding dress out of her mother's bridal gown, which Mrs. Tavistock had kept carefully stored away for many years. It was full length silk and lace. Monica had suggested a pattern from *Vogue* which had worked to perfection. With long sleeves, peter pan collar, and the smallest of nipped-in waists, my best friend could have graced the pages of the magazine itself. More than that, she was a picture of serenity, a young woman absolutely safe in the knowledge she was marrying the best chap in the world.

"And may I congratulate you on your choice of bridesmaids," said Guy, saving the day before everyone melted into tears. "Very lovely, indeed."

"I'm the Chief Bridesmaid, and Emmy is Matron of Honour," said Marg. "It's because she's married. Not like a matron in a school or anything."

"That's a relief," said Jack.

"Cod liver oil all round," said Bunts and the two of them pulled faces at each other.

"There's some in the pantry," I said. "So, everyone had better behave. And no faces in church, either of you. Goodness, I sound like Mother. Now, are we all ready? Last minute inspection. Guy, very handsome. Margaret Jenkins, entirely gorgeous."

Marg smiled and, now all shy, looked at her shoes.

"Can you tell me if my tie is straight?" asked Jack, crouching down so Margaret could see. "I don't trust the others to say."

Marg studied his tie as if she had been hypnotised, then nodded, earnestly.

"Thank you," said Jack. He gave her the thumbs up, which she returned.

With everyone admiring each other while denying that they themselves looked anything other than an absolute wreck, we were all going in delightful circles when we were interrupted by a loud knock on the window. It was Stanley and George who were standing in the flower bed, George now pointing at his wristwatch and Stan dramatically miming a clock with his arms.

"Loads of time," said Guy. He went over to the window and opened it. "Don't panic, boys, we're leaving in just a minute. Shouldn't you be at the church?"

"Major Mayhew has been held up delivering Mrs. Tavistock," said George, making it sound as if Bunty's granny was a parcel stuck at the post office without the right stamp. "He said to hold fast, and he'll be back as soon as he can."

At that point Charles appeared behind the boys, slightly red faced and a little out of breath.

"Mrs. Tavistock is in place," he said, "and I've just broken the four-minute mile. Now we need to track down the groom. Anyone know where he's gone?"

Margaret's eyes became the size of dustbin lids. My husband was as bad as my brother.

"I despair," said Bunty. "Don't worry, Marg, it's fine. Thank goodness Guy is here, because the rest of you are dreadful."

"We said Bunty wouldn't fall for it," said Stanley.

Charles laughed. "Oh, all right then. Worth a go." He paused and then said, "Ladies, may I say that you look simply lovely. Bunty, Harold's going to keel over when he sees you. We'd better go and warn him in advance. Come on boys, as Harold's Best Men you're currently in dereliction of duty so we're going to have to sprint." Then he gave me the most dashing smile and belted off with the boys.

"See you at the church," I answered. As if my heart wasn't already full enough, Charles had just finished the job. I had very nearly missed our own wedding service, almost having to run up the aisle. The fact that Charles was here at all was nothing short of a joy. A year ago, I could only dream of him being home. Now, it was beginning to feel that we really were married. Soppy though it was, I couldn't wait to stand beside him in church today.

Bunty drew a deep breath.

"Right then," she said. "Marg, Em, Jack, I'm counting on you to make sure I get there in one piece. I have to not fall over, get anything on my frock, or start crying before the service has even started. Do you think you're up for the job?"

"Yes, Bunty, you can count on us," said Marg. Jack gave her a small salute.

"In that case, I'll be fine," said Bunts, with all the confidence in the world. "Now then, Guy Collins, how about you? Are you ready to give me away?"

"It will be my honour," replied Guy.

Of that, I had no doubt. Guy had been thunderstruck when Bunty asked him several weeks ago, but she had assured him that he was the only man she could possibly want for the job. Bunty's father had died when she was tiny, and even though there were other men she had known longer than Guy, he was the one who meant the most to her. Certainly, no one could have done more to help in Bunty's true hour of need.

In nineteen forty-one, when the German bombers had tried to do their worst in a terrible air raid, it had been Guy who forced his way through the chaos and confusion so that he and I could search for her. It was Guy who knelt with me in the rubble trying to dig Bunty out, and when the news came that Bill, her fiancé, had died, even though Guy hardly really knew Bunty then, he seemed to understand what she was going through better than anyone else. And when two years later, Bunty and I faced the nightmare of trying to make up for the loss of Thelma, Guy hardly left our sides. He was my brother-in-law, but as far as Bunty was concerned, he was just as much family to her.

Before all the excitement over the wedding preparations had started, Bunty and I had talked about Bill. Although I knew she was very much in love with Harold, the day would not be entirely without sadness. William had been killed just two weeks before they were due to marry. Everyone, including Harold, would understand if she wanted a smaller, swifter affair. But Bunty had thought about it and decided that having a proper celebration was very much the right thing to do. Harold had been through his own personal nightmare when a bomb had exploded before he and his team were able to defuse it. Neither he nor Bunty had thought they would ever get a chance to find a love like this. Bunty hoped Bill would understand. I told her I felt strongly that he would.

Now, I carefully helped Bunty arrange her veil and then Guy offered her his arm, and with Marg leading the procession, together they headed out of the door.

Jack and I hung back for a moment. For all the larking around, Bunty meant the world to him. There had been times after that air raid when neither of us had thought we would ever see her happy again.

"She's going to be all right," I said. "Much more than all right."

"I know," replied Jack, a catch in his voice. "Thank God. Harold's a terrific bloke. They both deserve this. Now we all just need to get to the end of this bloody war."

He smiled, but his blue eyes were thoughtful, and he looked so much older than his twenty-four years. Sometimes I worried more about him than any of us.

"We will," I said, taking his hand. "Come on. Or Marg will start to pine."

The church was only a short drive from the cottage, but Jack had seen to it that the bride would arrive in style. Bunty carefully took her seat in the back of the gleaming blue Hillman, which had been polished to a fault. With Jack and Guy holding the wedding posies, Marg and I slid ourselves in by her side, taking the flowers as the men then slammed the doors and got into the front.

While almost all of Mrs. Tavistock's estate was now turned over to food production, the beds at the front of the cottage had been allowed to continue to bloom, and as Jack cajoled the car into starting at the second attempt, hundreds of flowers waved their heads from side to side in the gentle late-summer breeze. Bunty's wedding bouquet was a mass of pale pink dahlias, white cosmos, phlox, and of course, roses. Marg and I had little posies of the same, which sat prettily next to our pale blue re-commissioned frocks.

"Chocks away," called Jack as he put the car into gear, and we were off. "We'll take the pretty route so you can be a bit late," he added, swinging the car in the direction away from the church.

The circuitous ten-minute trip turned into a stream of memories of childhood derring-do's as Jack drove slowly around the village, past the two-roomed school, and stopping first outside the bakery, and then The White Horse as we recognised people we knew. It was a good job Bunty wasn't a nervy bride, as the entire pub emptied out and we rolled down the car windows so that everyone could wish her the greatest happiness.

With what felt like the best wishes of the whole of Hampshire, when we finally drew up to the church Bunty was just a few moments late.

Doors were opened and hands were held as the bride was helped out of the car, and it was time. Our little party stood at the door to the church as Bunty thanked Jack once again and bent to kiss Marg and tell her how pretty she looked. Then, having smoothed the skirt of her dress and brushed away a petal that had fallen from her bouquet, Bunty reached for my hand and for just a moment, we looked at each other. Neither of us said anything. We didn't have to, and anyway, where would we have started? A lifetime of friendship. Of hopes and dreams and sticking together through this awful, awful war. Both of us knew that today's wedding was happening against all possible odds.

With no thoughts for creasing her dress or squashing her bouquet, Bunty threw her arms around me, and we gave each other the tightest hug.

"Go on," I whispered. "Go and get him."

Bunty nodded and sniffed, and Guy very gently took his handkerchief to wipe a tear from her cheek. "Ready?" he asked.

"Yes," said Bunty. She took a deep breath. "Without a shadow of a doubt."

Inside the little church, the aisle was lined with sprays of wildflowers at the end of each pew, and as our small procession made its way up to meet the groom and his two very dapper best men, the scent was simply lovely.

When Harold turned to see Bunty, the look on his face was even more of a picture than I had imagined it might be.

"Gosh," I heard him say and then he broke into the biggest smile ever.

Everything was perfect.

Marg and I slipped into our seats next to Charles and my parents, who were beaming with happiness for the bride and groom. Our fathers had been in the first war together and they had known Bunty since before she was born. They also knew how much she deserved this. Out of the corner of my eye I saw my mother gently take hold of my father's hand.

Thirty minutes later, after some of the couple's favourite hymns, a lovely sermon, and almost everyone in tears during the vows, Bunty and Harold were married. The congregation followed the new Captain and Mrs. Thomas out of the church and into the sunshine, where it looked as if half the village had turned out to throw rose petals and give the couple a cheer. Monica, effortlessly elegant in pre-war Chanel that she referred to as "this old thing," herded people together and took photographs for posterity.

"What's the point of gadding about with news photographers if you can't wrestle a whole roll of film off them?" she said, looking the least likely person to have had to wrestle for anything.

With the serious part of the day done, now everyone could loosen their ties and relax, and I could say hello to all the guests properly. Roy and Fred were the first to stride over, full of cheer and declarations that London was boring and rubbish without us. Mrs. Harewood had come in a large hat that had proved a trial on the train, and I was thrilled to see our friends Anne and Betty along with Anne's children, six-year-old Ruby and Baby Tony, who was now a gigantic four.

"Hello, my lovely," I said to Ruby, giving her a hug.

"Don't tell anyone, Aunty Emmy, but that big boy's got a rat," replied Ruby, at the top of her voice.

I glanced over at Stan. During the service, I had noticed an odd scuffling noise from the direction of one of the best men, which I was fairly sure meant Stanley had brought along Monty, his recently acquired pet rat. In the spirit of the Lord God making all creatures great and small and therefore hopefully not minding, I had remained quiet.

"I think it's time for the sandwiches," I said, as I could see Miss Peters looking alarmed.

Best of all on the guest front was the fact that Hester's young man had been given twenty-four hours' leave from the army to attend. Bursting with pride, Hest brought him over to say hello.

"Miss Lake, Major Mayhew, you know Gunner Boone of course," she said, clearly feeling the need to formally introduce one of my favourite people in the world. Taller than ever, with the same gentle eyes and enthusiastic smile as when I had seen him last, Clarence Boone had swapped the uniform of the Launceston Press post room for that of the British Army. I remembered when we had first met, me a part-time junior at *Woman's Friend* and Clarence a very young fifteen-year-old who could hardly manage to speak to girls.

"Gunner Boone," I cried, as he saluted Charles and then gave me a small and very respectful bow. "Please say you'll still let me call you Clarence and that you're going to call me Emmy?"

"Oh yes," said Clarence. "If you're sure that's all right."

"Of course it is," I said, throwing caution to the wind and kissing him on his cheek. "Honestly, Clarence, you look wonderful in uniform, you really do. Please tell me everything about what you've been up to as I'm dying to know."

"It's all very small beer really, compared to what Major Mayhew does," said Clarence, glancing slightly nervously at Charles.

"Not all," said Charles. "Gunner Boone, the army only works because of the determination and courage of men like you. We're winning this war together. And anyway, I bet you've been doing far more interesting things than me as I'm now an old man stuck behind a desk."

Hest looked as if she would burst with pride. Encouraged, Clarence began to tell us all about his new role.

Soon it was time for a very happy procession to walk back to Rose House, Jack driving Mrs. Tavistock and Mr. and Mrs. Brand. Charles and I walked hand in hand alongside Hester, Clarence, and the children, together with my parents. Everyone was saying what a super chap Harold was and how the idyllic day was thoroughly deserved. Even when a trio of the RAF's finest flew over us as a reminder that there was no such thing as truly idyllic just yet, the promise of a slap-up tea and dancing in the garden meant spirits were high. The war could wait for one day at least.

At the house all the effort and preparation had done everyone proud. With the sheep lending us their lawn for the weekend, Mr. Brand's artwork panels provided a backdrop that turned the already quintessential English garden into something that by the early evening would take on an almost ethereal quality. The trestle tables were now covered with Mrs. Tavistock's best linen tablecloths and little posy vases were filled with flowers that echoed the bigger displays in the church.

The carefully saved rations and home-grown bounty provided more than enough cucumber, tomato, and even the thinnest ham for sandwiches. Cauliflower tartlets and tiny Cornish pasties lined up beside mini-cheese and potato pies. There were even scones with jam, and cream that came as a present from the farm. And of course, a wedding cake. Not the traditional fruitcake, but layers of Victoria sponge, filled with mock butter cream and strawberry jam.

With pear and raspberry wine flowing and an equal amount of sloe gin for those sturdy enough to take it, it was a carefree, drowsy party that raised toast after toast to the happy couple, to family and friends, and to the King. And then to the Allied advances in France, to the liberation of Paris, and to Victory, of course. That raised one of the biggest cheers of all. It wouldn't be long now.

The previous day, Harold and Mr. Newton had engineered a kind of loudspeaker system, which meant gramophone music could be played loudly in the garden, and after the wedding tea it took hardly any encouragement for everyone to take to the lawn to dance.

From slightly rusty folk dancing to dignified foxtrots and enthusiastic efforts at the hokey-cokey, everyone found something they liked. As the afternoon turned into evening, I stood for a moment on the terrace, happy to just watch as the people who meant the world to me could forget the world's troubles just for this night.

Roy was dancing like Gene Kelly with a delighted-looking Monica, while Fred was whirling Marg around and making her laugh. Hester and Clarence had eyes only for each in the way very young love always does, and Jack, who had gallantly danced with nearly every woman at the party including a captivated Margaret, was now talking to Mrs. Tavistock, who was patting his arm. I knew she would be telling him to take care. My parents were dancing as they loved to do, and Guy was driving Stan barmy by swearing blind he didn't know where Ruby was even though she was sitting on his shoulders, shrieking with excitement.

In the middle of it all were Bunty and Harold, he with his arm around her as she leant into his chest. He said something that made her laugh and look up at him, her eyes shining. Then Harold leaned down and they kissed, surrounded by love and in their own world at the same time.

I felt an arm around my waist as Charles came to stand with me.

"Happy?" he said quietly as I put my head on his shoulder.

"Utterly," I said. "I wish we could stay like this forever. Can you imagine?"

I felt him breathe in deeply.

"All the time," he said. Then he kissed my hair. "It won't be long now, my darling. We just need to keep going."

Someone put on Anne Shelton singing "A Nightingale Sang in Berkeley Square." It was one of our favourite songs.

"Shall we dance?" asked Charles.

"In a minute," I answered, softly. "I know this is silly, but if we don't move, it feels as if everything can stay entirely perfect. Just a few minutes more here."

Charles held me tighter.

"I love you, Emmy Lake," he said.

CHAPTER 7

A Request from the Ministry

The excitement and romance of the wedding lasted far longer than the day itself. Whether it was the flowers now on the breakfast table or the way that just when you thought we'd all re-lived every lovely moment, someone would remember a new snippet—the way someone had danced to a particular piece of music, or told a funny story nobody else had heard, or how someone from the village had thought that one of the cakes was particularly memorable. And in the way that all the best occasions end up, the stories became even better when they had been told several times. That was the thing about weddings. They were smashing on the day, but after all the re-telling and re-living, it was like getting the value out of it, again and again.

Best of all, it carried everyone through the reality of being back to the grindstone. It was now September and there was a definite feeling of the summer coming to an end. There were so many more signs than when we lived in London. The hedgerows were full of blackberries that now became a welcome element of every pudding Mrs. Whiteley made, while the start of work each morning was accompanied by the autumnal view of heavy dew outside on the lawn. The entire team ran to look out of the windows the first time we heard a flock of geese chatting to each other as they flew in formation over the house. It took Guy finding a six-hundred-page volume on the migration of birds to convince Stan that they had just travelled thousands of miles. He was used to pigeons that always stayed put.

Stan, Marg, and George had been enrolled at the local schools. The children had taken to the country like ducks to water, and while they missed their London friends, Bunty and I had decided that they should remain in Hampshire for the rest of the war. The national newspapers reported that during August, London had been bombarded with a hundred flying bombs every day, and the Government's Minister of Health had said that evacuated mothers and children should not return home. We were more than happy to comply, especially when Marg's old school friend and now pen pal, Ginger Belinda, wrote with a detailed description of her cousin's school after the playground had been destroyed. Bunts and I were grateful that George, Marg, and Stan had loved the summer and needed no persuasion to stay.

As far as the *Woman's Friend* team was concerned, no one had raised the question of leaving, either. We had always left it open, and for now at least, our team seemed to be content where they were. I knew that Mrs. Mahoney worried about her grandchildren, and Miss Peters sometimes fretted that her landlord was getting chummy with the temporary tenants in her flat, but otherwise things appeared fine. Hester even said she'd rather we never went back. She said now that she'd left home, she didn't want to go back to her mum's.

I could see her point. Hest had come on leaps and bounds over the summer. From being an organisational whizz during the move to Rose House to taking the children to the pictures or accompanying Mrs. Tavistock to church in the village, she had thrown herself into everything and, in doing so, had thrived.

"It's like having a younger version of you around the place," said Guy one evening over a game of draughts. Hester had just persuaded everyone to take part in a darts league and had now gone to bed armed with a pile of fashion magazines as she said she wanted to be able to help Monica more.

"Is that a compliment?" I asked him. "You once told me I was exhausting."

"Yes, it is, and yes, you still are," said Guy with a smile. "But it means life is never dull."

He was right there, not least as the *Woman's Friend* workload was fast becoming almost unmanageable. Over the summer we had been lucky to have extra help when Mrs. Newton and Mrs. Brand said they couldn't possibly sit around doing nothing while we were all working so hard. They asked if it might be all right if they did some filing or letter opening, or helping out Monica who was still horribly short staffed.

Then it turned out that Mrs. Newton was quick as a flash on the typewriter and Mrs. Brand had read maths at Cambridge even if in her day they hadn't allowed women to be awarded degrees.

"I may be slightly rusty," said Mrs. Brand, before promptly sorting out the company's first year's accounts in just over an hour.

I wondered if we could persuade them to stay on if we went back to London. There was certainly plenty of work for us all.

Mr. Langley's requirements, or "Dickie's Christmas List" as Monica wrote at the top, was copied out in triplicate and pinned to the temporary noticeboards that were rigged up by our desks. I had been travelling around the country interviewing women in the services and factories for several years, but since our meeting I had been dashing about even more. My diary was a juggle between hitting the problem page's copy deadlines, catching trains to places I couldn't disclose, and frantically writing articles on the way home for Hester to type up as fast as she could.

From promoting child inoculations to vegetable pickling or avoiding VD, there was no subject that was either too mundane or too personal for the Ministry to promote. Every section of *Woman's Friend* had to pull its weight to support the big push to the end of the war. Guy even wrote one of the weekly romance stories about a shy but conscientious girl who signed up to clean the wards in a sanatorium. She ended up being proposed to by a young wounded officer who was so terrifically attractive Mrs. Shaw said that if it were her, she'd have shot him in his good leg just to make sure he wasn't sent back to the front.

"Is it too unbelievable?" asked Guy. "I can do some edits if so."

"Don't you touch a word," said Mrs. Shaw, forgetting herself but speaking for us all.

"This is an odd way of doing one's bit for national morale," mused Guy.

"It's a good way," I said, firmly.

I was serious. We asked so much of our readers, the least we could do was to provide some entertainment at the same time. It was a definite juggle, but we kept trying. Monica was on a particular mission, and when an enthusiastic Mrs. Newton volunteered for the job of testing readers' recipes for home-made beauty preparations, we all became familiar with handwritten notices warning bathroom users to beware. At one point the entire first floor of the house smelt of a rather terrifying bleach preparation submitted by a reader who claimed it helped with dark circles under her eyes.

"Mrs. Newton, I think we might leave that one out," said Monica. "I'm worried we'll blind someone, starting with one of the staff."

In the end Bunty suggested using one of the sheds as a beauty laboratory just in case something blew up.

The eagerness was indicative of everyone wanting to play their part, whether on *Woman's Friend* or in general. The children loved helping Mrs. Tavistock's estate manager with the animals and on the land, and as all spare hands were gratefully welcome during the harvest, the staff had been mucking in as well when they could.

One Wednesday afternoon, Hester and I were sitting in the nook in the library trying to prioritise a very large pile of work.

"Fire away," I said. "I have a horrible feeling I'm behind on everything."

"Honestly, it's not that bad," said Hest, with enviable confidence. "First off, 'Yours Cheerfully.' The next two issues are fine, but Mrs. Mahoney says we're short on room in the one after that as Eno's Fruit Salts have taken a half page. So, you either need to do shorter answers or we can print fewer problems."

"Is it just that week?" I asked.

Hest shook her head. "Mr. Newton has agreed they can alternate with Fairy Soap for six weeks."

"Right-oh," I said, "leave it with me."

"Thank you. Next is, 'Women's War Work.' I've put three more interviews into your diary. The laundry workers, the military hospital in London, and the rubber dinghy girls. And we've had lots of letters about your piece on the orderlies at the Air Evacuation Centre." She handed me quite a bundle. "They're lovely, especially from readers whose boys have been sent home. One says her son has never flown before, but she feels a bit better about the transport plane now she knows how kind the girls are. Isn't that nice of her to write?"

"Thanks, Hest," I said. "Yes, it very much is. I'll read them properly tonight and write back then. It'll give me something jolly to do while I sit all sad and lonely by the phone, hoping Charles will call." I put the back of my hand to my forehead and gave a melodramatic sigh.

"Have you not heard from him?" said Hest.

"Not for days. He was lucky to get leave to come to the wedding but since then he's said not to expect much from him as they're all working flat out. I can't complain. He was here for two entire days and nights. Your Clarence only had twenty-four hours."

Hester beamed as she always did when I called him "Your" Clarence. She had been chuffed to bits that his appearance had been one of the highlights of the day. Almost all the staff knew and loved Clarence from the Launceston Press days, and to see him in his uniform, arm in arm with Hester both proud as punch, had melted everyone's hearts.

Monica had insisted on using precious film to take photographs of the young couple, one of which was now in a frame by Hester's bed. The other, of Hest and Clarence together with Charles and me, was pinned up in pride of place on a noticeboard in the office.

"Clarence said thank you again for asking if he could stay with Mrs. Whiteley," said Hester for at least the twentieth time. "He's still going on about the breakfast. She gave him a real poached egg."

"I hope he thanked her chickens," I laughed. "I'm sure she'll have him again when he visits."

"He's not allowed leave at the moment," she said, in a small voice.

"Then we're in this together," I replied, gaily. "We can start our own club. The 'We Won't Care, We Know They're Still There' club. We can have meetings and go to the cinema, ping-pong, day trips, you name it. It'll be great fun. What do you say?"

Hest smiled and was about to answer when Monica walked in.

"Sorry to interrupt, ladies," she said. "Emmy, Richard Langley's on the phone. Might he have a word?"

"Of course," I said, jumping up. "Excuse me, Hester, I'll be straight back."

I raced over to Monica's desk and picked up the receiver.

"Good afternoon, Mr. Langley, it's Miss Lake speaking," I said.

"Good afternoon. I trust all is well with you." He sounded most chipper. "A couple of things. First, well done on the articles. Spot on, and a note from the ladies in Censorship who say your work is always clean as a whistle, which is much appreciated."

"Thank you," I replied. "That's very kind."

"It's very true," said Langley. "Now, the other is your piece on the RAF Transport Station—the evacuation centre. Your report has gone down very well here, and we would like something more from you."

"Of course," I said. "I've just been discussing the upcoming sanatorium workers interviews."

"That's fine," he interrupted. "Actually, there's been a slight change of plan. We'd like you to report from another hospital. How are you fixed for next week?"

I was used to requests changing, so there was no need to flap.

"I'm sure I can be available. Am I allowed to ask where it is?"

"Yes," said Mr. Langley. "We want to send you to Belgium."

———

Our Ministry man spoke for some further time, during which I wrote hurried notes in shorthand while not quite believing my ears.

I was to join a flight to an aerodrome just outside the newly liberated Brussels, at which point I would be taken to where a new base hospital was being set up. I would meet and interview the British servicewomen working there, from nurses and NAAFI workers to drivers.

I hardly knew what to say.

"We want to show your readers how their efforts over here are enabling us to win the war over there," he said. "You can tell the women working in factories that you've seen what they've produced in action, with your own eyes. If you can come into Senate House tomorrow, you can pick up your accreditations and I'll give you more details then. You'll need to sort out your uniform while you're up in town, too," he added.

"Uniform?"

"It's compulsory. You're an official war correspondent now, Miss Lake," Langley replied.

I said, "Right-ho," as if this were all perfectly normal and agreed a time to meet at his office. Then I thanked him profusely, and we both said goodbye.

An official war correspondent.

I had written it down, not in shorthand, but in standard script, and now there it was, bold as brass. Ever since the war started, it had been my dream. It was why I had applied for an office junior job at Launceston Press in the first place, not realising the position was at their women's magazine. And now here I was.

"Everything all right, Emmy?" asked Monica.

"Did he tell you?" I managed.

Monica smiled. "Yes, he did. He wanted to check we'd be happy letting you go. Guy said he didn't think a double-decker bus could stop you, let alone us." She marched over and, as I rather slowly got to my feet, gave me a huge hug. "Congratulations. Did he tell you that no one else has been asked? None of the other magazines. And don't for a moment think this is preferential treatment. He says you're the best writer he knows."

"What's happened?" asked Hester, who had been patiently waiting for my return.

"I'm going to Belgium," I said. "Next week."

Within seconds the entire office was in uproar, with questions coming thick and fast. When exactly was I going? Would I get to go in a Dakota? How long would the flight be? Where would I be staying? How long would I be there? Would I be allowed to speak to the Belgians? What would my uniform be? Were they sure it really was safe?

"It's so exciting," said Bunty. "A proper war correspondent. Emmy, I'm so proud of you. It's what you always wanted to do and now you are. Charles is going to burst with pride. Can we phone him now? Are you allowed to during the day? It almost counts as military information. We could call his commanding officer."

"I don't think the CO would be very impressed," I said. "They're probably planning actual battles while I'm just going to talk to people for a few days."

It was lovely that everyone was so thrilled, but I didn't want to come across as The Big I Am.

"Well, I agree with Bunty," said Guy. "Charles will be thrilled, just as we are. You'll be carrying the flag for us all."

"I'll work through the weekend to get ahead before I go. On my own," I added, firmly. "You all do enough."

"We'll see about that," said Monica. "First off, tell me the uniform brief. I have it on good authority they're impossible to get hold of, so let me start making some calls."

"Thank you," I said.

How are you fixed for next week? We want to send you to Belgium.

Richard Langley had listened. He couldn't send me to the front line, but he was getting me to Brussels just weeks after it had "belonged" to the Nazis. Or so they had thought. As the buzz of excited chatter continued around me, Mr. Langley's call began to properly sink in.

Emmy Lake, Official War Correspondent. A schoolgirl's dream was about to come true.

CHAPTER 8

A Smashing Rig Out

Monica was as good as her word, speaking to her tailoring contacts to find out where I might find the necessary garb. As she had feared, stocks of everything were low, but she was able to produce a list of those shops most likely to be able to kit me out. In the meantime, I had a ton of *Woman's Friend* work to do before I collected my instructions from Richard and swotted up on the women I was to meet.

Before anything else though, I had some calls of my own to make. That evening, I tracked Charles down at his quarters.

"Darling, I am so very proud. Bloody well done," he said down the phone. "And well done the old Ministry for being clever enough to send you. Marvellous news."

Charles had always understood how important my career was to me. He didn't see women's magazines as just a silliness, and he had never minded that I had kept my maiden name for work. Not many men were like that. But Charles was modern and didn't think career girls were sad or suspicious or trying to take men's jobs, unlike far too many of the husbands that readers wrote to me about.

"I wish I could see you before you go," said Charles. "Dammit. I'll see if there's any way I can get out of here, even just for a few hours."

"That would be lovely, but I do understand," I replied. "I know you have a lot on your plate." The truth was that I would have loved to have seen him, especially once I was all togged up in my uniform, but I'd been spoilt by having Charles for a whole weekend at the wedding and there was, after all, a war on. It was no time to be a demanding spouse. "I'll get Monica to take a picture so you can see me looking important. Holding a notebook. Investigative yet thoughtful, that sort of thing."

"Chewing a pencil?" asked Charles, joining in.

"Definitely."

"Excellent," said Charles. "I shall carry it at all times and show off my brilliant wife to everyone I meet. They'll secretly call me obnoxious, and I won't give a fig."

"That's the spirit," I said. "We'll talk again before I go of course. I need to get handy hints on how not to be sick on the plane."

"Jack's probably your man for that," said Charles, "but I'll do my best." Then he paused. "God, I would love to see you."

"Me too," I replied. He sounded terribly serious. "Darling, I hope you're not worried. I'm only going for a few days. I'll be back boring you to death with it all before you know it. Now I'd better call my parents. Mother is going to go crackers with excitement. In fact, if I tell her where the aerodrome is, I've a feeling she'll probably try to come too. Don't tell her if she tries to interrogate you."

"Your secret is safe with me," said Charles, being chipper again. "Em, I really am awfully proud of you. And I could not love you more."

"I love you too," I said. "To an embarrassing degree. Just in case I haven't made that clear. Shall we speak again after I've told Mother?"

"Yes," said Charles. "Let's speak as much as we possibly can."

But when I phoned him back later, I was told he had been called into a meeting and would not be able to talk.

———

At eleven o'clock the next day I was sitting opposite Richard Langley in his very ship-shape office at the Ministry of Information. In front of me was a pile of papers, all vital parts of the jigsaw that would get me out of the country and into Europe.

"And here's your accreditation," he said. "Once you get to Brussels, you'll need to show it to get your accommodation slip. I can't tell you where or what that will be, as everything's being requisitioned as I speak, but first reports suggest you'll be fine. We're taking on buildings the Germans have been using so you can assume they're decent. I'm sure the Nazis were not prepared to slum it." The contempt in his tone was obvious.

"I'm very happy anywhere," I replied.

"Good approach. And finally, these are your official orders. Don't lose them. They're the ones that mean if you're captured you'll get prisoner-of-war status, and they'll have to treat you all right." Now he smiled. "I don't think there's much to worry about. You'll be in the thick of the women's services and not in danger. Guy would have my guts for garters if anything happened to you."

I knew he was joking about Guy, but I didn't want anyone to think I needed wrapping in cotton wool.

"That's very kind," I said, "but if I was a soldier and fighting, he'd have to put up with it the same as everyone else. Just as he does with Charles."

Langley smiled. "Point taken. Now, feel free to ask all the questions you want. I think you know the sort of coverage we need. Upbeat, encouraging, positive. And most of all, reassuring to everyone back home. You'll find people there will want to grill you about everything in dear old Blighty. You'll probably come home with more pen pals than you can keep up with."

"That's all right, I'm good at letters," I replied.

"Indeed. I must say, your office is quite something. The village post office must be exhausted."

"They're being very decent about it. You must come and visit us again, if I'm allowed to say that on Government property."

Mr. Langley laughed. "I'd love to. I enjoyed my visit immensely. And contrary to popular belief, we are allowed personal lives. That's if Guy and Monica are happy for me to elbow in."

"Oh yes," I said. "It was their idea. Guy says he's found a particular Beethoven on 78 conducted by someone I've never heard of, but he says you'll know them."

"I wouldn't bank on it," said Langley, breezily.

I had decided that I liked Richard Langley. He was modest in his bearing, and, while he spoke in the usual careful Ministry way that meant you always wondered if he knew more about things than he let on, he was approachable and, out of hours at least, good fun.

As we finished the meeting and I carefully put the documents into my bag, I thanked him again and assured him I would do the best job I could. Then, clutching my bag to my chest as if it held my entire career in it, which in a way it did, I left the labyrinthian corridors of Senate House and, now on strict instructions from Monica, headed to Oxford Street and Austin Reed.

Several hours later, I was the proud owner of an almost identifiable, if hotch-potch, uniform of a member of the Auxiliary Territorial Service. Monica had been right. Uniforms, even from private tailors, were extremely hard to find. Half of mine would have fitted an all-in wrestler with very long arms. But it was nothing that two evenings of re-pinning, re-cutting, and re-sewing couldn't sort out. By Saturday my friends and colleagues declared that I looked the part.

"Chin up, eyes towards me," ordered Monica, adjusting her tripod as I stood outside the house for my War Correspondent photograph. "Got it. Now, everyone else to positions please. Thank you. Is Mr. Whiteley here? Good."

We had decided to use the occasion and still-decent weather to have an official picture taken of the *Woman's Friend* Wartime Team,

Rose House Division. From the regular members of staff and our temporary helpers to the children, Mrs. Whiteley, and Mrs. Tavistock herself, we stood outside the front entrance of the house as Mr. Whiteley recorded our summer in the country for posterity.

For a moment I thought of how things were likely to change after the war. Very much for the better, of course, but I wondered if there would be things that I would miss. It seemed almost boorish to think it. There was nothing good about war in itself. But the people around me that I had met because of it had become a cherished part of my life.

I looked down at Margaret, who was standing between Bunty and me. Marg's heart's desire was to become a nurse, and she was proudly wearing her Junior Red Cross uniform for the photograph. The boys were also appropriately turned out: George in his Army Cadet uniform and Stan standing tall in his position as a Cub.

The three of them had all been so good about everything. They'd lost their mum, their dad had been away for over three years, and then when the buzz bombs in Pimlico killed and hurt countless people who they all knew, they were put on a train and expected to start a new life in the country. Undoubtedly, compared with the vast majority of evacuees, in terms of where they had moved to, they had been extremely lucky. Being surrounded by people they knew who would keep them safe while they were allowed to gallop around acres of their own country estate was by anyone's standards a dream. But my goodness, they'd earned it. There wasn't a person among us who didn't wish more than anything that they could have carried on their previous life with their mum. Every night I prayed that Arthur, their dad, would come home safely.

I put my arm around Marg's shoulders. If you asked me what the best thing had been in the past four years, I was more than grateful to have a long list. Meeting Charles was definitely at the top. But the children also meant more to me than the world. I would not sleep well until Arthur was back.

The photographs now done, Bunty clapped her hands together and announced glasses of elderberry cordial all round.

"You do look smashing in this rig out," she said as we walked inside. "Charles will go mad for you in that."

I sighed. "That's a nice thought," I said. "I suppose he'll have the photograph."

"It's such a shame he can't sneak out," said Bunty. "In the middle of the night, like in the films."

"We're not in the films," I said, firmly.

Bunty was not in a mind to give up.

"Why don't you go and see him?" she asked.

"Because I wouldn't be allowed in," I replied. "And he isn't allowed out. He's in operational meetings day and night anyway."

Bunty snorted. "You're being terribly defeatist for a top-flight investigative war correspondent. I remember the days when you would talk your way into an armaments factory as a matter of course."

This was true. Even if I had ended up getting thrown out. And I really did want to see Charles. I thought for a moment more. Then I smiled at my friend.

"Bugger it," I said. "Why not? When's the next bus?"

CHAPTER 9

A Highly Irregular Visit

It took two buses, two trains, and then several miles on foot.

But by early evening, I was standing in a telephone box in a picturesque village somewhere in Wiltshire.

"Hello, love," I said, when Charles came to the phone.

"Hello, darling. You sound funny. Are you in a telephone box?"

"Yes. Are you anywhere near . . . hang on." I opened the door slightly and looked around. "A pub with a red door?"

"Em, you've just phoned me. You know where I am."

"Well, I'm near there. It's a white building by a stream. I'm dressed as a war correspondent."

My husband was very bright, but it was taking a while to sink in. Finally, the penny dropped, and he started to laugh.

"You're near The Coach and Horses?" he managed. "Are you on your own? It must have taken you hours."

"Yes, I am. I thought you might want to see me in my service glad rags. I can just say hello at the gates and then leave. Although I do have Monica's camera with me as I thought it would be rather nice if we could find someone who might take a snap. If that sort of thing's allowed. But I'm not sure where you are."

"Well, this is my kind of turn up," said Charles, sounding extremely cheerful. "Don't move. I'm on my way."

Ten minutes later, a motorcycle roared up to the phone box.

"Good evening, Major," I said as he sprang off it. "Should I salute?"

Apparently not.

"Gosh," I said, a few moments later. "I hope you don't greet all the new recruits like that."

"You, Miss Lake," said Charles, his arms still very tightly around me, "are a lunatic. Adorable, but a lunatic."

"What do you think of the kit?" I asked, adjusting my cap. "Do you think they'll let me in?"

"Belgium or our security chaps?" he said, grinning widely. "I should of course mention that this is a vitally important military establishment protected by highly trained personnel, so as a member of the press you shouldn't be allowed anywhere near, but we'll worry about that when we get there. Up for it? Come on then, hop on."

I crammed my cap down onto my head and climbed onto the bike behind Charles before we roared off back up the road. This was tons better than sitting on the bus.

"Don't mention the journalism," Charles whispered, as he stopped the motorcycle at the guard house. "It won't help. Just show them your basic identity papers. You're here as my wife."

Now it was proper salutes and serious voices. I stayed by the bike under the watchful stare of a guard as Charles went inside and a phone call was made. I could hear him say, "Thank you, sir. No, not a thing. Yes, sir, I will. Thank you." It sounded as if he was speaking with someone high up.

Charles gave nothing away, but as he had clearly been given the OK, the gates were opened, and we were allowed through, riding on up to an impressive red-brick building that would have dwarfed Rose House. Leaving the motorcycle outside, Charles took my hand and led me towards the heavy doors.

"You won't get into trouble?" I asked, quietly. "I know this is highly irregular."

"This entire place is irregular," replied Charles. "But I'd argue seeing my wife at this point is more than acceptable. Come on in. After you, darling."

There was more security to go through, but this time it was straightforward, and we passed into an imposing reception hall, still with the trappings of an aristocratic hunting lodge. Crossed swords and stags' heads lined the walls, and the darkest red-brown mahogany furniture stood shoulder to shoulder with glass cabinets full of stuffed birds.

"This is what we use as the mess," said Charles. "You'll be OK here. Just don't go anywhere without me." He squeezed my hand and gave me a rather knee-buckling smile.

"I really didn't think I'd be allowed through the gates," I said as we began to climb the stairs. "It was Bunty's idea." I sounded as if we'd been caught scrumping.

"Tell her I owe her a drink," said Charles.

Charles' quarters consisted of a spacious room with an ancient wooden bed at one end and an occasional armchair next to a radiogram at the other. Heavy curtains had not yet been drawn across the latticed windows.

"Have you eaten? You must be starving. I can get someone to rustle up a cold supper for us if you want. Or we could just stay here. I have whisky. You're not thinking of going home tonight or anything awful like that, are you?"

This was turning out to be lots better than Bunty's plan to deliver a parcel and then leave.

"Absolutely not," I said. Charles poured two glasses of Scotch, while I sat down on the bed and bounced on it a bit. It was rock hard. "I'm so glad they've let me in."

"This is quite good for my reputation, actually," smiled Charles. "It's not every day a fellow's extremely gorgeous wife turns up at a high security army base."

He handed me my drink and sat down beside me as we clinked glasses, and then after a slug of the single malt we propped ourselves up on the pillows, lying where we could see out of the window. The sun was setting behind some towering oaks, and I was sure whoever had built the house had known exactly where the inhabitants would enjoy the most romantic view. Now, the corrugated iron of a long row of Nissen huts meant it wasn't quite so picturesque.

Neither of us cared.

As the whisky warmed the back of my throat, I regaled Charles with the full story of my week, from Richard's call to the meeting and the scramble for kit. Then I broke all security regulations and told him where I was going and who I was going to see. He had heard most of it on the phone but was happy to listen, laughing at the funny bits and asking questions about Monica's photography and how Stan was getting on in the Cubs.

Hours went by as we enjoyed the rarity of being alone together and hidden away. It was a thrill to be confined to barracks, but with the person you loved and wanted to be with more than anyone in the world.

"When the war's over, can we do this sort of thing all the time?" I asked, laying my head very comfortably on his chest.

Charles, who had been stroking my hair, stopped for a moment. "Mmm," he said.

"It might even be this Christmas," I said rather dreamily. "Imagine. Somewhere like this, only a hotel, with a tree and everything decorated, and there might be snow. That would be so lovely."

"Yes," said Charles.

I could feel his heart beating more quickly now.

"And even if the war isn't over, we could still go away if you can get leave. Do you realise it will be our first ever Christmas Day together? Oh, Charles, I can't wait."

When he didn't answer I twisted my face round to look at him. Even though it was now dark, and the room was only dimly lit, I could see his eyes shining. He didn't look back at me.

For a moment I waited, and then as a cold feeling began to creep up my spine, I pushed myself up and sat beside him, cross-legged as if I were a child. I had seen this look on his face too often.

When he took hold of my hand, I could hardly bear it.

"Darling, I'm being sent back," he said, now sitting up too. "There's a whole load of us going. I can't tell you anything about it. Em, I'm so sorry."

My heart crashed to the floor.

Down the hall, other officers were wishing each other goodnight as doors then slammed and somewhere a radiogram was switched on, no doubt for the news.

This was the part where I was to put on a brave face and say how it wouldn't be for long, and then come up with something plucky about it being perfectly all right and what with me going to Belguim, how we might even cross paths in the air. But this time I couldn't find it. I needed a moment more.

"Damn it," I said. "I thought you were going to be a boring old major stuck behind a desk." It didn't come out in the light-hearted way I had hoped.

"Not this time," said Charles. "But this *will* be the last time. I'm going to find something else after the war. Non-combat, at least."

It was the first time he'd ever said that, and I knew he wouldn't have if he didn't mean it.

"But you love it."

"I do. I did. But one last sortie will be enough. It's you I love, Em. And it's been a bloody long war."

Now I found the brave face, a deep breath, and then a smile, even though my eyes were full of tears. "You don't have to give this up for me. We'll talk about it when you come back."

Charles nodded, his eyes full of concern.

"I'm sorry to chuck this at you. We should be celebrating the news about your assignment. It's just I could go quite soon."

"Do you know when?"

"I don't know, or at least . . . Darling, I can't even tell you that. It's classified, especially with you going overseas. Not that anything's going to happen now they've been liberated, but it's better you don't know." I could tell he was struggling as much as I was. "But we may still get this Christmas together," he managed. "And if not, then the next one. Christmas '45. That's a promise."

We both hated this. It seemed to get worse each time.

"Deal," I agreed. Then I lifted my chin. "We'll do that. Christmas '45. Good. Right. So, thinking out loud." Now my voice was bordering on hearty. "I imagine you can't say, but will you still be here next week when I get back?"

"I was hoping I would be, but . . ." The slightest shake of his head.

"Then it's a good job you've sneaked me in, isn't it?" I moved closer to him, the smallest act of defiance in the face of having to say goodbye once again.

Even if Charles could have said anything more, I wasn't going to ask. Since the Normandy landings, for all the advances being made and the real hope that the war would soon end, everyone knew that the cost was appallingly high. My jaunty report from the evacuation transport station had been full of "splendid"s and "terrific"s and "our excellent girls." It had also left out almost everything I had seen of the wounded men being brought home.

"What time do you start work tomorrow?" I asked.

"Seven, I'm afraid," said Charles. He pushed a strand of hair away from my face.

"Well then," I said. "That gives us the whole of the night."

———

We got up very early the next day, both with the intention of being buoyant in the extreme. First off, I did my best to look respectable. I was Major Charles Mayhew's wife, and I was not going to slink out as if I had done something wrong. As we walked through the reception area, we met one of the junior officers, who looked somewhat shocked until Charles introduced me and explained my visit.

"I say, Mrs. Mayhew," said the lieutenant heartily. "I do admire your initiative. If I were in charge of the British Army, I should suggest we offer you a job. Don't you think, sir?"

Charles told him not to encourage me, but I grabbed the bull by the horns and said I'd only really come for a photograph with my husband, and might he be able to help?

"I'd be honoured," the young man replied. "I wish I'd thought of this myself. I may telephone my wife."

Now I knew that Charles was about to go back to Europe, I wondered if this was why the rules had been significantly bent. I was grateful, but the idea he had perhaps been allowed one last night with me made me shudder. Smiling for the camera, I pushed the thought to the back of my mind.

Then it was time to leave. Charles took me to the railway station, claiming it was just to ensure I had left the premises.

Saying goodbye was awful. It always was.

"Cheerio then, darling," I said, sticking to the accepted etiquette of sounding as if one of us was off to the shops. Then I veered off script. "Let's never say goodbye at a station again," I said to him, trying to keep my voice light. "After the war, let's only ever go near a train when we're jaunting off somewhere together. Shall we promise?"

"I promise," said Charles, holding me tightly. "I'll see you again soon."

"Yes, you will," I replied with absolute certainty. "And I promise too. Now, go and give those Nazis what for." And then, in the most determined voice I could muster, "Don't forget how much I love you."

"I won't. Ever. I love you too. My darling girl."

We kissed each other goodbye, and then he was gone.

CHAPTER 10

Emmeline Lake, War Correspondent

Four days later, Charles was already somewhere in Europe when, kitted out in my uniform, with pencils sharpened and notebooks ready to be filled, I set off for the aerodrome. A small rucksack held everything I thought I might need, while safely in my jacket pocket were two of my most prized possessions, a matching set of an art deco silver-plated notebook and a visiting-card case. Charles had given them to me on our wedding day. When I said they were so lovely I might be scared to use them for every day, he said that especially now when "every days" were often hard going, if something nice could bring cheer on that front, then all the more reason to make sure it was used.

Since then, they had come with me on every assignment I had done.

It was only a few weeks since I had last visited the RAF airfield out of which we would be flying, so that was a boost as I knew where to go, and so felt more of an old hand. Everything appeared just as it had on my previous visit, but as I showed my identification documents, I felt entirely different. Last time, it was an interesting, but not out-of-the-ordinary assignment. I knew what I was doing. Whether an evacuation centre, a visit to a timber operation in the middle of nowhere, or talking to war workers in the lunchtime canteen, my approach was the same. Arrive well prepared, put people at their ease, and then listen. Blend in, don't make a fuss, get on with it. For the next few days, I would be trying to do exactly that. Only this time I wouldn't just get to sit in an RAF Dakota. Now it was going to take off, and I would be flying into the unknown. I found myself taking deeper breaths than normal. I would be lying if I said I did not feel a certain amount of nerves.

"So, you're leaving us via the fast route today," said the woman in charge of administration, who I was pleased to recognise. "The girls were thrilled with your article about them. One of them cut it out and put it in a frame in the bunk room. It's nice to see them getting the recognition. We'll all be reading your next one." She gave me a friendly smile. "Good luck. We'll see you when you get back."

Ten minutes later, I was perched on a metal bench in a transport plane on the runway, talking with a group of servicemen and WAAF nurses. They were all used to travelling this way and they chatted as casually as if we were on the number twenty-four bus. I admitted I had never flown before, and when I explained that my task was to show what Britain's servicewomen were doing for our boys overseas, I was welcomed warmly. An affable Canadian Army officer insisted that I sit in the best position to see out of the window.

"Just tell me if you're going to throw up, and I'll make sure I duck out of your way," he said with a laugh, and then a thumbs up when I said I had brought my own paper bag.

Although Richard Langley had warned me that flights had been affected by fog that week, today we were lucky, and the sky was clear enough for me to have my first sight of what England looked like from the air. I must have been the thousandth person to remark that the fields looked just like patchwork as we took off. For the whole journey, it still didn't seem real that I was thousands of feet up in the air, especially when we flew over the English Channel.

Just as I was beginning to get used to the idea, the plane began its descent, finally landing with some bumps that made me hold my breath as I braced myself against the very new sensation. A short while later, once we had come to a halt, the plane door was opened. Following my fellow travellers, I hopped down the flip-out steps and for the first time in my life, stepped onto foreign ground.

"Well done, kid," said my Canadian friend with a warm smile. "Welcome to where it all happens. Take care of yourself."

I thanked him and wished him the same as I looked around, feeling a surge of excitement to be here. Less than two hours from Britain and I was actually in Europe, the place I had only ever seen in newsreels. It took longer to get from Pimlico to Rose House if the trains were having a bad day. Had I really been chatting with Hester just hours ago? It seemed a world away. I had always wanted to travel but had never thought it would happen during the war.

The aerodrome on this side of the Channel was even busier than the one at home, a Piccadilly Circus of Allied troops, vehicles, and activity. I was pleased to be able to report to my first contact and be directed to a staff car used for the press.

In the short journey to Brussels, my head constantly moved from side to side as I looked out of the car windows trying to see as much as I could, part journalist, part tourist, with a mental checklist of what looked different and what might be the same. The main road was very wide and straight and lined with trees that were tall and thin like lollipops, while burned-out vehicles littered the side of the road. A horse and cart loaded high with hay would not have looked out of place back home as it plodded along. Then an ancient village with cobbled streets and a bedsheet strung between windows on a terrace of houses with a painted-on message that read, "Bienvenue aux libérateurs." That was when it felt real.

As we made our way into the city, flags hung from beautiful buildings with grand windows and ornate balconies. Slowing down through a handsome square, I noticed two fashionably dressed women chatting outside a shop. Its windows were full of clothes that wouldn't possibly have been available at home. Richard Langley had told me that everything here would be enormously expensive, but anyway I doubted that I would have time to shop. As the women talked, a group of children spotted the staff car and waved enthusiastically. I smiled and waved back as a small, frail man in a dark cap trudged past them, not looking up.

Used to the bomb-damaged scars of London, I thought Brussels looked well. Or at least, the part that the Germans had decided to enjoy for themselves. I was not naive enough to think the same could be said for the people whose country and homes had been taken and whose lives had been irrevocably changed.

When the country had been liberated, the Germans had left fast. They had tried to burn down the Palais de Justice, but for the most part they had simply run for it.

The hotel that was to be my initial base was almost majestic, the sort of high-class affair that in peacetime Charles and I might have thought about staying in for a special occasion, before moving to more modest accommodation that was gentler on our purse strings. Perhaps one day I would return here with him. Now though, as I walked into the imposing foyer, I was part of the British military mechanism, my credentials at the ready and my heart thumping. My itinerary was packed, my mind focused on showing the readers back home what their fellow women were doing to help win the war, and most of all, help the British boys.

"We want them to see that our men are in the best possible hands," Langley had said. "We know the second front has meant significant losses for the public. We want you to show how women are softening the blows. And mention anything made in Britain. Your readers need to see the impact they're having."

I could have told him that.

I had time to throw my rucksack down on the bed in my small but very comfortable room on the fourth floor before dashing back downstairs to where I was introduced to two staff nurses from the Queen Alexandra's Imperial Military Nursing Service, who were to be my first interviewees. QAs Alice and Winnie had come to Brussels to set up the hospital directly from Normandy, where they had been stationed since the landings in June. They were decent sorts, a little younger than me, bright and attractive, and clearly very good friends.

On the first evening we sat together on high-backed chairs in a luxurious restaurant that was now being used as a canteen, a vast chandelier the size of a car hanging above our heads.

"Stick with us," said Alice, who was slim as a reed and a picture of elegance, even though still in her uniform. "We'll have you changing dressings and doing bed baths by the end of tomorrow."

"I think the men probably deserve better than that," I said. "I'm just a ham-fisted reporter."

"You'll be surprised," said Winnie, kindly, in her soft Edinburgh accent. "If you're cheerful and efficient it goes a very long way."

"And smile," said Alice, her expression serious. "I don't mean that in a silly way. It's awfully important. I'm assuming you're not squeamish, because if you really want to know what's going on you'll see some pretty roughed-up cases. But however badly wounded the patient is, you *must* not show how you feel. It's not fair on them and it's the one thing we'll be very firm on. Some of our men have already been through hell on earth and most of them have a very difficult time ahead. They don't need reminding of it."

Alice may have looked like someone out of a magazine, but you could tell she was made of stern stuff and was very protective about the men. I scribbled down notes as she and Winnie spoke, which they said they didn't mind, as long as I didn't write anything that might worry people at home.

"I'll be telling everyone that their boys are in the best hands," I said. "It will be a very great comfort to our readers. It's why I'm here."

"I'm glad," said Winnie, tucking a dark curl behind her ear. "One day, once we've won, I hope people will listen and know the truth, but at the moment, telling them the worst won't help anyone. We have to push on."

"It wouldn't get past the censors if I did," I said. "But I do want to make sure our readers get a proper idea of what you're doing. Setting up a completely new hospital is some feat."

"Oh now, stop," said Alice, holding up her hands. "You'll make us big-headed."

"And anyway, the hospital was here already," added Winifred. "When the Germans scarpered, they left everything. When we moved in the tea was almost still warm."

"What did you do?" I asked, my pencil in mid-air.

"Threw it in the sink," said Alice, deadpan.

I laughed a little. "I mean, how did that feel? To move in and just get on with things, knowing the enemy had been here, running everything?" I looked around me. "Sitting in these seats only a matter of days before you arrived?"

"Just getting on with it is what we do," said Winifred, calmly. "The boys turfed out the Germans, then we came in, disinfected the place, and started putting it to decent use." Then she smiled. "Although it does make a nice change to have a proper roof. I've had my fill of tents."

I had interviewed dozens of servicewomen over the last years, and I could safely say that none of them thought they were doing anything special. Alice and Win were in exactly the same vein.

"What made you become a nurse?" I asked.

"Well, I was all set up to do the season," said Alice. "Presented at Court and all that business. I was never expected to work. And then my brother joined the RAF, and I thought, if he's doing that, I should probably do something useful as well. I suppose I'll marry someone once this is all over, but I'm rather fearful it's going to be dull after this."

"We might get sent out to the Far East," said Winnie. "Or we'll stay on here after Victory. There's going to be an awfully big mess to clear up and a lot of people to look after."

"You don't want to go home?"

"It's not about that," said Alice. "We'll stick it out. You'll under-stand once you've seen the people we work with. The medics are remarkable. The things they can do now to patch up the boys are extraordinary. And the wounded men are some of the bravest you'll ever meet. I hope people will remember that when they go home. We should be awfully proud of them."

"We're awfully proud of *you*," I said.

"Don't be daft," said Win. "We're all doing our bit."

When I pressed them about their experiences on the Normandy beaches back in June, Winnie said you couldn't imagine how quiet it was. Hundreds of ships and not a soul saying a word, just waiting for the go ahead to get out. She and Alice had been two of the first nurses to set foot on the French sand.

"Some of the boys were surprised to see women in a bunker," said Alice. "I think it cheered them up."

"That and penicillin," said Win. "It's like magic. You'll see it on the wards tomorrow. In fact, we'd better turn in. You need to get your head down. It's a long day if you're not used to it."

I slept fitfully that night, excited about getting down to things, but I had to admit I was also disquieted by my surroundings. If walls could talk, I wondered what the fancy wallpapered ones of the hotel room would say. This grand old building had once welcomed monied Belgians, then been home to German fascists, and was now just briefly putting up a British woman in a cut-down uniform asking questions and writing the answers down for a magazine. I thought about Charles, wondering how near he might be. He hadn't been allowed to say where they were going, but Guy had hazarded some guesses. It didn't take a brainbox to see where our boys were now being sent. If Charles was part of the big push in Holland which had been all over the newspa-pers, he could be just an hour away from Brussels. I pulled the bed covers closer around me. I wished he were here now.

The next morning, I joined the two staff nurses as they showed me around the wards. They were all equally pristine, the long rows of beds fully occupied with not one free. When an orderly gave Alice a message, she excused herself and said she would see us shortly, so I followed Winnie as she set to work, taking patients' temperatures, checking dressings and administering medication, rearranging pillows and getting the men to sit up if they could. She asked each one how he was feeling and how their night had been, nodding in response or assuring them she would speak with the doctors if anything raised a concern. It was all done with a kind smile and an air of calm efficiency that would make anyone feel safe in her hands.

Win quietly explained to me how each patient had sustained his injuries and then introduced me to them as she went, although I had said that she must tell me if I was in the way or intruding.

"Don't worry, I will," said Win with a twinkle in her eye. "And if we see Matron, just stand up straight and wait to be spoken to."

But it seemed that I was not intruding. When the men were told I was from *Woman's Friend* magazine, if they were able, most were happy to chat, pleased, they said, that their wives and girlfriends and mums would get to know they were well looked after.

"Are you going to put our picture in then, miss?" asked one. "Because if you do, can you leave out all the nurses or my wife's going to think I'm just putting this on." He tried to wave a broken arm at me.

"If I do, I'll make sure it's a very fierce doctor holding a great big syringe," I replied.

"That's the ticket," he said. Then he gestured for me to come closer. "Don't tell them I told you, but our nurses are the best thing about this whole bloody war. Make sure people know that, won't you?"

I nodded. "I will, I promise."

"Don't believe a word Private Reynolds says," said Winnie, coming over. She gave him a tiny smile and looked at her watch. "We need to push on."

"Goodbye, Private Reynolds," I said. "Don't forget, you have my word." Then I followed Winnie out of the ward.

"Are you getting what you need?" she asked.

"Very much so," I answered.

"Good. I need to join Staff Nurse Evans," she said, referring to Alice formally. "She's on the critical ward. You're very welcome to come, but this is where you may need to brace up."

"Absolutely," I said. "I've been to several military hospitals back home, so I hope I'm not too lily-livered."

"Right you are. Sorry if it sounds as if we're trying to put the frighteners on you. We're quite protective of our lot."

Winnie led me to the critical ward, which had the same layout of sixteen beds, eight on each side. It was far quieter however, and only one or two of the men were sitting up or smoking. She introduced me to a corporal who she said was from near Southampton. He was keen to hear anything about life back in Hampshire, so we talked for a while as I told him about my summer.

"What I'd give for a pint in that pub," he said when I told him about The White Horse.

"It won't be long until you're back in your own local," I said. "You'll see."

The corporal began to tell me about the pub in his village when the ward doors opened and, led by Alice in a mask and gown, two orderlies wheeled in a patient on a trolley. He was covered from head to foot with spotlessly clean bandages. I excused myself from the corporal and joined Winnie.

"The patients with burns have saline baths," she explained, quietly as Alice settled him in. "They're very effective for recovery and pain management. Private Lorne was caught in a firebomb with the rest of his unit. He was the only one to get out. He has ninety percent burns and is one of the bravest boys here. He's not twenty yet."

"Oi, Lorney," the corporal called. "They've sent a pretty journalist who's looking for a scoop."

I looked at Winnie, who gave me a small nod.

"Hello, I'm Emmy," I said, going over to Private Lorne. "I don't know about pretty, but your pal's right about the scoop. I'm from a women's magazine and I want to know if your staff nurses are look-ing after you properly. I hope they're not gadding about or leading you all astray?"

Most of Private Lorne's face was covered, the rest swollen and raw, but I thought he gave a slight smile. "They say I'll be all right," he managed.

"I'm sure you will," I said, with conviction. "They really know their stuff. I hear this saline business is helpful?"

Private Lorne didn't answer that. "Will my girlfriend read this?"

"I hope so," I answered. "I'm from *Woman's Friend.* We do have quite a few readers."

"I don't want her to see my picture."

My smile didn't drop.

"There won't be any pictures," I said, gently. "But I could men-tion you if you want. She might see your name in print." This wasn't part of my brief whatsoever, but that was hardly the point.

"Can I ask you a question?" His voice was hardly more than a whisper.

"Of course," I said. "If chatting won't tire you out."

"Will she still care?"

I didn't know. Of course I didn't. But what I was sure of, was that everyone needed a reason to fight.

"I have absolutely no doubt that she will," I answered. "What's her name?"

"Dorothy."

"That's lovely. Like in *The Wizard of Oz.*" I paused for a second. "Do you know, Private Lorne, I run the problem page at the maga-zine, and in all the thousands of letters I read, the thing that the girls say the most is that they just want their boy home. So, I reckon, your Dorothy is probably hoping like mad that you're well enough to get on a plane as soon as possible. That's the main thing. That you con-centrate on getting better." I gave him the biggest smile I had. "For what it's worth, my husband is somewhere over here, and all I care about is that he comes back. It's all that matters."

The young man moved his head just slightly, I hoped perhaps in a nod, as Alice came over.

"I trust you're not exhausting my patients, Miss Lake," she said with a grin. I took the gentle hit.

"I'd better let you get some rest," I said to Private Lorne. "Bye for now. It's been lovely to meet you."

I went to take my leave, but then turned back.

"I'm Emmy Lake," I said again. "From *Woman's Friend*. If you ever feel like letting me know how you get on, please write to me. I'd love to know how you are. Good luck with getting home as soon as you can."

"Thank you," he said.

Alice walked beside me as we left.

"We'll make a nurse of you yet," she said, under her breath.

It was the biggest compliment I'd ever had.

CHAPTER 11

Immeasurable Bravery Required

The nurses had not exaggerated what many of the patients had been through. When a press photographer came to take photographs for the article, he was not invited to the critical ward. I understood his job, but I was also beginning to appreciate why Alice and Winnie felt so strongly about protecting their men.

The next morning, I had breakfast with Winnie and Alice in the canteen at the hotel and then we made our way back to the wards. They were going to introduce me to some orderlies before I moved on to meet the girls who drove ambulances with the First Aid Nursing Yeomanry.

"So, Emmy," said Winnie. "Do you fancy swapping magazines for nursing?"

"Actually, I can't wait to write about all of you," I replied. "And it won't be propaganda. I can tell everyone with my hand on my heart that no one could possibly take better care of our boys."

"Ahh, everyone's doing their best, whatever their job," said Win.

"Honestly, though," I said. "It matters such a lot. Everyone is so busy putting on a brave face, but we don't really know how the men are. At least now I can tell our readers that if something horrible happens, there are girls with them like you. They should take comfort from that."

"I hope so," said Alice. "It's a rough old time. Speaking of which, well done with Private Lorne yesterday. I thought you handled the question about his girl very well. It's always terribly hard to answer something like that."

"I hope she stands by him," I said. "He's not much older than a young friend of mine, Clarence. I hate the thought that if the war doesn't end soon, he could go through what Private Lorne is. Even though I know his girl will stick with him through thick and thin."

It was too awful to contemplate.

"Do you want to call in and say hello again?" asked Alice. "I think Private Lorne might like that. Then we'll send you off to the second floor for your next initiation."

"I'd love to," I said.

The three of us set off as Winnie filled me in on the women I was to meet next. But as we reached the critical ward, rather than the relative calm of the previous day, shouts of "Medic!" could be heard and the corporal I had met came limping out of the door.

"Nurse," he shouted when he saw Alice and Win. "Come quick. It's Lorney."

The staff nurses were already on their way. As I began to follow, Alice half turned and shook her head at me.

"Get Major Carrick," she ordered. Then she and Win disappeared with the corporal into the ward.

I had never moved so fast, running down the corridor to where I remembered the commanding officer was based. I was sure running was forbidden, a hunch that was quickly proven when I saw the sister coming from the opposite direction. The look on her face stopped me in my tracks.

"Pardon me, Sister," I managed. "Staff Nurse Evans has sent me for Major Carrick. There's an emergency."

The sister gave a curt nod and left me standing. Moments later, staff came from all directions. I did not follow them. I knew I would only be in the way. After a moment I retraced my steps until I was nearer the ward. I could hear the sound of the medical staff speaking but could not work out what was being said. A medic came out of the ward, shot off, and returned with some equipment in hand.

I had never felt so useless. I couldn't help. I could only write about it.

Ensuring I was well out of the way of the entrance to the ward, I took out my notebook and began. It was all I could think of to do. I wrote about the first shout I had heard, of the panic in the corporal's voice, of the look on Alice's face. I wrote down *Private Lorne* and underlined it. Then I stopped.

Writing was no use to anyone. Instead, now I prayed for him.

Minutes passed, each one taking forever. I hated every second.

But what on earth had I thought would happen at a military hospital in the middle of a war? That it was all friendly chats and promises of the pub?

Some war reporter I'd make. I wasn't even anywhere near the front. I thought back to the beginning of the war when I would imagine myself as a Lady War Correspondent, charging around London in an air raid, showing immeasurable bravery if required. Even then, I should have known better. There was nothing glamorous or exciting about any of this.

Finally, Winifred came out of the ward.

"Let's walk down here," she said, leading me away. "Emmy, I'm afraid we lost Private Lorne."

"Oh, Winnie," I said. "I am so sorry."

Win nodded. "That poor boy," she said, her voice flat. "It was always going to be a battle for him, but we wanted so much to give him a chance. We really did. At least Major Carrick can tell his family that we were all at his side. He wasn't alone." She stopped walking. "You won't write about this, will you?"

I shook my head. "No, of course not," I said. "But I'd like to write about you and Alice. Win, I know you play it down, and I understand. But you do an extraordinary job. I want people to know that." My voice shook a little as I spoke. "I'm sorry," I said. "I only spoke to Private Lorne for a few moments. I really should be more professional."

"Being professional doesn't mean you don't care," said Win. "You were kind to him yesterday. He even managed to smile. Remember that."

"I wish I could tell his mother what a smashing young man I thought he was," I said. "And Dorothy."

"I'll speak with Major Carrick," said Winnie. "I think it might be nice if you wrote to them too."

———

After I said goodbye to Alice and Win, I did what everyone did, which was to get on with my job. It would have been remiss to do anything else. We exchanged addresses and Winnie promised to be in touch as soon as she had asked the major about me writing to Private Lorne's mother.

I spent the following three days in Brussels as I had started. Notebook in hand, I watched, interviewed, and marvelled at the servicewomen, as well as the men they both worked with and helped. Each night I slept somewhere different, sitting up in whichever bed I had been given, reading through the day's notes, and frantically scribbling ideas for how I would organise them into articles for *Woman's Friend*. There was enough to fill the entire magazine for a month. I wrote to Charles, wishing I could pick up a telephone or get on a bus so that we could speak. I thought about Private Lorne too and wondered how many other young men Alice and Win had helped, doing everything they could, to give them a chance.

There was so much I wanted to say, to report back to the readers. How the women here were as committed and hard-working as all the girls back home. How it wasn't just propaganda—we really were all part of the same effort. You might be in a factory working night and day to churn out metal parts, but those parts could end up in an aeroplane that flew someone's husband to hospital. And at that hospital another woman would help him, using the medical instruments yet another might have engineered in another factory a hundred miles away. It was a jumble of connections, all of us trying to make this wretched war end.

When I climbed up the steps into the plane that would take me back to England, I knew that *that* was what I was going to write about in *Woman's Friend.*

I had been doing what I loved—talking to people, finding out about them, what they did, how they felt. My remit was to tell the stories of the women, but I wanted to include some of the men I had met, too. I knew the censors wouldn't let me mention Private Lorne, even if his family had wanted me to. But somehow, I would find a way to show how brave the boys like him were.

This time, the flight was full, with both walking wounded with whom I sat near the front and more serious cases stretchered onto the plane. One WAAF nurse was in charge of them all, spending the flight over the Channel checking on the most severely injured patients and graciously letting me chat to the boys who were well enough.

Some of them were in transit for evacuation and were facing extremely long journeys, in some cases, thousands of miles. At least for the British boys I could promise them that in just a couple of hours they would be back on home soil.

"You'll be reading the paper by the fire before you know it," I said. I was relentlessly upbeat. Being able to go home now seemed more precious than ever.

We arrived back at the RAF aerodrome by mid-morning, and as I took the bus to the nearest railway station, I looked out of the window at the recently ploughed fields and the trees that were on their way to the spectacular gold of autumn. I'd been gone for a matter of days, but I had visited another world entirely. Then I took out my notebook and continued to write, a sense of urgency now, to capture it before I returned to my friends.

The walk from the station to Rose House gave me a chance to quietly gather my thoughts. I knew how excited everyone would be to hear all about the trip, and equally, I was looking forward to seeing them too. I would tell them about Alice and Winnie. And I would tell them about Private Lorne, a brave young man who had given everything in this war. I would hold the memory of meeting him very carefully in my heart. A small place for a stranger I would not forget.

When I finally opened the front door to Rose House and walked into the office, within seconds I was surrounded by the whole team, who greeted me as if I had returned from a conquest. Any tiredness I felt after the whirlwind of the previous days disappeared as I took off my cap and put my rucksack down. I ran my hand through my hair.

"What was the plane like?"

"How was the food?"

"Did you look around Brussels?"

"Did you meet any Belgians?"

"Did you see any Germans?"

"Is it all run on the black market?"

"What were the girls like?"

"What were the men like?"

"How did they treat you?"

"Will they send you again?"

"One at a time," said Mrs. Mahoney assertively. "Let Emmy speak."

Everyone was watching with bright eyes, eager to hear the details about my adventure.

"Do you mind if I sit down?" I asked. "It's hard to know where to start." I looked for the right words. "I met the best people you could dream of. All the girls, the women, were wonderful. The way they look after the men . . . they're so well trained and capable and so kind, too. And the men . . . the patients were . . ."

They were wounded, brave, cheerful, angry, frightened, friendly, and invariably in great pain. They were dads and sons and brothers and uncles and best friends. They were all those things to people like us. Young men just like Mr. and Mrs. Brand's grandson serving overseas, Mrs. Mahoney's son-in-law, Miss Peters' brother. Perhaps soon, Clarence. And, of course, Charles. I didn't need to give my friends every detail of what I had seen.

For all that propaganda could be abused or misused, today I embraced it, perhaps even finally understood it. As Winnie had said, telling people the worst wouldn't help anyone at the moment. We had to push on.

"The patients were good men," I said. "All of them. They and the women are doing us very, very proud."

"Well, Emmy, we're proud of you," said Monica. "*Woman's Friend*'s first ever overseas war correspondent. That's one for our history books."

"Hear, hear," said Mr. Newton.

"Honestly, I just chatted to people and watched," I said. "I'll tell you about some of the boys another time. Although a Canadian officer on the plane called me 'kid' like they do in the films."

"Fancy that," said Mrs. Shaw.

"And he talked about 'throwing up,'" I added. "That's what they call it in Canada."

"Oh," said Mrs. Shaw. "He sounded nice until then."

"That's air travel for you," I said as everyone laughed, and I pulled a face. "Goodness, listen to me. I've become full of myself overnight."

"I don't blame you," said Guy. He had been quiet until now, but I thought he looked pleased for me too. "Well done."

"Thank you," I said. "Now then, I know you all wanted me to look for chocolate, and there *was* chocolate. But I think it was probably black market and it was horribly expensive. An awful business all round."

There were several unenthusiastic noises of agreement. I opened my rucksack.

"Would anyone like some?" I asked.

It went down a storm.

Everyone had a small chunk as I sneaked upstairs for a quick bath and to wash my hair. Two inches of tepid water woke me up nicely, and I returned to my desk eager to catch up after my time away from the office.

Stacks of letters had been lined up on the table, tied in garden twine as rubber bands had become a rare commodity. Slips of paper from the salvage box had been tucked into the twine, with Miss Peters' neat handwriting outlining which pile was which.

URGENT

UNUSUAL

FREQUENT

YOUNG

REPEAT REQUESTS

END OF THE WAR PLANS

I reached for the *END OF THE WAR* pile and slipped off the twine, opening the first envelope.

Dear Miss Lake

I have been married for five years and we have a girl and a boy. I love my husband very much but every time he comes home on leave, we quarrel terribly. I'm worried that he's fallen in love with somebody else and if so, what will happen when he comes home for good?

Please can you help?

Yours,

Worried, Shrewsbury

Poor Worried. She was far from alone. Miss Peters could have put her into the *FREQUENT* stack.

Some women on the other hand, had the opposite concern.

Dear Miss Lake

My fiancé is overseas, and we're getting married when the war ends. At the same time, one of my mother's lodgers is being very attentive to me even though he knows I'm engaged, and I find I lose my head whenever he is around.

What should I do? He's ever so handsome and nice.

Miss Smith (that's not my real name), Penge

In my view, the lodger wasn't that nice if you were Miss Smith's fiancé, and possibly neither was Miss Smith. Particularly in the light of the preceding days, I was confident I could come up with a pithy answer to it that would help with Mrs. Mahoney's concerns over lack of space.

"Emmy?" I looked up to see Hester, standing in the doorway. "Could you come, please?" she whispered, looking concerned. I followed her out to the reception hall. A young boy in a navy-blue uniform with red trim was waiting, his hat in one hand and a brown envelope in the other.

"Mrs. Charles Mayhew?" he asked.

"Yes," I said. "How can I help?"

He held out the envelope.

"Telegram for you, ma'am," he said.

ON HIS MAJESTY'S SERVICE—PRIORITY

SINCERELY REGRET TO INFORM YOU THAT YOUR
HUSBAND MAJOR CHARLES MAYHEW IS MISSING
PRESUMED TAKEN PRISONER FOLLOWING
OPERATIONS IN ENEMY OCCUPIED TERRITORY.
LETTER TO FOLLOW.

LT. COL. A. BURNS

CHAPTER 12

Missing Presumed Taken Prisoner

Nothing immediately changed. The typewriters did not stop. A telephone began to ring. Monica called out to ask if Mrs. Brand knew where a spread on winter frocks had gone. And still the typewriters went on.

I thanked the telegraph boy, who nodded and left as fast as he could. Then I stood there, staring at the piece of paper. Hester waited, not daring to speak. Everyone knew what telegrams could mean.

"It's all right, Hest," I said, calmly. "Everything's fine. I'm going to get Guy."

To her eternal credit, Hester was quicker witted than me. Walking through the office ashen faced and holding a telegram was not a good idea.

"Emmy, I'll go," she said. "Do you need to sit down?"

I didn't know.

Regret to inform you.

I glanced out of the window as if the answer might be there. It was beginning to rain.

"Thank you," I said. "I'll be in the sitting room. Please find Bunty and Harold too." I was speaking awfully slowly, like someone trying to work out a very difficult equation.

Hester nodded and headed back into the office as I got my bearings and walked into the other room.

Missing presumed taken prisoner.

Presumed was the vaguest of words. I'd never thought of that before. Did it mean highly likely, or was it just a vague notion or even a guess? My job, my career, my every hour of the working day was about words. Ludicrous though it was, all I could think was that *presumed* wasn't good enough. Because if he *hadn't* been taken prisoner, the alternative was even worse.

Within moments Guy rushed into the sitting room, his face drawn. I said nothing but handed him the telegram and watched as he read it and flinched. Then he bit his bottom lip for a second, before looking up and then putting his arms around me in a brief, fierce embrace.

"Emmy," he said, "this means he's alive."

The noise of the typewriters had stopped.

Guy stepped back, his brow furrowed in concentration.

I said nothing.

Then Bunty hurried in, followed by Harold and Hester.

"What is it?" said Bunty, her voice breaking the silence.

"Charles has been captured," I said. "They think."

"Letter to follow," said Guy, reading the telegram again, then handing it to Bunty.

She took it but didn't read it, instead rushing to my side and grabbing my hand, squeezing it for all she was worth. I didn't know what to say.

It was Hester who brought me to my senses. She looked very young and very scared and had hung back from the rest of us as if she didn't want to intrude.

"Oh, Hest," I said. "He'll be all right." I opened my arms as she ran into them, bursting into tears and burying her face in my hair. She was awfully fond of Charles. "You know what he's like," I said, trying to soothe her. "Tough as anything. He'll be home before you know it. Won't he, Guy?"

Hest's fear was what I had needed to shake myself out of the shock. All I wanted to know was where was Charles?

I love you Em, very, very much.

I love you too.

I felt it so strongly it was almost as if he were here. We loved each other too much for things to end now. I spoke to him in my head as if he were listening.

I'm all right, my darling. Know that I will be fine. Come home. We are here.

"Guy?" I said again.

"Damn right he'll be home," he said. "Charles is as strong as an ox. Don't worry, Hester. We'll get him back."

There was no way any of us could get my husband home of course, but that wasn't the point. We were setting out our stall, determining our position, and declaring our strength. Charles belonged to us, not to the Germans, or the Nazis, or Hitler himself. He was ours and they had no idea how strong we could be.

I hugged Hester again. "You're my right-hand woman," I said, as I found a handkerchief in my skirt pocket. She took it from me but dried her eyes with the back of her hand and said she was sorry for crying.

Harold leaned over and whispered that he felt exactly the same as her and not to worry as it was all a very big shock.

Bunts gave them both the kindest smile before turning to me. "What about the children?" she said. "They'll be home from school soon, and I know they are dying to hear all about Belgium, so they'll be racing back to see you."

It was another prompt to brace up. I didn't want them to find out with everyone here.

"Shall I go to meet them?" I asked.

"Let us go," replied Bunty, taking Harold's arm. "You need to let this sink in. All the staff will want to help once they know. We'll go back to Granny's, and maybe you and Guy can come over later? Hest, would you like to come too? We could have supper together."

The plan was unanimously agreed, just as there was a soft tapping on the door and Monica appeared.

"Is everything all right?" she asked.

As Guy told her the news, I thought how waking up in Brussels this morning seemed a hundred years ago. Since the telegram, the trip had gone from my mind. Now a horrid realisation crept over me. Had Charles already been captured when I was talking to Alice and Winnie?

"I might have been so near to him," I said. "He could have been a motorcycle ride away."

Guy was the first to speak, trying to reassure me.

"Emmy, he's been captured. It doesn't say wounded or handed over or evacuated. We don't even know where it happened. We have to wait until we get confirmation."

I turned to the coffee table and picked up a newspaper. "*British tanks on their way through Holland . . . difficult position for the British Airborne Division . . . counter-attacks launched by the enemy.*"

"I wish we'd known for sure where he was sent," I said, again. "The base hospital had boys coming in from Holland all the time. Someone might have seen him. If the telegram had come yesterday, you could have got word to me."

I was making no sense at all. The excitement of the assignment was now entirely gone.

"Don't do this to yourself, Em," said Bunty. "You might have been on the same side of the Channel, but that's all. I know it sounds awfully harsh but Emmy, I don't think Charles would have been anywhere near Brussels. If he is a prisoner of war they'd have taken him to one of the POW camps. There's nothing you could have done."

She was the first one to spell it out. Guy nodded silently in agreement.

I had been hearing from the wives of POWs since I had joined *Woman's Friend*. Through their letters I had learned about the enormous challenges that they faced. Of coping with financial difficulties, of endless bureaucracy, and the pain and fear of not hearing or knowing, especially about the men held in the Far East. We had tried to help them as much as we could, digging for information, and in the absence of one central organisation for the families, building contacts in countless Governmental departments.

If strength came from loving Charles, then it could also come from knowledge. I may have wanted to run back to the aerodrome and beg to be on the next flight to Europe, but that was pie in the sky. At least here, as the wife of a prisoner of war, I knew where to start.

"You're right of course," I said. "I'm sorry, I'm not making sense."

"Don't be silly," said Bunty. "It's a horrible shock."

"I think we should tell the staff," said Guy, gently. "You two get the children."

Before we split into our teams, we all hugged each other. It was a comfort, but also felt significant, as if we were on a mission together, combining resources and sharing our kit, even if we didn't yet know where the mission would take us.

The *Woman's Friend* team's response to the news was no different. Shock, concern, and then an irrepressible determination to help. The Letters Ladies immediately began to plan Red Cross parcels while Mr. Brand said he had friends who had contacts in the Foreign Office. Mr. Newton quoted part of the Geneva Convention about prisoners having all sorts of rights and then Mrs. Shaw spoke for us all as she went into a spirited verbal decimation of "the filthy coward Nazis."

I wished Charles could have seen them. Guy and I thanked everyone again and again, both of us saying how nothing would get Charles down. Then Mrs. Mahoney sent us off to Dower Cottage to make sure that George, Margaret, and Stan were all right.

Never was *Woman's Friend* better named.

Bunty and Harold had done a very good job too. Harold had gone straight into bat, filling their heads with tales of POW camps that resembled a rather cheerful boys' boarding school. Charles would be so busy playing football and ping-pong and learning to paint and do wood carving and probably conversational Spanish and French that he wouldn't have time to worry. He'd be miffed that he wasn't part of the fight any more, but even that didn't matter as it wasn't his fault and anyway, he'd already done his bit in earlier campaigns.

No wonder Captain Thomas was so persuasive with the advertising clients. It all sounded an absolute wheeze. I wished I could believe it as well.

"Honestly, Em," he said to me, "he's an officer, so he won't even be allowed to work. They'll put him in some Oflag halfway up a mountain, and he'll be bored out of his mind until it's all over and he can get home. I know it's rotten news, but once you've heard where he is and that he's well, things will feel a lot better."

"It's the 'presumed' part that scares me," I finally confessed to Guy as we walked back to Rose House after supper, safely out of range of young ears. It was easier to voice my fears in the dark. "What if he isn't lolling about in an Oflag? What if he's wounded? Some of the men on the wards in Brussels were in a wretched way."

"We'll know more, soon," Guy replied. "And you know we'll all be using every contact and pulling in every favour we possibly can. We just need to hold firm."

We had nearly reached the house. It had been a very long day. At the front door, Guy paused.

"I have something I need to give you," he said. "It's a letter from Charles."

Dearest, darling Em

I'm sending this to Guy so he can keep hold of it and only hand it over if I'm rather a clot and manage to get myself captured. So, if you're reading this, then I imagine that's what has happened, and I'm holed up somewhere on the Continent.

As I write, I am still in dear old Blighty, sitting in my bed which of course you now know well, having broken in here last night! Thanks to young Carter (our helpful photographer friend) the story of your espionage has already done the rounds among the chaps. You should know that they all think you're quite splendid and have told me I am very much outclassed by my wife!

Anyway, now you know exactly where I am sitting as I write this, complete with the view of those ghastly Nissen huts. They may not have given us the most romantic of settings, but I promise that while I am stuck in a German clink, I will think of being with you here, every day and night until we are together again.

Until then, please promise that you will not worry about me. Guy will tell you that they have to treat POWs all right or the chaps from the Red Cross pile in and start waving rule books at them.

I know you will be on top of everything back home. You're far better genned up on the drill for POW wives than I am, and I bet Mrs. Tavistock already has the knitting circle in full battledress. It makes me very happy that you have so many terrific friends around you.

Darling, could you do me one favour? The men in my battery are a very good bunch. Some of the chaps might be having a far stiffer time than me, so if it comes up, and any of the men's wives get in touch, would you tell them how very highly I regard their boys? If I'm stuck in a camp, I'll be limited in how much I can do, but I should so very much like them to know how proud I am to serve by their side. It might raise a smile.

In the meantime, know that as you read this, I'll be safe and well fed and I may already have taken up writing poetry if things get too frightfully dull. Not sure it's my bag as I can't think of something to rhyme with "Emmy Lake, I love you more than anything else on earth." Which happens to be true.

Well, I'd better get some sleep as things are about to get busy. I will write as soon as I can.

Please know that whenever you think of me, I will feel it in my heart and be thinking of you too.

Chin up, my dearest darling. I know you can do it.

I love you,

C. xxx

PS: When this is all over, I am never bloody well leaving your side again.

CHAPTER 13

Dear Miss Lake

By the next morning, I knew his letter by heart.

I was up terrifically early and surprised to find I was far from the only one. By eight o'clock the office was a hive of activity, noisier than normal, which was perhaps only the tiniest hint that the Business as Usual atmosphere was at all forced. Bunty had even slipped a small note into my To Do folder, which meant that when I opened it the morning after the telegram, the first thing I saw was, "IN YOUR EAR, ADOLF," written in large capital letters in red ink. I couldn't agree more.

I decided to look at the "Advice for Families of Prisoners of War" booklet. We had sent out hundreds, if not thousands of copies, and it had been updated and reprinted several times whenever new information became available. For the first time, I truly understood how it felt to need the advice, and most peculiarly, to feel a tingle of hope that it would contain something that might help.

Of course, I knew what was in it, the step-by-step guide that took a reader from when they first received the news, through to when to expect official confirmation, and the joy, at least if he was in Germany, of the first Kriegsgefangenenpost from their boy. Although I was feeling blue, I counted my blessings that Charles wasn't missing thousands of miles away in the Far East. Things were far less predictable and even harder if the prisoner was in Japanese hands.

We'd done our best to explain what to expect from the International Red Cross, what to pack in the initial next-of-kin package—the most popular items and how cigarettes were essential currency whether the prisoner smoked or not. We listed the endless organisations and advisory departments families had to navigate, trying to help make sense of a situation no one wanted to be in.

And now here I was. Step One: sit tight and hope for news. It wasn't my strongest suit. The reality, which wasn't in the booklet, was that until the arrival of that confirmation of Charles' status we would be stuck in a sort of civilian's no man's land of not knowing where or how he was.

Keeping busy became my priority. There was no shortage of work to do, and I eagerly extended my office hours well into the evenings. I re-wrote and edited my articles about Brussels until they were as good as I could possibly make them. Then I sent them to Richard Langley and hoped the censors would approve.

Three days after the telegram, as promised, a letter arrived. It was from Charles' commanding officer, Lieutenant-Colonel Burns.

Dear Mrs. Mayhew

I am writing to convey my sincere sympathy regarding the news about your husband, Major Charles Mayhew, missing presumed taken captive. I understand the great concern this will cause and join you in the keen hope that there will be good news as soon as possible.

While I am sure you will appreciate that I cannot go into any detail in terms of the mission itself, please be assured that Major Mayhew has been part of an operation of much significance to the war effort, and his service has been exemplary throughout.

It has been my pleasure to have your husband under my command. I am also able to say that he is a greatly respected officer in command ("OC") in his own right. Informally, he is what his men call "a good bloke." Please excuse my colloquialism: I would like you to know it is meant very well.

I know this is a difficult period while you wait for news. As you may know, this can take several weeks, or months. However, the International Red Cross will do all they can and are an excellent source of help.

In the meantime, there is a possibility that you may hear from other members of Major Mayhew's battery, or even from your husband himself. Should you do so, I would be grateful if you could communicate this to the appropriate organisations, including me, the IRC, and the War Office.

Again, on a personal level, I join you in looking forward to hearing what we all hope will be good news. In the meantime, may I reiterate my very sincere best wishes.

Yours sincerely

Lieutenant-Colonel Andrew Burns

The letter was handwritten and almost two pages long, and while it gave no further information than the telegram, it made a difference. I added it to my armoury of good wishes and high hopes.

That evening at supper, Mrs. Shaw had an idea.

"Excuse me for asking and I don't want to intrude, but Miss Peters and I couldn't help but notice that the Major's next-of-kin package hasn't had much of a start."

Miss Peters, who was enjoying a slice of savoury flan, nodded in agreement.

"That's true," I replied. "I haven't done anything yet. It could be weeks until we know where Charles is."

"You never know," said Mr. Newton, joining in from the other end of the table. "The Red Cross are very good. They tracked down your nephew ever so quickly, didn't they, Florence?"

"They did," said Mrs. Newton. "My sister had a smashing woolly all ready to go."

"Miss Lake, I think we'd all like to help, if that would be all right," said Mrs. Brand. "As we're all here."

"Oh yes," said Miss Peters. "We really would."

"And winter is coming," said Mrs. Shaw, darkly. Then she rallied. "We could do you some of those socks that we do for the navy. With our own wool of course. You could even have a go at something yourself. I know you're not confident, but how about a scarf, if one of us started you off? I'm sure Major Mayhew would be pleased."

This was a kind, if bold suggestion. Charles had witnessed my struggles with wool in the past. He'd said it felt cruel even to watch.

"Perhaps I could get him some paperbacks," I said. "That would be safer."

"Good idea," said Guy, a little too quickly. I gave him a look. "What?" he said, all innocence.

"Thank you, everyone," I said. "That's very kind. I would love some help. Guy, how are you off for cigarettes?"

"Please have as many as you can fit in," replied Guy. "I'm going to cut down. Possibly even give up."

"Oh Guy, please don't," said Monica. "I know you mean well, but you're awful if you don't smoke. Look at the other week when you ran out. You were quite murderous until Miss Peters came to the rescue with a packet of Craven A."

"You still owe Mr. Newton as well," I said, ganging up on him for fun, which was the first time in days.

"I'm beginning to think we've all been living together too long," said Guy, melodramatically.

"No need to owe me, Mr. Collins," said Mr. Newton. "A pleasure to share."

"It would be jolly to start putting things together," said Monica. "What other sorts of things do you think he'll want?"

I looked around the breakfast room, where we had all spent so many happy mealtimes together over the past months.

"Perhaps something from everyone?" I replied. "I think he would like that, very much, indeed."

So far, and in the absence of any definite information about Charles, our main activity had been to go through all our contacts and make a list of who could possibly help. Mr. Brand's friend in the Foreign Office had given us the name of a top man in the POW Information Bureau, and Bunty had listed several people she knew in the Home Office. Guy had remembered an old pal he was pretty sure had moved to the POW Central Enquiry Bureau, and Monica had an old boyfriend who was now at the Soldiers', Sailors', and Airmen's Families Association. Everyone who knew anyone anywhere lined them up. For my part, I had been through every organisation I had ever visited or interviewed that had anything to do with POWs. It all turned into quite a significant list. It was amazing how many people one could think of when the stakes were so high.

I wrote back to the lieutenant-colonel by return of post, thanking him for his consideration and kindness. It meant a great deal, I said, to know that Charles was popular with his men. If there was anything I could do to be of help to their families, as Charles' representative, I would very much like to pitch in.

I wondered how the other wives and families were coping. At Rose House, it was hard not to become jumpy. Deliveries or an unexpected pull of the great clanging doorbell now came with an edge. Emptying the huge sacks of post also took on a new urgency as now every delivery might include a letter from Charles.

"Post's here," became the twice daily call to action around which I planned my days. At first the Letters Ladies joined me, but very quickly, without comment or fuss, the rest of the staff all began to help. Anyone who wasn't on a phone call to a client or supplier would simply put down their pen or stop typing or sketching and quietly begin to sort through the hundreds of letters that came in. There was no hubbub, just the occasional question of what went where, or request by one of the more regular sorters for a new pile to be started.

Anything that looked vaguely official was given to me. Within days we became the most efficient machine.

Two weeks after we heard about Charles, a letter arrived in the second post that did not look at all official, but when Hester saw it, she handed it to me.

"Emmy, look at this," she said, leaning over the wide table that we used as our sorting office. "What do you think?"

It was a small envelope, handwritten and addressed to *Miss Lake or Mrs. Mayhew, wife of Major Mayhew, c/o* Woman's Friend.

I quickly opened it and unfolded the paper inside.

Dear Miss Lake

I hope you don't mind me writing to you. May I ask, might you be Mrs. Mayhew in your real life, as I have reason to think that you are?

I hope I don't sound like a crank. Please keep reading.

You see, my husband is currently missing, presumed taken captive in Europe. His name is Lieutenant Thomas Carter and his officer in command is Major Mayhew.

Please forgive me if I have the wrong person, but I am writing to you because one of my friends is also married to a man in their battery. He has been evacuated back to England from Holland as he was seriously wounded at Arnhem. I understand our boys came in for a pretty stern time of things there. Anyway, my friend's husband said he saw a group of the men when they were taken by the Germans, and Major Mayhew was one of them. I must tell you that when he saw him, the Major was definitely unharmed.

My heart was hammering. I hardly dared to read on.

Tom was with him, and I am very much hoping they are perhaps still together. My husband always speaks very highly of Major Mayhew and said that if anything happened, they'd be all right.

I believe Thomas may have met you before they left England. He told me a funny story about meeting the Major's wife at the crack of dawn and not knowing quite what he should do, but you were very nice and later the Major said off the record that you answer letters for a women's magazine. I have bought all of them this week and looked at all the pictures of the ladies on the letters pages, trying to guess which one might be you. (I am sending this letter to two other ladies as well, just in case.)

If you are Mrs. Mayhew, I know you must be awfully worried about your husband as I am about mine. So, I wanted to find you to share what I think is good news.

I do hope it is not rude of me to contact you like this. May I ask that if you do hear from Major Mayhew, you might be kind enough to let me know, please. It would mean Tom may be safe too.

Yours very sincerely

Mrs. Wallace Carter (wife of Lieutenant Thomas Carter)

It was the first, even if slightest, hint of real news.

Since the arrival of the telegram, I had managed put on a brave face, in public at least.

Now, I sat down and cried.

CHAPTER 14

In the Same Boat

Mrs. Carter had included a telephone number in her letter, so after I had assured everyone that it was the most hopeful news, I pulled myself together and called her.

"Hello, this is Mrs. Mayhew, or rather, Miss Lake. Both really. Mrs. Carter, I've just read your letter. I can't thank you enough."

"I'm so sorry to hear about Major Mayhew," a bright, youthful voice replied. "I'm so glad you didn't think I was interfering. Tom always says that if the Germans get you, they do have to play by the rules."

"I am assured they do," I said. "And I'm very grateful I ran into Lieutenant Carter that morning as I have a lovely photograph. I'm afraid I rather shocked him. We had to do some very fast talking to spare everyone's blushes."

"Oh, not at all," said Mrs. Carter. "Tom said you were a terrific sport about it, as was the Major. I very much admire you. I wish I'd had the gumption to break in there, myself."

"It wasn't really planned," I admitted. "Mrs. Carter, I'd like you to know that I don't usually go around sneaking into military establishments. Although given half a chance I'd probably try again now if I knew where Charles and the men are."

"Rather a lot of us would be right by your side," she replied.

"Are you in touch with many of the other wives?" I asked.

"Yes, quite a few. Almost everyone is waiting for news. We're the lucky ones. Some of the boys had an awful time. I understand that quite a few of them were lost. I wish I knew what to say or how to help."

It was just as Charles had said might happen in his letter, and I felt poor indeed that while Mrs. Carter had been keeping in touch, I hadn't even tried. Meanwhile, it was clear that Wallace Carter was not the sort to sit around.

"I wonder if there might be something we could come up with together?" I said. "Would you perhaps like to meet? I saw in your letter you have a London address so it would be easy for me to come up on the train."

"Gosh," she replied, sounding a little surprised. "That's terribly kind. I'd love to."

We arranged to meet the following Saturday in Clapham, near where she lived, and both agreed that we felt rather buoyed by our chat.

Later, when I went to bed, I picked up the framed picture of Charles and me that Lieutenant Carter had taken. We both looked hopelessly tired, but we were grinning like Cheshire cats. It always made me smile, but tonight as I kissed the glass of the photo frame and wished Charles goodnight, I felt sure he would know I was thinking of him.

. . . whenever you think of me, I will feel it in my heart and be thinking of you too.

———

It had now been nearly three months since we had moved to Hampshire and so the night before meeting Mrs. Carter I took the opportunity to stay at the house in Pimlico. The house had not been left empty. While we had locked the offices, the bedrooms and upstairs flat had all been put to good use as temporary accommodation for neighbours after the rocket bomb attacks. As promised, Mrs. Harewood next door had made sure all was well, so I called in to see how she was.

Mrs. H was glad to see me, and over hearty plates of rabbit and pickled pork pudding, we updated each other with our tales. She listened with concern about Charles and then apologised as she said her grumbles were very small beer. She was, however, struggling to manage her own boarding house and to ensure that everyone was happy next door. Now that two of the families had found accommodation, she asked if Bunty would mind if she moved the remaining elderly lodger to her own house. The lady was struggling with the stairs, and Mrs. Harewood had a vacancy on the ground floor.

"You'll be back soon, anyway, won't you?" she said. "You are missed. Everyone's always asking in the queue at the butchers or when I'm getting my paper."

"That's very kind," I replied. "Though I'm not sure. The children are in school now. But I'll ask."

The next day, as I sat on the bus heading towards Clapham, I thought about returning to London. The summer had been a wonderful break, and we had been very lucky to be able to escape from the devastation of the flying-bomb attacks on the city. But Charles going missing was a gloomy reminder that the war would find you in the end.

I got off as the bus stopped at Clapham Common and checked the address of the tearoom I had written down. Mrs. Carter had described herself as short, blonde, and currently embarrassingly shabby, to which I replied that that applied to nearly everyone now, including myself. I hoped she wasn't expecting quite the polished appearance of my picture in *Woman's Friend*. I had let my hair grow long during the summer and now it was squashed under a felt hat that was feeling its age. We always told the readers that wearing clothes

that had seen better days showed that you were doing your bit and
not falling for the black market, which was true, but it was still hard
going when one felt permanently drab.

As well as the elderly hat, I had put on a long-serving frock that
I had updated with a new collar made from one of Mrs. Tavistock's
best blouses, last worn, she said, in nineteen twenty-eight. There was
nothing I could do about my handbag, which was way past retire-
ment age, but it would have to do. I was here to talk, not launch a
fashion parade. A minuscule dab of lipstick applied while on the bus
and I was prepared.

The little tearoom was tucked between an antique book shop and
a rather sad hardware shop that had almost nothing to sell. The bell
jingled as I opened the door and was immediately greeted by a pretty,
fair-haired young woman who waved at me and shot out of her seat.

"Good morning, Mrs. Mayhew," she said, offering her hand, "I'm
Wallace Carter."

"How lovely to meet you. Do call me Emmy," I said, shaking her
hand. "Thank you for meeting me. I hope your mother doesn't mind
having to babysit?"

"Not at all," said Mrs. Carter. "And please call me Wallace. Mother
was so pleased that you phoned and even more that you suggested
we meet. And she loves looking after Baby Daphne." She hesitated.
"I was worried Tom may have been rather cheeky when you met. He
said to me, 'Oh Wall, you're not going to believe this, but I offered
the Major's wife a job.'"

Wallace looked so mortified that I burst into laughter.

A waitress had come over, so we ordered a pot of tea and two
scones before I continued.

"Was that why you hesitated when I suggested we meet up?" I
asked. "You must have thought I was an old rat bag."

"Not at all. Tom said you were lovely. But you are the OC's wife,"
said Wallace. "And sometimes, well . . ."

"They're rather intimidating?" I interrupted.

"Yes." Wallace looked relieved.

"Don't worry. I completely agree. When I first met Charles, I found it all terrifying." I shook my head at the memory. "And anyway, on the OC's wife front, Charles has only been a major since he came back from Italy. He's not like the ones who spent the last war sitting on a horse and now think that all women should be banned."

For a second Wallace stared at me and then started to laugh.

"You've just described my father," she said. "He thinks our generation is awful."

The bell on the door jingled again as a middle-aged lady with a small child came in. I glanced over at her and then back at Wallace. For the first time since I arrived, her face was serious.

"Do you read the newspapers?" she asked. "Or do you prefer not to know? The reports from Arnhem were horrible," she said. "My friend told me she heard that our boys ran out of ammunition. She's the one that had awful news." She looked at the tablecloth and scratched a mark on it with her finger.

I hadn't asked Wallace how old she was, but I guessed in her very early twenties. She and her boy should be larking about, enjoying being young and in love. But then, I supposed, so should Charles and I.

I reached across the table and took her hand. "I'm sure they're well," I said.

"I just want to know where he is, don't you?" said Wallace. "We've only been married a year."

"We'll have been married three years at Christmas," I said. "But we've only spent about six months of that together. Wallace, I met your husband briefly, but I liked him very much. And when you do get to write to him, please tell him he wasn't cheeky. He was kind and jolly when I was feeling quite low about going home. He's very good with a camera, too. I must show you the photograph he took, one day. It's my favourite. I talk to it all the time. There, now I sound mad."

Mrs. Carter looked a little happier. "You're very kind," she said. "You can tell you're used to sorting out people's worries. I'm afraid this is a busman's holiday for you."

"Not at all. Wallace, we're in similar boats. I'm feeling cheerier just having met you. Now, let's have tea and perhaps you might tell me what you've heard from the other wives? I'm sure we're not the only ones worried about things."

I said "we" on purpose. I liked Wallace and hoped she liked me, but I was still aware that I was the boss's wife, old-fashioned and silly though that was.

"I have heard from some of them," said Wallace. "You know, you're chums with one or two girls, and then they know someone else, and suddenly if you were all in one place, you'd make up rather a party. But we all live in different places and everyone's working or looking after children or parents. We write and share notes about things we've heard, more so now of course. I'm keen to find someone who knows Johnny Bagley. Lieutenant Bagley, that is. He and Tom are as thick as thieves, but Johnny's missing as well."

"Is Johnny married?" I asked. "Do you know his family?"

"No, I don't," said Wallace. "He's not married and doesn't have a girl. Johnny's a bit of a dish actually and I think probably enjoys playing the field. He's only twenty-one. I mean I'm only twenty-two but I'm an old married woman with a baby, while John's still rather a boy. I do hope he's with your husband. He'll be all right if he is."

It was a lovely thing for Wallace to say, but it made my heart ache. I was only a handful of years older than her, and Tom and their friend, but I felt so much older. Even though I was desperate to hear that Charles was safe and well, I could hang on to the knowledge that if anyone could cope with being a prisoner, it was him. He'd been through Dunkirk, and the North Africa and Italy campaigns. He had ten years on young Lieutenant Bagley.

"He will," I said. "They're probably playing cards as we speak. Would you like me to write to the CO? Lieutenant-Colonel Burns sent me a very kind letter about Charles. I could ask how you might get in touch with your friend's family."

"Goodness, would you?" asked Wallace. "Won't he be rather busy for this sort of thing?"

"I should think so," I admitted. "I'll have a word with someone at the Red Cross too. I interviewed a very nice lady there earlier this year. Leave it with me. I should really know the answer off pat. Honestly, we get letters about everything under the sun. Is there anything else you might want to know? I would like to help if I can."

Wallace picked up a crumb of scone, thinking for a moment.

"Actually," she said. "I think there is."

Over the next two hours Wallace asked questions, both her own and on subjects that had come up amongst her friends and the other wives she had mentioned. I was pleased that I could answer most of them, from what she might expect once she heard about Tom, to her friend whose husband's injuries would mean significant changes to their lives, and to the saddest question of all about the widow struggling to make sense of the financial maze she now faced.

"I'm going to start noting these down," I said, after a while. "Then I'll write to you with the details so you can send them on to your friends. Honestly, I have lists and lists of organisations that might be able to help."

By the time we parted, Wallace said her head was fuller than it had been since her School Cert.

"This is awfully kind of you," she said for the tenth time. "The next time you're in London, could I take you out to lunch or do something nice to say thank you?"

"I'd like that very much," I said. "Let me get on with everything as fast as I can." Then I paused for a moment and smiled. "And when you do write to Tom, tell him I'm going to hold him to that offer of a job."

CHAPTER 15

A Quandary and an Idea

The trains back to Hampshire were sticky that day, not least as a bomb had fallen on the line, and it was early evening before I got back to Rose House, where it was quiet and nearly deserted. Mr. and Mrs. Brand were listening to a concert on the radio in the living room and reported that Hester and Guy were at Dower Cottage. Mr. and Mrs. Newton were playing Ludo together in the breakfast room. The others were away visiting family or friends.

I had become very proficient in riding bicycles in the pitch black, or at least with the very dimmest of torches, so I made my excuses and headed back out to go over to Bunty's. There I was greeted by the welcoming scene of my friends all squashed into the living room and playing an animated game of charades. It felt like coming home.

While the children wanted me to pick sides, Bunty got to her feet and insisted that I eat. I followed her into the kitchen, which hadn't changed a bit since we were children and used to sneak down to eat marmalade cake with Mrs. Tavistock's estate manager and his wife. It was one of those places that transported you back to a time when you were looked after, and happy and safe. I plonked myself down at the worn oak table, wondering if I could curl up in the dog's basket and stay there all night.

A plate was being kept warm at the bottom of the oven, and Bunty took it out to reveal a large slice of tomato and onion pie with boiled potatoes and crumbed runner beans. It was just the job after three hours of standing up on the train.

"There's fruit pudding, too," said Bunty, wiping her hands on a tea towel and sitting down opposite me. "Now eat up, before you fall asleep in your pie."

"Do I look that bad?" I said, tucking in.

"Yes, you do," said my friend.

"I'm keeping busy," I said, my mouth full. "This pastry is a dream."

Bunts nodded but said nothing more and the two of us sat in silence as I worked my way through the generous helping.

When I'd finished, I put my knife and fork down and sighed. I felt like an old man who had come home to his long-suffering wife and scoffed down his dinner without saying a word.

"Thank you," I said at last, reaching for the glass of water Bunty had poured. "That was perfect."

"Was it a good trip?" she asked.

"Yes, it was. I'll tell you about Wallace Carter properly tomorrow when I'm a bit more awake, but she was super. Mrs. Harewood was well. She sends her regards."

"How's the house looking?"

"Still standing. I popped into the office and then went downstairs. Silly really, but I found myself feeling rather sentimental and thinking about when Charles and I got married and we had such a lovely party there afterwards. And the first time Harold came to see you, and Thel and the kids and I were all smitten by him and I knew you were too although you tried desperately to hide it."

Bunty smiled. They were good days—war-defyingly happy times.

"Being out here does almost make you forget what a pummelling London has taken, though," I added. "The journey down to Clapham was sobering, even though the sun was out. Mrs. H was full of stories of people who have been bombed out for the second or third time. We could let out rooms five times over. And, on that point, Mrs. Harewood says the Browns and Mulligans are both leaving, and she would like to take Miss Nichols in as she can't really be left on her own. To be honest, I think Mrs. H has had enough of being a temporary landlady on our behalf."

"I can understand that." Bunty took my plate away and replaced it with a bowl of the pudding. "I'm fattening you up," she said. "You're too thin."

"I'm hoping to fit into some of Monica's Chanel," I grinned. "I'm fine. Honest."

"You're running yourself ragged. Everyone's worried about you."

I stopped for a moment, my spoon in midair. I put it down before it dripped.

"I'll be fine once we know about Charles," I said. "What do you mean about *everyone*?"

"Maybe not everyone," said Bunts. "But Mrs. Shaw and Miss Peters for a start, and Mrs. Mahoney. And Monica. And Harold who said Mr. Newton had said something to him. Mrs. Brand said you're too thin as well."

"Hmm. That is everyone, almost, isn't it?" I said, picking out a piece of apple.

Bunty smiled. "Yes, it is really. Guy and Hester are permanently concerned so they're on the list too." She folded the tea towel. "Em, I'm in a quandary and I don't know what to do. Can I ask your advice?"

Now I woke up. "Yes, of course. Are you all right? Is it the children?"

"No, nothing like that. We're all OK. It's about the team. Emmy, I think they're ready to go home. Back to London that is. They all insist they don't mind staying indefinitely, but Guy reckons they're saying that because they think you and I want to stay."

"What does Guy want to do?"

Bunty pursed her lips. "I don't think he cares where he lives as long as you hear that Charles is safe. Mind you, he has said that in

London he knows what's going on because the press chaps get hold of all sorts of hush-hush information."

"That's a good point, too," I said. "Although I have loved being here. Your granny has been so generous."

"She's enjoyed it," said Bunts. "The company has done her the world of good. But that's not my main concern."

"What's the quandary?" I asked.

"Well, in terms of *Woman's Friend* and the staff, I think you should go back to London. Harold says Mr. Newton is spending half his time on the train as now summer's over clients don't fancy the trip. Mrs. Mahoney's worried about her daughter as the baby's nearly due, and Miss Peters thinks she's going to lose her flat. I can tell Monica's getting bored, but she'd rather die than admit it. Where the quandary comes in, is that the children are happy and settled in school, which means they, and Harold and I, would need to stay here." She frowned and bit her lip.

"I agree entirely," I said, straight away. "With everything you've said. Truly. No dilemma at all."

"There is though, Em," said Bunty. "I don't think you should live in Braybon Street on your own. You know how we rattled around when it was just us two. It'll be horrible by yourself, especially at the moment."

When I'd thought about us all moving back, I hadn't really considered the fact that after *Woman's Friend* shut for the day, I would be on my own in the house in Pimlico. Spending the winter there would be very glum indeed.

"Yes," I said. "I think you're right. I could see if Mrs. Harewood has a room?"

I didn't really love the idea of that, either, despite her excellent pickled pork.

"That would be dreary as well," said Bunty, "especially as Buzz and the girls have been moved."

Our friend Beryl "Buzz" Berkeley and several members of her All Girls Big Band had been billeted with Mrs. Harewood for over a year and been huge fun, but they had changed billets back in the spring.

"True," I said. "Move in with Roy?" I tried to make it into a joke.

"Actually, that would be fun," said Bunts. "But we've got another idea."

I could read her like a book. "Is this what you've been building up to with all the preamble?" I asked. "And the pie?"

"Perhaps. Anyway, here's the idea. Guy and Hester move in. Guy in the flat, Hester in the room next to you. That would mean my room and the children's would be free so Harold can stay a couple of nights a week if he's in town for meetings. And when Arthur comes back, there'll be room for him and the kids if they all want to stay." She opened her arms with a flourish. "What do you think? Hest's the only one who doesn't want to leave here as she loves having moved out of her mother's home, and Guy is so worried about you and Charles that he'd live in the shed if he had to. The only thing is I know how much you'll miss George, Marg, and Stan."

It was a very well thought-out plan. I had wondered if the others wanted to get back to their old lives and homes. It didn't matter how hard Hitler tried to break them, you could only take Londoners out of London for so long. There was also something about being back in the middle of everything that felt right. I would be near to the organisations and officials who might be able to help Charles if that was required.

But it was true about the children. It was the only thing against the idea, but it was a very big one.

"I'll come back," I said, "at weekends."

"Every weekend," said Bunty, almost fiercely. "You have to promise."

To my surprise, her eyes had filled with tears.

"Bunts?" I said, standing up and pushing my chair back so it scraped across the stone floor. "Whatever's the matter?"

Bunty wiped away a big tear as I went over and crouched down by her chair.

"I'm being an idiot," she said, but the tears kept coming. I hadn't seen her this upset in an age. "I just feel terrible saying you should go back, and then I'll stay here and not come and help. I can't bear the thought of you being on your own. That's why it only works if Guy and Hester move in too. We haven't heard about Charles yet, and you're being so good about it and it's all horrible. I'm just so sorry."

"Oh, Bunts," I said. I put my arms around her and as she was hugging me back, she dissolved into sobs. "You silly thing, you'll start me off. And anyway, you've been propping me and everyone else up for years."

This wasn't her at all. Just like everyone else, she and I had been through so much. Perhaps that was it. For almost all of it we had been together. The one time when we hadn't had been the hardest to bear.

"I'll just be up the A30," I said. "Or on the ten past nine to Waterloo."

Bunty nodded and sniffed. "Of course. I don't know what's come over me."

"You can't be Boadicea all of the time," I said, gently. "I've tried it, and it doesn't work."

"Are you sure you'll be all right?" she asked.

"I am," I said, meaning it. "And well done on the idea of Guy and Hest moving in. The three of us will have fun. Now how about we share being Boadicea? What do you say? I think together we've got her in the bag."

———

A week later, *Woman's Friend*'s stay in the country officially came to an end with a large, happy farewell dinner. Bottles of elderberry wine led to heartfelt speeches, including one by Mrs. Tavistock, who said we had brought the sun back to Rose House and she would miss us all very much. The next morning, it was time to leave. Guy and Hester had gone on ahead to Braybon Street to take the dust sheets off the office furniture and to move themselves into their new digs. When Guy and I had asked Hest if she really could

bear living with two very old fogies like us, she had been adamant
that she could.

"And it's really only one very old fogey, isn't it?" she said.

"Thank you," said Guy. "Is it too late to change plans?"

"Undoubtedly," I said. Hester just beamed.

Helped by the children, Bunty, Harold, and I tackled the last of
the tidying as we waited for our friend Roy to arrive. Roy had managed to get his hands on one of the vehicles the Fire Service used to
pull the smaller pumps, and once loaded up, he and I would head
for Pimlico and home.

We made an industrious party as Harold and Stan went through a
checklist of boxes in the reception hall and the rest of us diligently sorted
the final post that had come in. Everything needed to be ship-shape back
in London and continuing to work meant any threat of melancholy
would be staved off. Now and then, someone would tell a favourite anec-
dote from the summer or look out of the window and remember something lovely from the day of the wedding. I began to reminisce about
Mrs. Shaw getting run over by Monica and Roy during the quickstep.

"Harold picked her up," I said, laughing, "and Mrs. Shaw told
him he was like a young Douglas Fairbanks in *The Private Life of Don
Juan*. Roy got a telling off for calling her flirtatious."

"What does 'flirtatious' mean?" asked Margaret, putting an arm-
ful of letters into a box.

"Ah," I said, treading carefully. "How would we define 'flirtatious,' Bunty?"

Bunty didn't answer. She was staring at the last few letters and
cards that had been emptied into an untidy heap on the table. Then
she picked one up, and thrust it towards me.

"Emmy," she said, almost in a whisper. "Look."

I saw it printed boldly across the top of the card before it was even
in my hand. One single, very long word.

KRIEGSGEFANGENENPOST

Darling Em, I am being held as a prisoner of war. Don't worry as I am in excellent health, and they are treating and feeding us very well. Tell the children there's football and Ludo but no guinea pigs.

Please send cigs and thick socks. I am sorry if you've been worried, darling, but no need now as it's all very good, I promise. How are you?

Write soon as I can't wait to hear from you. I'll write properly soon.

Love to everyone. Cheerio my darling, I am thinking of you.

All my love. C.xxxx

CHAPTER 16

The Show Will Go On

The brief, wide-lined card the prisoners were given to send a handful of precious words home was the best news in the world. Charles was safe.

I phoned Guy straight away. He could hardly say anything other than, "Good man, good man," over and over again.

Then I called Wallace, hoping she might have heard from Tom, but she hadn't. I tried to sound measured—pleased but not over-excited. She was terribly brave and said how happy she was for me. I told her I would ask Charles straight away if he had any news of Tom and that I was coming back to London so I hoped she and I would meet up soon. Wallace said she would like to and that she would phone me if she received any news too.

Tidying the rest of the house was now forgotten. We went straight to The White Horse to celebrate, drinking watery beer as I wrote my first letter to Charles. It was a rushed, probably indecipherable, and definitely giddy affair, but it was stamped, addressed, and in the letterbox within an hour of knowing where he was.

By the time Roy arrived, we were all well away, and once he had happily joined in a drink to Charles' health, we went back and loaded up the van, if slightly haphazardly on my and Bunty's part. After a far more cheerful goodbye than any of us had imagined, I climbed into the van with Roy and sang all the way back to London.

Now, I could take a deep breath and begin to live with what was my new normality. I would still wish a thousand times a day that Charles was in England with me, but I thanked my lucky stars that his situation was far better than it could have been. For all the optimism of the summer, the fighting in Europe was brutal. We were winning the war, but the Germans were not giving in, and even the newspaper reports admitted that Allied losses were horrendous. Now, no one thought it would be over by Christmas. There was no doubt that Britain would still be at war in nineteen forty-five.

Amid all of this, Charles was safe enough in an Oflag in Germany. In the normal world his card might have appeared unremarkable and brief, with minimal information or emotion. But to anyone who knew how these things worked, it spoke volumes. Prisoners had just a handful of lines to fill and Charles could not risk writing even the smallest detail that a German censor might deem unacceptable. So, while the details were few, the important thing was that the message was written in his own hand, strong and immediately recognisable. And after all, who else would have mentioned Stan's guinea pigs?

It was more than enough for me. Charles was alive and I felt sure he was well.

I returned to Pimlico with renewed energy and heart, flinging open doors all over the house and moving everything back into the office. Guy and Hester shared the same spirit, and when an unsuspecting Monica arrived to help out, she was met by a team of people who felt they could take on the world. As we emptied boxes and put everything back in its usual place, the four of us were full of ideas for the magazine and the readers, chatting about how we could help them for what was going to be a long haul towards Peace. We may have been cock-a-hoop at hearing from Charles, but there was still a huge job ahead.

By the next day I had made three separate lists and pinned them up. Unsurprisingly, the first was entitled CHARLES. I had written to Lieutenant-Colonel Burns immediately to tell him the news, as well as to the War Office as I had been instructed, and most importantly the Red Cross so that I could push on with sending Charles his next-of-kin parcel. It was a far cry from our romantic plans about saving up to go to the Ritz, but the opportunity to do something for him, to show him I was here and thinking of him, was enormously important to me.

Guy and I would also now go back to our contacts with the sole objective of keeping Charles in the front of their minds and unsubtly hinting that we would welcome any news they could share about the Oflag in which he was held. Nothing ventured, nothing gained.

The second list was labelled WOMAN'S FRIEND, and we all added ideas to this. We may have just worked our way through a bucolic summer, but it was highly unlikely any of our readers had. Top of the list was a series of editorial pieces under the banner of "It's Asking a Lot, But Let's Finish the Job." It was tempting to add AGAIN in big letters underneath.

The final one was called WALLACE. This was because I wasn't exactly sure what it was going to involve. All I knew was that even before hearing from Charles, meeting Mrs. Carter had made me feel better. There were others in the same boat too and I wanted to do something for them. I had meant it when I said we were in this together. Charles would be trying to look after his men. It was my job to do the same with their families.

I had put together a package of information for Wallace to pass on to the others and sent it straight away. At the top of the list were ways I could help her try to find Tom.

On Monday morning the *Woman's Friend* team returned to work, arriving for the weekly editorial meeting as if it were a new school term, full of jokes that the daily commute was now far harder and that they'd woken up to find no one had laid out the breakfast.

"There are spare rooms upstairs," I said, "and you are always welcome. By the way, we've had some news."

It was some time before the meeting got going after telling them about the card from Charles. But when it did, Guy explained the idea for "It's Asking a Lot, But Let's Finish the Job."

"We obviously need a proper, decent name for it," he said, "but I hope you get my gist. We all know we have to keep pushing, but I am absolutely sure our readers are sick to death of being asked to give more. We know everyone's had enough and can't wait for the war to end. Personally, I've found the last few weeks of waiting for news of my brother quite ghastly."

Everyone sat up. Even Monica looked surprised.

"That's right," he continued. "Awful. But do you know, how it was made bearable?" Now he looked around the room. "It was because of all of you, here in this room. And some notable absentees of course." He took off his spectacles for a moment and studied them as if looking for dust. Then he put them back on again and added, "I was extremely fortunate to be surrounded by people who cared, and who showed immense kindness. That is something I shall never forget. Thank you, all."

This was the first time I had ever heard Guy say something so personal in public, and certainly during a meeting.

It was Mr. Newton, usually the quietest one in the room, who finally spoke first.

"We wouldn't have had it any other way, sir," he said. "If I might speak for us all."

"Hear, hear," said Mrs. Shaw in a slightly choked voice.

"Hear, hear," echoed Mr. Brand.

"We're just jolly pleased that he's safe," said Mrs. Mahoney.

Hester looked as if she was about to burst into tears. I felt much the same.

Guy cleared his throat. This was uncharted territory for him.

"Thank you," he said, again.

"It was a lovely summer," said Mrs. Shaw. "Despite the worry."

"I must say, I found it very quiet in my flat last night," said Monica. "There was no one to play vingt-et-un."

"Mrs. Brand is very happy she's going to come into the office to help out now and then," said Mr. Brand.

Mr. Newton nodded. His wife would be doing the same.

"I thought we'd end up getting on each other's nerves," said Mrs. Shaw, never one to beat around the bush. "But I don't think we did. Even planning Major Mayhew's Red Cross parcel was cheerful, in the circumstances."

"It certainly was, Mrs. Shaw," I said, gratefully.

The editorial meeting was now well and truly derailed, but Guy didn't seem to mind.

"I'm going to miss the knitting circle," said Mrs. Mahoney.

"Oh, I *did* enjoy that," said Miss Peters. "And we made so many socks. I'd like to think there's a battleship somewhere full of men wearing them."

"We could all continue in our own homes," said Mrs. Mahoney. "And then package them up together."

"It won't be the same," said Miss Peters, sadly.

I wondered if I should suggest continuing the circle here at Braybon Street, but I knew that was a dud. At Rose House we would all have dinner together and then the knitters would convene and have an agreeable evening in comfortable armchairs until bedtime. That wouldn't work at all now. There was nothing agreeable about having to head off in the blackout to go home.

"Mrs. Newton said to me last night that now we're not in Hester's darts league we might have to go and play in a pub," said Mr. Newton, looking aghast at the thought.

"I'm sure it was said in jest," said Monica.

"Either that or you'll end up down The Sailor's Rest, surrounded by men with tattoos," said Mrs. Shaw unhelpfully. "Can you imagine?"

Mr. Newton looked as if he certainly could.

"Well, now," said Guy, as the constructive start to the meeting appeared to have taken a turn, "at least you won't find yourself being coerced into communal activities on top of your jobs. I know how hard you all worked, despite the very pleasant surroundings at Rose House."

"We didn't mind," said Miss Peters.

"I liked them," agreed Hester.

"What we need is another wedding," said Mrs. Shaw. "Something to organise and look forward to."

"There is the end of the war," said Guy, still doing his best to lead the positive charge. "That's definitely something to look forward to."

The sighs and hmms from around the room spoke volumes.

"I'm with Mrs. Shaw," said Monica, which was a surprise. It was highly unusual for her not to back Guy to the hilt. "I think that's the problem we all have. Everything is so up in the air. We know we have to keep pushing on to Victory, but it's like a race where they keep moving the finish line. I'd bet a penny to a pound that our readers feel much the same." She paused, narrowing her eyes thoughtfully. "Do you know, I think this is what we should look at for 'It's Asking a Lot, But Let's Finish the Job.' We shouldn't tell them to work harder or keep chipper, or any of that. They've had it for five years. Let's give them suggestions for nice things to do, or to plan or look forward to, regardless of when the war ends."

As soon as she said it, I understood.

"Things they can have some control over," I said. "That make you feel a little bit better even if yet another mile gets added to the race."

Monica nodded. "That's right."

Guy was listening intently. He had been in this business long enough to know a good idea when he heard one. "They need to be simple, available to everyone, easy on time or money if you're short on either," he said. "Saying to the readers that we know you're all pushing hard so here's how you can have a moment for yourself. Yes. I like it."

"'Pick You Up' home tonics," said Monica. "Comforting recipes you can whip up in a flash."

"Like Mrs. Whiteley's crumbles," said Hester.

"Exactly."

One by one, ideas began to be offered as the team cottoned on to Monica's point. Anything that could bring cheer.

"Christmas will be here before we know it," said Mrs. Shaw. "We should think of ideas that perk people up when the war still isn't over."

"How about a fayre?" said Miss Peters. "We could suggest people put one on." She looked bashful. "It was the organising I liked best at Rose House. Helping with the wedding. That sort of thing."

"Everyone loves a fayre," I said.

"We could do our own," said Hester, her voice high with enthusiasm. "A Christmas fayre. Then we could tell the readers what we're doing every week to plan it and suggest they might like to do one too. We'd all be in it together."

"Oh yes," said Miss Peters. "I should like that very much."

"Might I suggest it could be in aid of a charity?" asked Mr. Brand in his quiet voice. "That might be rather a nice gesture."

"Hear, hear," said Mr. Newton, which was echoed by everyone.

"Tombola!" said Mrs. Shaw, loudly, as if she'd just won. "I have my own drum."

"I do love a tombola," said Monica. "One spends a fortune trying to win tins of peas."

"And a lucky dip," cried Hester. "With sawdust and you have to dig for the prizes."

"And it sticks to all the children's cardigan sleeves," smiled Miss Peters. "We've done them at church."

"Pin the tail on the donkey?" said Mr. Newton, as if it was a request.

Guy glanced at me and then Monica. He raised an eyebrow for just a second as one by one everyone joined in with their favourite stalls and games.

"The *Woman's Friend* Christmas Fayre," he said, thoughtfully. "It does have a ring to it. But are you quite sure about taking it on? You're all working your socks off as it is."

Guy was immediately pooh-poohed.

Suggestions began to fly around for committees and working parties, and how if they wanted, readers could get together with chums to turn "Finish the Job" into some fun. Forty-five minutes later, serious plans for both the magazine and an event were beginning to form, and Mr. Brand had already sketched out a yuletide inspired poster.

With everyone in full agreement, the deal was sealed.

"I will get to be in charge of the tombola, won't I?" asked Mrs. Shaw, as a final word on the subject. "I have experience."

"My dear Mrs. Shaw, there can be no one else," said Guy, wisely agreeing. "Now then, unless there are any additional suggestions, may I suggest we move on to other business. Mr. Newton, an advertising update if we may?"

But Monica raised her hand.

"There was just one thing," she said. "I hope no one will mind if I add this in, but it's really about Mr. Brand's very nice suggestion of raising funds. I'm going to ignore both Mr. Collins and Miss Lake on this one and just put this to the rest of us. Would anyone mind if we use the Christmas Fayre to raise money for the Red Cross Prisoners of War Fund? I think that might . . ."

Monica got no further. As Guy and I watched on, her voice was drowned out by a torrent of cheers from the best and very dearest team in the world.

CHAPTER 17

Wallace Carter Joins In

I spent the rest of the day hard at work. I finished an article about answering the call for home helps, and wrote up an interview I had done at a house in Surrey that ran rest breaks for war workers who were feeling the strain. Then I launched into a stack of readers' letters. By five o'clock, as the rest of the team were putting on their coats to go home, I was up to date, with just a tricky letter to write to a pregnant nineteen-year-old who was scared to tell her parents. My letter would go to her friend's address as she couldn't risk being found out. I sat chewing my pencil. There were no stock answers and invariably I had to guess at whether the parents in such a situation would be as angry as their daughter feared. Sometimes the girl could be surprised. Much of the time, however, sympathy was in very short supply.

I was saved from having to make an immediate decision by the arrival of Wallace Carter, whom I had invited round for a cup of tea and a chat. I knew she was keen to see what a real-life magazine was like and thought it might give her just a small boost.

"I hope you don't mind, but I wondered if this might be of help," I said, handing her a piece of paper. On it I had listed all the organisations I knew that might be worth writing to in the absence of any news from her husband.

"Mr. Gorman at the Prisoner of War department at the War Office, Miss Smythe at the Prisoner of War Information Bureau at the Foreign Office . . . the Directorate of Prisoners of War . . . the . . ." Wallace stopped reading and looked up. "Goodness, Emmy, I didn't know about half of these."

"Officially it's still not long since they were captured," I said. "Forgive me for putting it like that. I know every hour feels like a year. But as I've heard from Charles and we think they were together, it's worth you writing, just in case. I'm also a big believer in making oneself known."

"I'm a fast typist if I can be of any help." Hester had appeared and I quickly introduced her to Wallace.

"Hester's young man, Clarence, is in the Royal Artillery as well," I explained.

Hest beamed.

"He's still in England," she said. "I'm secretly glad, even if Clarence isn't. I'm ever so sorry about your husband, Mrs. Carter. I do hope you hear from him soon. The picture he took of Emmy and Major Mayhew is lovely."

It was just the right thing to say, and so very like Hest. I knew from experience that some people shied away from even mentioning it when your boy was injured or missing, and especially if they had died. I found it made things far worse. Hester was not like that, and sometimes she was wise beyond her years. Now I saw Wallace warm to her straight away, asking if Hest had a picture of Clarence, which of course made Hester's day. She said she would go and get one as soon as she'd finished the last of her typing.

"It's past five o'clock," I said, mock sternly. "Hester, just because you now live above the shop doesn't mean you should work late. I'm going to take Wallace to meet Monica. Come and join us and do bring a photograph."

With Hester promising that she would, Wallace and I headed upstairs to Monica, who always ignored standard office hours.

"How super to meet you," she said, shaking hands with Wallace. "Sorry about the mess. I'm trying to sort out a feature on re-using swagger coats."

A number of photographs from a recent fashion shoot were laid out on the floor of what had once been a front bedroom. It still had the floral wallpaper and heavy velvet curtains so did not exactly shriek "Fashion."

"How exciting," said Wallace, who did not seem to notice the reality of wartime accommodation.

"They have so much fabric in them," explained Monica as Wallace crouched down to look. "If anyone has one left of course. Most people have already cut theirs up. I do like your blouse, Mrs. Carter. Did you make it yourself? Beautiful stitching. Now, can I make you girls a cup of tea?" she asked as she headed toward the door. "I won't be long, and then I'd love to hear which of the snaps you think might work best."

When Monica had left, Wallace turned to me with big eyes.

"Is that *the* Monica Edwards?" she whispered. "From *Woman Today?*"

"It is," I replied. "Monica helped us buy *Woman's Friend* and then became our publisher. When we needed a new Fashion and Beauty Editor, she stepped in."

"And she's going to make the tea?" Wallace was goggle-eyed.

"We don't stand on ceremony much, here," I smiled as we sat down in the occasional chairs by Monica's desk. "This morning Monica was fighting over who would run the tombola. We're having a Christmas Fayre," I added, as Wallace looked lost. "We're going to raise money for the POW Fund."

"What fun," said Wallace. "If you need any help, please let me know."

"That would be super," I said. "There's masses to do, if you're sure. Everyone got rather carried away and we haven't long to organise it. We're hoping to get the church hall. I thought about asking some of the other wives to come if they're in London. Do you think they might?"

"Absolutely," replied Wallace. "I've written to some of the girls whose boys are missing and told them you've heard from Major Mayhew. I'm hoping they might have heard too."

I nodded. "I asked him about your friend Johnny Bagley in my letter last night and of course, I mention your Tom all the time. I don't know if it will get past the censor though or how many of the letters they actually receive. I wish Charles and I had worked out a code or something. My friend in the Red Cross says sometimes the information about prisoners just gets lost and people don't hear for ages, even though their boy is quite safe. I know they'll be doing all they can to find him."

"That's ever so kind," said Wallace. "It's nice to know we're all trying, isn't it? Doreen Townsend said to say how grateful she is for your advice about her husband's wages. I don't think she quite believed that the major's wife would go to all that trouble."

"It's the least I can do," I said. "Please tell the others I'm nothing fancy. I just work here so I have lots of leaflets."

Wallace looked at me and then around the office. On the front of the large wardrobe a pre-war Burberry overcoat had been placed carefully on a hanger with Monica's favourite Schiaparelli scarf draped over the top. The current issue of *Vogue* lay open on her desk next to several swatches of new utility fabric and a large pad with notes in her beautiful handwriting.

"I don't think that will help," said Wallace. "Your photo is in a magazine every week. That's very swish."

"Honestly, Monica's the swish one," I said. "And as you've seen, she's as down to earth as anyone. Wallace, I'd love to be able to help the other women and their families if I can. We were saying this morning that things always feel a bit better when you're not on your own, and I know Charles would be pleased if I could be useful." Now I paused. "I probably shouldn't say this, but in my job, I have to be quite careful what I say in the magazine. *Woman's Friend* tries to be helpful and encouraging, and if you read it, you wouldn't know that we get just as frustrated about some of the Government's rules and endless departments as everyone else. And don't start me on war work. I once got thrown out of a factory for asking awkward questions about shifts."

"Good for you," said Wallace, clasping her hands together. "Does the major know?"

"Charles? Oh yes. Remind me to tell you about our wedding day some time. It was quite fun. The thing is, at *Woman's Friend* we're careful about how often we mention war widows or how bad their pensions are, or the difficulty in finding out about the men missing in action or wounded. I suppose that's the grimmer, sad side of war. And while it's not taboo to write about it, and we do try, we're a popular magazine, not a political one. If I could do something separate to my job to try to support you and the others, I'd be awfully pleased. Perhaps you and I could even work together in some way?"

"Careful how you answer that. Emmy's a devil for getting people to volunteer." It was Monica, returning with a tray of tea. "Before you know it, you'll have a job here and no trace of a social life."

I knew Monica well enough to know that this had already crossed her mind. Wallace smiled back, still slightly in awe of her, which I entirely understood.

"Most harsh," I said. "Although I have mentioned the fayre."

"Perfect," said Monica. "We need all the help we can get. Can I steal you if you fancy helping out on the costumes? I understand there's been a development that involves some sort of a show."

"I'd be absolutely delighted," said Wallace. "I'm not bad on the machine."

"I knew it the moment you said you make your own clothes," said Monica. "Those pin tucks are a dream. Now, I'm stopping you two from talking about business. Ah good, here's Hester." Hest had appeared, shyly holding her framed photo. "Come on in. Emmy, might I listen in on your plans with Wallace? If there's anything I can do, I should very much like to be of help."

Darling C

How are you? Are you well? I do hope so. I've just sent you another parcel. I shan't tell you everything that's in it so that there are some surprises, but you'll be glad to know tobacco (Wallace says she's heard this is better for currency than cigs?) and a vest and gloves (don't worry—made by Bunts, not by me—they'd have 27 fingers!). Also, razor, soap, 2 x paperbacks and tin opener. Everyone wanted to put something in.

I know I mention him every time, but Tom's wife Wallace Carter has been here for supper with Hest and me. (Guy is out with Richard L whom you met. He's nice. I like him.) She is a smashing girl but so worried. She and I are starting a sort of round robin letter for the other wives/families. They all write with questions or news—mostly to W—re the boys and we are going to put them all in a letter once a fortnight + with tips etc. It's nice to do and Wallace says it's cheered her up already being part of something. You should know this new venture is all your fault for saying in your letter to pass on that you are proud of the men. I did and they were so pleased and now it's led to this. So, thank you darling and hurrah!

Plans are also getting going for the Christmas fayre—the gang are crazy about it and it's turning into Pimlico's answer to the Ziegfeld Follies. I've signed up to do waitressing on the teas. Black dress, white cuffs, and all! I'll try to get a photograph for you. The children desperately want to come up to London for it but we'll see how things are. They are writing to you. Stan wants you to know he got his Signaller badge at Cubs. He's very proud.

Well, I'd better go to bed. I'll have a chat with the photo of us first. I know that makes me sound rather mad! I always do at half past 10 every night so if you're awake your time, you'll know and can chat back. They can certify us both when you get home. I won't mind a bit as long as they lock us up together. More tomorrow. I love you. We all do. But you know I do the most.

All my love. E. xxxxxxxx

CHAPTER 18

A Dignitary Steps Up

The next weeks were a busy jumble as Guy, Hester, and I found our feet in our new household together and I settled into a routine that took up almost all my waking hours, which was exactly what I needed. It was full steam ahead on *Woman's Friend*, with Mrs. Harewood back in her old role on the letters page and Mrs. Newton and Mrs. Brand now permanent part-time members of the staff. The only challenge was fitting us all in. Monica, who was an old hand at spotting talent, had asked Wallace if she might help out with the fashion and beauty pages, which had been a marvellous move. With her mother looking after little Daphne, Wallace now came in several mornings a week. This meant Monica could reclaim the odd hour or two for her social life, Hester was thrilled to have a young chum on the team, and I was able to keep up with the news from the other wives. Best of all, Wallace was delighted.

Evenings were cheerful too, even if some of them were spent in the air raid shelter. Rumours were everywhere about attacks from new bombs that were even bigger than the V-1s.

"Let's just say there seem to be an awful lot of gas mains blowing up recently," said Roy, cynically. "At least that's what everyone's being told."

We tried not to think about it and, like everyone else, just kept going. Guy insisted on doing his share of the cooking, which was always rather an event, even if his nights involved a level of culinary perfectionism that meant we would eat just before bed. These became known as *Soirées Parisienne* due to Guy saying that late dining was de rigueur when he lived in Paris as a young man.

"Oh dear," said Monica, in mock despair. "It's Montmartre all over again."

"What happened there?" I asked.

"Nothing at all," replied Monica, wide-eyed with innocence to make Hester laugh.

"Ignore Mrs. Edwards, Hester," said Guy, calmly. "She wasn't even there."

Hest and I looked at each other.

"I bet they were awfully dull," I whispered, rudely.

I didn't believe that at all.

When we weren't pretending to be in nineteen-twenties France or trying to beat each other at Monopoly, I wrote to Charles, planned work articles, or worked on the round robin news. Sometimes letters now came directly to me from the other wives and mothers.

Dear Mrs. Mayhew

Please excuse me for writing. Mrs. Carter says you won't mind. My son is a gunner in your husband's regiment and was taken prisoner at Arnhem. I haven't heard from him yet and no one can tell me where he is. Would it be all right if you ask Major Mayhew if he has heard of him or knows where he might be?

I have enclosed a photograph with Geoffrey's details and service number written on it should you wish to send it on. I have many others, so I don't mind.

Thank you in advance.

Yours sincerely

Mrs. C. Barber

I wrote to both Mrs. Barber and Charles that night, pretending in my letter to Charles that Mrs. Barber was an old friend who happened to ask after Geoff. I hoped Charles would read between the lines. I hoped even more that the German censor would not.

———

Ideas for the inaugural *Woman's Friend* Christmas Fayre had grown at a rate of knots. The vicar at St. Gabriel's had kindly given us the church hall in early December, and when he said that the building was ours until midnight, within seconds we were putting on a daytime fayre followed by an evening talent show. Or as Guy put it, "Mrs. Shaw has got carried away."

None of us minded. It was nice to have another cheerful thing to plan. As December loomed, several members of the organisational committee arranged to meet at the hall for the first time. Monica and I were to go straight from a meeting with the Ministry at Senate House. Along with a small group of other editors from the women's press, we attended a regular briefing where the Ministry informed us of what they wanted our magazines to focus on in the coming months. As ever, the invitees were a mix of well-turned-out women, confident-looking men, and Ministry employees with the serious air of people who were busy winning the war all on their own.

Today we had started with seasonal vegetables and progressed to an assistant deputy director giving a lecture about encouraging our readers to keep going as The End of the War Was in Sight. There were lots of references to lights at ends of tunnels, but equally how we must ensure our readers knew that the final push was going to be hard and it was their duty to be up to the mark.

"What the hell does he think we've been doing?" said a statuesque features editor to me as we were dismissed. "Gadding down to Monte Carlo and having a lark?"

Before I could answer, Richard Langley appeared, marching towards me with a friendly smile.

"Miss Lake! Good afternoon. Do you have a moment, please? Just a very quick chat on a couple of things. Good afternoon, Mrs. Edwards."

Monica greeted him and then said that she would meet me downstairs.

"Might as well nip into my office," said Langley, which as the building was enormous made it sound more than a very quick chat, but I followed him as he enquired after Charles.

"Have you heard anything more?" he asked as we headed along to the stairs.

"Just the card so far. Hoping for a letter soon," I replied, brightly. "Several of the other wives are still waiting, though."

"Difficult times," said Langley. "But I'm so glad your husband is safe. I could see Mr. Collins was very relieved."

It was surnames only when in the confines of this building.

"We all are," I said, trying to keep up with his long stride without trotting along like a faun. "Now we just need the war to end so he can come home."

"Of course."

When we arrived at his office, he became a little less formal.

"I wanted to thank you again for your reports," he said. "The ones from Brussels were excellent. The top chaps liked them, and I'm told they went down very well over there too. I hope you're happy to do more. Britain based though. If you could continue to focus on our war workers, especially domestics, that would be much appreciated."

"Yes, Mr. Langley. It's top of the list."

"Good, and we're not as concerned about post-war careers articles, so don't worry about those."

The previous week's issue had included a column answering readers' questions about jobs they might do after the war. I had mentioned joining the post office or the police.

"Actually, I think our readers are keen to look beyond Victory," I said, politely. "They'll still need to pay the rent and feed their families, even after Hitler's done in. Many women will still need to work. And it's a modern world now," I added, with my best diplomatic smile. "It's not just the men who have done their bit to win the war and now want a better life."

"Yes, of course," replied Richard. "Now, there was just one other thing." He sounded slightly hesitant. "Not a big point, but we noticed you ran a letter from a reader whose husband has recently been reported missing."

"That's right."

Now Langley looked awkward. "I'm speaking very informally here, but just to say, it was noticed that the lady was quite spirited . . . negative even about her situation."

"Well, unsurprisingly, she's very worried about him, and on a more practical level, she has no money coming in," I said. "Until he's found, his wages are stopped. She and her family get nothing until her husband is confirmed to be either a POW, or dead. It's grim."

I looked him directly in the eye and he frowned.

"I do understand," he said, "and please know that I'm with you in your sympathy for this lady. I also understand that this has a personal resonance for you now." He paused for a moment. "Look, Emmy, this is just an off-the-record tip. Perhaps when you answer this sort of query, you could mention how hard the Government's departments are working, how we all stand together with our servicemen's families. You know the sort of thing."

I knew that Richard was doing his job and trying to make sure I didn't get into hot water, but none of this was going to help the reader feed her family.

"Mr. Langley . . . Richard. She has written to eleven different departments, all of which have a remit for POWs but none of which appear to be able to help. Can you see how worrying this is for wives in her position?" I sighed, knowing that it had nothing to do with him. "I do appreciate your candour and of course will have your comments in mind. Thank you for giving me the tip."

Richard looked relieved. "No, thank *you*. I'm sorry I have to toe the party line," he said. "It must be especially hard for you now."

"Not at all. I'm fine," I said. "And unlike lots of people I have a job, accommodation, and only myself to support. And it does make all the difference that I know where Charles is and that he's safe. I must admit that waiting to hear was quite a strain." I smiled at him. "But I can deal with anything anyone throws at me, now."

"I don't doubt it," he replied. Then the slightest twinkle appeared in his eyes. "Hitler doesn't know what he's up against."

"That's true," I agreed with gusto. "But I'm no tougher than most women. You should meet more of our readers, then you'd understand." A thought occurred to me. "I say, Mr. Langley. How is your diary for next month? It's just we're looking for a local dignitary to open our fundraising event."

"*The* Mr. Langley?" Mrs. Shaw was incredulous. "From *the* Ministry of Information? Well, I never. That *is* something to write home about."

"Nice catch," boomed Harold from the other end of the church hall where he was measuring the stage. "You bagged a good one there. We should get the evening paper down. Have a picture of Richard with one of the champion pets." He put his tape measure in his pocket and came over. "There's plenty of room up there for Buzz and the girls," he added.

Buzz and some of the All Girls Band had kindly agreed to make the trip to Pimlico and provide the music for the evening dance. They were a guaranteed hit so now we just had to make sure the rest of the day would go well. The committee was being led with military precision by Mrs. Shaw and Miss Peters, with additional input from the rest of the team. This evening, they were allowing Guy to pretend he had even the slightest control over any of it by making him chair the meeting.

"He brings real decorum to everything, doesn't he?" said Mrs. Shaw.

"And he's got a nice speaking voice," said Miss Peters. "Don't tell him though," she added.

A semi-circle of chairs had been set up so that we could both discuss and survey at the same time. Almost everyone had come along, other than Hester who had taken the day off to go all the way to Wiltshire to watch Clarence in an important parade. She would join us later if the trains didn't play up.

"Mr. Collins," said Mrs. Shaw, ceremonially. "If you would."

"Thank you," said Guy in his nice voice. "So, lots to do. Shall we start with Captain Thomas, who I believe is in charge of pets?"

"Representing Masters George and Stanley Jenkins and Miss Margaret Jenkins, who send their apologies," added Mrs. Shaw when Guy forgot to mention them.

"A career high," grinned Harold. "In a nutshell the pet show is bound to be mayhem. Good fun all round."

"Is that your full update?" asked Guy.

"More or less," said Harold, calm as ever. "We've had a very good response regarding entries although I've had to turn down the python on grounds of safety. On the upside, PC Monroe is coming with his Alsatian dog, which should be fine although it isn't keen on cats. That should add some jeopardy. Oh, and we have some very good prizes. Over to you, Mr. Newton."

Mr. Newton sat up to attention and cleared his throat.

"Thank you, Captain Thomas," he said. "Mr. and Mrs. Bone from the newsagents have sponsored the Best in Show Championship with a commemorative cup and a three-month subscription to *Animal and Zoo Magazine*."

"Oh, I say," said Mrs. Shaw, looking impressed.

Mr. Newton knitted his brow at the interruption but kept his composure.

"Please go on, Mr. Newton," said Guy.

"Thank you, Mr. Collins. Dickie Durton has provided a two-shilling postal order for the Best Caged Bird, excluding pigeons or we'll be overrun with the things, and finally, for the Juniors, Benny the cat-meat man has donated a pound of undisclosed offal and a ride on his barrow if the overall winner is under ten."

There was a collective "ooh" at that. Benny Cat Meat was a favourite with the local children as he was always followed on his round by a cavalcade of animals, all hoping for snacks.

"He'll be good with the Alsatian," added Mr. Newton. "Dogs and cats never fight when Benny's around."

"A metaphor for us all," said Guy. "Very generous indeed. Thank you, gentlemen. Emmy, how is the evening looking?"

Now I began my update.

"Buzz is sorted as you know. Fred and Roy assure me that the bar will be well stocked, and I think we can trust them on that. We've had lots of entries to the talent show, and Guy has kindly volunteered to act as accompanist on the piano, which is exciting. Sadly, the fire-eating act has had to drop out as Roy said the station boys would prefer not to have to put him out if they're manning the bar. It's disappointing, I know," I added as there was a loud tut from Mrs. Shaw, "but we can't have someone setting fire to the Girl Guides. Other than that, it's just the costumes. Mrs. Edwards?"

"All in hand," confirmed Monica. "A big thank-you to Emmy and Hester, who have been sewing their hearts out, along with our newest member of the team, Mrs. Carter, who has the patience of a saint. All the costumes are finished other than Mr. Trevin's, who has asked for more embroidery on his bolero."

The look on Guy's face shrieked, "Of course he has," but he said nothing.

Mr. Trevin was *Woman's Friend*'s zodiac expert whose column, "Your Stars, My Pleasure," was hugely popular with the readers. He was very nice but prone to showing off. Guy, who thought astrology a fabrication of the highest order, found him a struggle.

"It is quite intricate," admitted Wallace. "But I really don't mind. I believe Mr. Trevin has a background in treading the boards."

"Classical guitar," breathed Mrs. Shaw, who was something of a fan. "And as a younger man, flamenco dance."

"Marvellous. I think that's everything, isn't it?" I said, quickly, while avoiding looking at Guy.

To my relief, a diversion was created by the arrival of Hester, who was looking very smart in her best frock and a little black hat with bows on the front. Her hands were clasped to her chest, and she was wearing the biggest smile in the world.

"Hello, Hester," I called out. "How was Clarence? Did it go well?"

"Yes, thank you," she said, her eyes shining. "It was all lovely. He looked ever so handsome, and the sergeant major said he did very well."

She looked as if she was about to explode.

"Is everything all right?" asked Monica.

"Oh yes, Mrs. Edwards," said Hester, her smile even wider. "Private Clarence Boone and I are engaged."

Mrs. Shaw gasped, Miss Peters made a squeaking noise, and Monica clapped her hands together.

Everyone leapt to their feet as Hester was surrounded by the whole team wanting to offer their congratulations.

"Well done, Hest," I said, hugging her as hard as I could. "And well done, Clarence. It couldn't happen to two nicer people."

"Thank you," whispered Hester, overwhelmed.

"Now we need to make the Christmas Fayre an even bigger party than ever," said Monica.

Now, I thought to myself, we need Clarence to stay safely where he is until the end of the war.

———

My darling Em. This is my first proper letter to you! Forgive the squashed writing as we don't get much room. Thank you so much for your wonderful parcel. Cigs and chocolate! Please thank everyone and send my best regards. I have rec'd lots of letters from you—keep them coming as when I read them, I can hear and see you and can pretend we are together. Thank you for taking the wives under your wing. I am very well but pls can you send brushes and socks and vests as the temperature is dropping a bit. Love to all. Take care, darling. Your own, C.xxxxx

CHAPTER 19

A Festive Success

While a sixth Christmas at war was the last thing any of us wanted, I knew I had much to be grateful for. If the Germans played by the rules, Charles should be able to write several times a month. We could send him as many letters as we wished, and of course parcels, which was now my main concern. It was highly likely that whatever kit he was wearing when he was captured would not be adequate for a prison camp in the winter months. Everyone I knew wanted to help, to knit, to give me precious coupons for supplies, or even spend long hours roaming the shops in search of elusive provisions to send to Charles.

The *Woman's Friend* generosity of spirit wasn't just about me. Wallace had been warmly welcomed into the team. Everyone knew about our newsletter and how we were trying to pull together with the other women whose husbands, brothers, and sons had been sent to Europe with Charles. They heard about their stories, and the uncertainties they faced, and they saw for themselves how brave Wallace was in the absence of any news about Tom.

Without exception, everyone had thrown themselves into organising the Inaugural *Woman's Friend* Christmas Fayre in aid of the Prisoner of War Fund. Wallace and I had told the other women about it, and to my delight, some of them from London and even farther afield said they were going to come.

Bunty and I had also thought long and hard about letting the children return to London for the event. It had not been a lightly taken decision, not least as Mr. Churchill had confirmed that the "flying gas mains," as Roy put it, were in fact, Hitler's V-2 rockets, a bigger, nastier version than the V-1s. But the children had begged and begged, and finally, when Roy and Fred assured us that they and the boys from the station would not let the kids out of their sight, we had relented. The church hall was next to the air-raid shelter. If a warning sounded, we all knew what to do, and fast. The children were elated, and promised they would not leave our sides.

Now the day of the fayre had arrived, and with a quarter of an hour to go before the Grand Opening, Stan's main concern was a million miles away from the V-2s.

"You said no to a snake? A real, live snake?"

Harold had let himself down.

"Correct."

"But that would have made this the best pet show ever."

"Stan," said Harold, "it's still going to be the best pet show ever. It's just that pythons are very big anima—"

"It was A PYTHON?"

Harold had just made things worse. "I'm sorry, old chap," he said. "Don't be cross. It was probably hibernating anyway. Terribly dull."

"You mean brumating, Harold," said Stanley, in the sort of polite voice you use for someone you feel sorry for.

"We're not cross, really," said Marg, trying to help.

"I am a bit," said Stan, who was a stickler for telling the truth.

"Not to worry," said Bunty, coming over from the tombola stand where Mrs. Shaw was looking on top of the world. "By the way, Mrs. Shaw says there's a tin of Nescafé, but don't say a word."

"Very wise," said Harold. "We don't want a riot." No one had seen a tin of coffee in ages.

"Did someone say Nescafé?" shouted Roy from the other side of the hall.

"No," said Bunty, trying to avoid Mrs. Shaw's eye.

I looked at my watch. There was just about time to make sure everything was under control. The church hall had been transformed into a yuletide fayre of delight. Every piece of red fabric anyone could get their hands on had been made into bows and tied to tables. Someone had even lent a tree covered in ribbons and glass baubles that an American GI had given them the previous year. Hester and I had spent the week staying up making paper chains from scraps out of the salvage bin, and sacks of holly and fir had been brought up from Rose House so that Mrs. Brand and Mrs. Newton could turn them into festive displays for the Christmas Fripperies stand.

Mrs. Shaw's tombola stall set the standard in terms of prizes, and some of the parcels in the Children's Lucky Dip were actual Quality Street sweets that Miss Peters' aunt had been keeping for Victory Day. There was even a Pin the Tail on the Hitler stall where Mr. Brand had painted a perfect likeness of old Adolf as a very fat pig.

Miss Peters' Tea Room was ready for business, where she and I, and to everyone's delight, Monica, were ready to serve in black frocks and white pinnies. The whole thing had the look of a Lyons' Corner House. Just past Mrs. Mahoney's book stall, a huge, over-confident parrot called Norman added an exotic touch, even if he did keep shouting "Not now, Colonel" whenever anyone walked past.

Everything was perfect. I wished so much that Charles were here. It had been the most tremendous effort all round.

"It's quite something, isn't it?" said Guy, quietly. "Would you like to say a few words before we start? I can if you prefer but I think it should come from you."

I nodded and cleared my throat.

"Can I have everyone's attention, please?" I called. "I just want to say thank you for everything, especially the generosity to the Prisoners of War. You've all worked so hard. Charles will be chuffed to bits to hear about it." I stopped, a lump in my throat. "Thank you."

There was a very kind round of applause as Guy said, "Hear, hear. And may I introduce our dignitary? I believe most of you know him. This is Mr. Langley from the Ministry of Information, who has generously given his time to open our event."

Everyone clapped as Richard, who was standing beside me, nodded graciously. Smartly turned out in a dark three-piece suit, he certainly looked the part.

"It is my pleasure," he said, but unfortunately moved too close to Norman, who let himself down and shrieked, "Shut your cake hole, Big Lad."

"Good luck, Langley," said Guy in a stage whisper. "It's too late to run now."

"I'll find his owner," I said and with a last-minute stomach flip of nerves headed to the exit.

A queue of people stretched right down the road.

By half past two, the hall was full. With Miss Peters' Tea Room in high demand and Monica purposely letting slip about the chance of winning the Nescafé on the tombola, everyone was doing a roaring trade.

I had just served tea to Mr. and Mrs. Bone when Wallace came up to me with a group of women, several of whom had children who were wide-eyed with excitement at the animals and stalls.

"Mrs. Mayhew," she said, "may I introduce you to some of the ladies from the newsletter? This is Mrs. Harris, Mrs. Kelly, Mrs. Franklin . . ."

Within seconds introductions were being made, shyly by some, but everyone said how jolly the fayre looked.

"Thank you very much for coming," I said. "And for helping with information for the newsletter. I do hope it's useful."

"Thank you for doing it," said a slight young woman carrying a baby. "I've met Mrs. Harris here because of it—both our boys got put in the same camp, but we didn't know each other before."

"We were so sorry the major got captured," said Mrs. Harris. She was a pretty woman, I guessed about the same age as me. But there were dark circles under her eyes, and she blinked anxiously. "I'm glad he's safe."

"That's very kind," I said, adding confidently, "It won't be long now."

I knew almost all the women by name. There were wives, mothers, a sister. Two had brought friends, both of whom had husbands who were being kept prisoner in the Far East, and those women had hardly heard a thing from them in nearly three years. I managed to grab a couple of empty tables in the tea area, and everyone began to talk about their boys. Some of them were in the same situation as me and had received a telegram or even letters. Others were like Wallace and had been waiting weeks for any news at all.

Mrs. Harris started to tell me about her husband. He had been wounded during the fighting but had written from the camp and said he was being treated well.

"I don't know if I believe that though," she said, her eyes full of concern. "My husband is the most honest man you would ever meet, but he wouldn't be allowed to put anything bad in his letter, would he? What do you think, Mrs. Mayhew?"

I was just about to answer her when Hester appeared at my shoulder.

"Sorry to bother you," she whispered, "but there's a reporter here from *The West London News*. He's taken a picture and wants someone to say something about us doing the fayre."

Mrs. Harris had shrunk back in her seat.

"Sorry, Hester, I can't come just at the moment," I said. "Can you ask Guy or Monica?"

"They're judging the Best in Show, and the man says he's got to leave in a minute," she replied, apologetically.

"Hest, would you mind having a word with him, please?" I asked. "Just say *Woman's Friend* is very pleased to be able to support the

Prisoner of War Fund as it's very close to our and our readers' hearts. You'll be fine, I promise. You've done a huge amount of the organising."

Hester looked slightly wide eyed at having to speak with the press, but *The West London News* was a small paper known for covering local events and I knew they would just want a line or two to go with a photograph.

"Right you are," said Hest. "I won't let you down." Then she raced off.

"I'm so sorry, Mrs. Harris," I said. "I understand about the letters. I've only had one and I looked between the lines for hours, trying to see if there were secret signs that my husband isn't actually all right. Then I realised that he would hate for me to worry like that. Perhaps Bombardier Harris might be the same? They don't want us to lose sleep, so I'm just trying my best to take it at face value." I tried an encouraging smile. I wasn't being entirely truthful, but that wasn't the point.

Mrs. Harris nodded. "Yes," she said. "Herbert won't want me worrying. I do trust him."

"Of course you do," I said.

At that point Mrs. Kelly, who had come all the way from Gravesend, joined in, saying that to take their minds off things, she and a group of wives who lived nearby were planning to hold their own fayre.

"Why don't you do one too?" she asked Mrs. Harris.

"I might," she answered. "There are quite a few girls near me who are in the same boat. I'll see what they say."

"If any of you do, we can put them in the newsletter," I said. "It will cheer things up. Whatever you're happy for us to share with everyone, or if there are questions someone may be able to help with, we'll put it in."

"They'll like that," said Mrs. Harris. "And it's nice to know you're not on your own. You read such frightening news in the papers. I always wonder, if what they're printing is bad, how much worse are the things they can't say?"

I nodded in agreement. "It's hard, isn't it?" I said. "We just have to keep going." It was an inadequate reply. "I do hope you enjoy today," I added, "and that it's at least a bit of a change. Will you keep me updated? I would very much like to know how Bombardier Harris gets on."

"Of course," said Mrs. Harris. "And it's been lovely to get out. We're going to have a go on the tombola," she added. "Everyone's talking about it. There's still a tin of coffee that's got to be won."

CHAPTER 20

My Name Is Mrs. Juliet Bagley

The day had been an enormous success. At five o'clock the tables were cleared and Hester and Bunty led the festive redecorating, with visitors to the fayre staying on to help. Within an hour we had a Christmas dance hall on our hands. Heavy curtains had been pulled across the windows, and with the help of some borrowed rescue lamps, a rather professional stage was set.

At six o'clock sharp the talent show began. First to go on was Mr. Parsons from the hardware shop, with a crowd-pleasing rendition of Gilbert and Sullivan's "He Is an Englishman." Then Mr. Trevin and his flamenco guitar gave a highly charged performance, which went well despite Mrs. Shaw jumping the gun and shouting "Bravo" during a prolonged pause for dramatic effect. Monica said she could die happy now she'd seen Guy accompanying PC Monroe when he did "O Jesus, I Have Promised" on the spoons, and in the end Sally from the wool shop, who sang like a lark, was declared the winner to unanimous acclaim. All the time, the cider flowed.

After the talent show, it was time for the dance, and within moments the floor was packed as Buzz and the girls took to the stage. As they began to play "In the Mood," I leaned back against the bar to watch. The children had loved every minute of the day. Marg was dancing with her old schoolfriend Ginger Belinda, Stan was jigging around quite happily on his own, and George was concentrating on his feet rather than look anywhere near Hester who had got him to dance. It had been worth the risk to bring them back. Nevertheless, an ever-vigilant Harold sat nearby, surreptitiously keeping track of where they all were.

For the next hour everyone danced their hearts out, clapping and cheering each song, switching partners, encouraging the reluctant, and making sure no one was left out. Some of the more local POWs' wives had stayed on, which was lovely to see. They were standing together and watching the dancing, so I grabbed Roy and Fred, and took them over to meet them.

"May I have the honour?" asked Roy, offering his arm to Mrs. Harris.

"Ladies, would you excuse me one moment?" asked Fred. "I know some other gentlemen who won't want to miss out."

When he told the rest of the firemen who the women were, not one lady was left on her own, whether dancing, or with company by her side if she preferred to just watch.

As the band took a break, to everyone's delight Guy went back to the piano, and some of the singers got up to do another turn. Monica even managed to persuade Guy to do "London Pride" on his own.

I never thought I would see my brother-in-law with his shirt sleeves rolled up, a glass of beer and a half-smoked cigarette smouldering in an ashtray on top of a piano as he played and now sang. I would have given my eye teeth for Charles to be there.

"He says he'll only do it if we all join in the chorus," cried Monica from the stage. Everyone cheered and enthusiastically did as they were told.

"Come on, everyone," called out Monica as Guy got to the last part. "Altogether."

At the end of the song about the city we all loved, everyone went wild.

"I'm not even from London," I yelled, arm in arm with Mrs. Kelly and Roy who was cheering his head off.

"Doesn't matter," Roy shouted back. "Anyone who's been through the last five years here like you have has earned it."

Guy got up from the piano and left the stage to a storm of applause. His tie was undone, and his hair was falling into his eyes.

"I've not sung in years," he said. "I think I need another drink."

"You're awfully good," I said, handing him the one I had half drunk. "I say, Richard, did you know Guy can sing?"

Richard had been the only one showing any decorum by watching from near the bar. He was from one of His Majesty's ministerial departments after all.

"Not a clue," he said, smiling. "Well done, old chap." He raised his glass.

As Buzz's girls broke into "Moonlight Serenade," an older dark-haired lady appeared and touched my arm.

"I'm so sorry to interrupt, Mrs. Mayhew," she said. "I've only just managed to get here. I've been visiting my sister, and the trains were absolutely stuck. My name is Mrs. Juliet Bagley. I'm Lieutenant Jonathan Bagley's mother. I just wanted to say thank you. You wrote to your husband for me, and I'm very grateful."

Buzz and the girls faded into the background.

"Mrs. Bagley, how nice to meet you," I said. "It's so good of you to come. Shall we find somewhere quieter to talk, and can I make you a cup of tea?"

"That would be lovely," she replied, and we made our way to where it was far easier to hear oneself think.

"I must tell you that we don't usually have parties like this," I said. "Please excuse us. Have you had any news?"

"It's lovely to see such happiness," she said, generously. "But no, I'm afraid I've heard nothing yet about John. I'm sure he's all right, but no one can tell me where he is."

I pulled out a couple of stools and motioned for her to sit down.

"He may be with Charles," I said. "I've only had one proper letter from him, and I don't think he'd had mine asking about your son. So, it is possible he's there. I mention him regularly in my letters along with Lieutenant Carter just in case not all of them get through, and I've written to some friends who are nurses in Brussels, just in case."

It was very much against the rules, but Alice and Winnie had searched for any records of both men and found nothing. It didn't mean they hadn't been through the hospital there, as some of the men had no identification, but it was worth a shot.

"Thank you," said Mrs. Bagley again.

"Not at all. There's been nothing from the Red Cross?"

Mrs. Bagley shook her head. She was in her forties, smartly dressed, and with dark-framed spectacles.

"They've been very kind," she said. "I've become quite a pest, I'm afraid."

"I doubt that very much," I replied.

"No, I think I have," she said, with a rueful smile. "I've sent letters to everyone. Anyone with a remit for the prisoners, or the boys who are missing." Now she began to count off on her fingers the names of multiple departments that were dispiritingly familiar to me. "I have a cousin in America who has been writing to international organisations there, and I can't tell you how often I sit through that awful Lord Haw-Haw on the radio, as sometimes he does mention names. Everyone must think I've gone mad, but it's better than just waiting, isn't it?"

"It very much is," I agreed. "Mrs. Bagley, I think you're doing everything you can to get news about your son. There's nothing mad about that at all."

"I saw Mrs. Carter earlier," said Mrs. Bagley. "She said there was a gentleman here from the Ministry of Information. I wondered if I might speak with him. Do you think he would mind?"

I didn't care if Richard did. I must have mentioned Tom Carter to him a dozen times since meeting Wallace.

"I'll introduce you," I said. "We'll both speak to him. He gets it all the time. Anyone in any of the ministerial offices is bound to. I don't know if he can help, but it is worth it, isn't it? *Everything* is worth it. Mrs. Carter says that all the time."

Mrs. Bagley nodded and took a sip of tea. For all her cutting an impressive figure, and coming across as awfully capable, I knew she must be worried sick.

"Johnny will think I've been making a terrible fuss," she said.

"Nonsense. If I ever become a mother, I hope I shall be exactly like you," I replied.

Mrs. Bagley smiled almost sadly. "We're all doing our best. I very much admire Mrs. Carter. She's awfully young for all this."

"She's as brave as they come," I said. "I admire her too. She has the baby at home and now she's throwing herself into work, despite all the worry."

"I do hope she hears from her husband soon," said Mrs. Bagley.

She continued to tell me of her efforts to trace her son, all of which had taken time, tenacity, and a confidence not everyone had.

"If one's not terribly keen on writing letters or becoming a sleuth, it must be impossible," she said. "Those are the mothers I feel for. I've met quite a lot recently. No wonder some of them say that no one is listening to them. There's nothing worse."

We sat in silence for a moment. Then I spoke.

"Some people are listening," I said. "And none of them will think you are making a fuss. Would you mind if we join you? There is a group of women I would like you to meet."

CHAPTER 21

Enjoy Every Second You Get

After the fayre, I stayed up late into the night writing to Charles, relaying all the details and telling him about meeting Juliet Bagley and the other ladies from the battery. I had taken great cheer that friendships had begun to blossom between women who found a comfort of sorts in knowing the others understood. It had also given me much food for thought, especially speaking with Mrs. Bagley. Her son Johnny was barely older than Clarence. He should have been enjoying himself, flirting with girls and breaking hearts. Instead, he was still missing, presumed captured, or, and neither of us had said it, worse. His mother was bearing it with more dignity and grace than I would have managed, but even though she spoke calmly, her point struck home. Was anyone actually listening to women like her?

In the office on Monday morning, I unearthed everything we had ever printed about prisoners of war. It wasn't a hard job as our filing system was excellent, but most striking was that if I compared the size of the battered buff file on POWs with those about having affairs or unwanted pregnancies or jobs or even queries about being too thin or too fat, the amount of coverage about challenges faced by the wives and families was significant by its scarcity.

I understood it. Our role at *Woman's Friend* was to encourage hope, not dwell on sadness and fear. But I couldn't deny that if your boy had gone missing, you could be forgiven for thinking that we either weren't listening, or that it wasn't important to us.

I wanted them to know that we *were* listening, and that it was very important indeed.

I went straight upstairs to see Guy and Monica.

"I want to write something to show the readers we understand," I said. "I want to tell them about Charles."

Guy raised his eyebrows. We never wrote about ourselves in the magazine. Only once, when it looked as if *Woman's Friend* might have to close, but never about our families or personal lives.

"Go on," he said.

"I haven't thought it through," I said, "so this may be awful. But we never admit that we're just like them—the readers. That we're worried about our boys, or that Hester's fiancé will get posted, or that we wish the war was over and are scared of losing even more people we love."

"We did say we should take a more personal approach," said Monica. "As long as it isn't depressing or self-indulgent. That wouldn't do."

I shook my head. "Definitely not. Sometimes I get letters saying we don't understand or it's all right for us as we're in swanky, safe jobs. I just want to say that we know we're extremely lucky on some counts, but we're still in the same war. We have exactly the same hopes and fears."

Guy had leaned his elbows on his desk, closing his eyes and rubbing his forehead as he thought. Finally, he spoke.

"Do it," he said. "We'll run it in the new year. One last push and all that." He looked out of the window, his face drawn and a million miles away from the carefree version on Saturday night. "Our last new year at war. It can't come fast enough." Then he slammed his hands down on the desk, making Monica and me jump. "Buck up, Collins," he said to himself. "Misery guts."

"That's the spirit," said Monica. "At least we know the Germans are on the run. It's not going to be long." As ever, she was right. The news reports were all about the Red Army moving in from the east and the Allies racing to push from the north and the west. "And you must write it, Emmy," she said, firmly. "We spend our lives answering letters and trying to help and I should hate it if it appears that we aren't listening or don't understand. Even if Mrs. Bagley meant it about the Government rather than us, or at least I hope she did."

I was glad they agreed. I was already planning the first draft.

A few hours later, as Guy had gone over to Fleet Street to meet up with some friends, I nipped down the road for fish and chips. It was a treat for a Monday, and I knew Hester would be pleased.

"Hest," I yelled, standing with the packages of warm newspaper and breathing in one of the best aromas in the world.

It was enough to make anyone hurtle downstairs, but instead Hester's answer came from the office. It was gone half past six and once again she was working late.

"Come on," I ordered, putting my head around the office door. "I got extra salt."

I made my way down to the kitchen, as ever grateful that Hest had moved in. The house would have felt so empty with Bunty and the children in the country. Harold came up two or three nights a week, but it wasn't the same. Putting the fish and chips on the kitchen table, I wondered what would happen after the war. Perhaps if he really did leave the army, Charles and I would live together here.

"What do you think?" I said, quietly, as if he were here.

Now I took two plates out of the cupboard and put them on the table, then placing the fish and chips, which were still in their paper, on top. Sometimes it was the best sort of cooking. I was taking off my coat when Hester came in.

"Thanks, Emmy," she said, going to the sink to wash her hands. She sighed. "It's my favourite."

"You deserve it," I replied, putting my coat on the back of a chair and removing my hat. "Although I must tell you, Miss Wilson, that this working late business just isn't on. We don't expect it and it's not necessary. Shall we eat this with our fingers? We can sit in the comfy chairs."

Hester nodded and looked guilty as charged, as taking our plates with us, we plonked ourselves down in the small armchairs in the corner of the room.

"I'm sorry," she said. "I forget the time. Oh, and Mr. Hill from *The West London News* called to check people's names. He's going to try to get us into their Christmas issue, or if not, at the start of the year. He was a bit vague. I hope that was all right?"

"Of course," I said, thinking that Mr. Hill didn't sound very on top of things.

"He was very nice at the Christmas Fayre," said Hest. "He asked what charity we were raising funds for and why that one. I didn't mention Charles or anything. I just said we thought it was a good cause and wanted to do our bit and that some of the ladies had come which was nice. He asked me my full name and who had been in the photographs."

"Good work, Hest," I said, smiling at her typically comprehensive report. "Your name will be in the paper."

"Gosh," said Hester. "I hadn't thought of that."

"It will be something to send your future husband," I said. "Get you, Mrs. Boone."

Hest giggled. "*Mrs. Boone*," she repeated, dreamily. "I can't wait. Clarence is hoping to hear if his CO will give him forty-eight hours' leave for the wedding. If he does, we can have a honeymoon."

"That's exciting," I said.

Hest blushed. "I'm not sure if he will," she said. "But when I stay with Clarence's aunty this weekend, we're going to talk about having a do after the registry office. I don't mind if we can't have a honeymoon. I just want to marry Clarence in case he goes. Meeting all the ladies at the fayre really made me think."

"You'll be fine," I said, trying to change the direction of the conversation. "Once the CO has given you a date, you'll be all right. It may even be a Christmas wedding."

"Just like yours," said Hester.

I nodded. "Yes. A good omen." I paused, feeling suddenly sentimental. "Hest, just make the most of every minute," I said. "Whether it's forty-eight hours or twenty-four, or even if Clarence is only given the morning off. Enjoy every second you get. That's all that matters."

"That's what Wallace said," replied Hester. "And Mrs. Bagley."

I thought for a moment of how, in peacetime, one always thinks there is all the time in the world. I knew I had when Charles was posted back to England. I'd let myself think we would be seeing the war out together, here. When I thought of the enormous job that was still to be done in Europe, that felt like pie in the sky now.

"You and Clarence will have all the time in the world together after the war," I said. "You'll be married for eighty years and still be under a hundred. But he might have to go to war, so honestly, Hest, just make the most of having him here for now." I smiled as brightly as I could, but I was thinking about the women I had met and how much they missed their boys. "Before you turn into a daft old lady like me who talks out loud to her husband even though he's not here."

"He'll be back soon, Emmy," she said, kindly. "They all will."

She was beginning to sound like me.

Upstairs, we heard the front door being slammed.

"That must be Guy," I said, looking up at the clock on the wall. "He can have some of my fish."

A few moments later, Guy came into the kitchen.

"Evening, ladies," he said, waving a parcel looking much like the one I had brought home. "Don't worry, I've got my own. Very boring drinks so I sneaked out."

He had taken off his outdoor things and now rolled up his shirt sleeves, before sitting down at the kitchen table and actually using a knife and fork.

"We've just been talking about Hester's wedding," I told him.

"How are the plans?" Guy asked. "Got a list?"

He knew Hester well.

"Can I ask your advice, please?" She looked at us both. "It's just that now we know the wedding is going to be very soon, I need to go and ask Mum if she'll sign the form because I'm under twenty-one." Hester paused. "Mum doesn't think much of Clarence."

This much I knew. Mrs. Wilson had not been impressed at the news of their engagement. She had not been slow to voice her view that Hester could do better than marrying a boy from the post room. Never the warmest of women, treading on Hest's dream had not endeared her to any of us, least of all me.

"Would you like me to come with you to see her?" I offered.

Hest didn't jump at the offer, and instead, hesitated, and looked awkward.

"Um," she said.

I took the hint. Mrs. Wilson was perhaps not a great admirer of mine, either.

"Guy," I said. "How would you like a trip to see Hester's mum?"

Guy said that nothing would delight him more.

"Are you sure?" asked Hest. "Mum's not very nice about Clarence. She says he's not exactly Clark Gable."

"Hest," I said. "No one's exactly Clark Gable. He was probably made in a laboratory for the good of international morale." Hester looked confused. "Guy, do you think you can turn on the charm and convince Mrs. Wilson to see sense?" I asked.

"I'll certainly do my best," said Guy. "Even if I struggle to quite reach Gable's dizzying heights. But it shouldn't be that hard. Clarence is a splendid young man."

Hester's face lit up. I was confident Guy would be able to ensure a signature. He had rather a way with middle-aged women despite being endearingly unaware of it, and if that didn't work, he could switch on a quiet but immovable resolve that I had never seen anyone get past. Either way, Hester was in very safe hands.

"Thank you," said Hest, looking at Guy with new levels of admiration. "Mum will like you."

Guy laughed. "Let's hope so," he said. "When would you like to go?"

———

My darling E. Happy Christmas! I have no idea when you will get this, so it will have to do as your card. Finally—news. Young Carter is now here. He took the scenic route and needs a wash and a sleep but do tell Wallace he is very well. You might get this before she gets the nod. I'm afraid I've still heard nothing re Mrs. Bagley. Please pass on my sincerest hopes for good news. All else well here. Chilly so many thanks for all the woollens. Food parcel delivery is a little patchy, but pls keep them coming. Also, toothpowder and brushes as they seem to disappear. Well, darling, not much more to say but I will be thinking of you the entire festive season. This time next year we'll be together at the Ritz. What a time we shall have! I think of that constantly. Happy Christmas my dearest love. Always, your own, C. xxxxxxx

CHAPTER 22

The Last Christmas of the War

Wallace said the news was the best Christmas present she had ever had.

Charles had been right that his letter arrived before she received the official notification or any word from Tom himself. The message from Charles was certainly the best present I had ever given anyone. With Christmas almost here, things were on the up, even if I did have the rotten job of letting Mrs. Bagley know that there had been no news about Johnny, from Charles at least.

A week later Wallace was still on cloud nine.

"A guest of the ghastly Germans, but safe," she said, full of smiles even though she had been up half the previous night with Baby Daphne, who was about to reveal a new tooth.

We were in the *Woman's Friend* office, where the celebratory mood was helped by the fact that half of the festive decorations from the fayre had now been put up. We knew this really would be the last Christmas at war. Hitler might still be sending his vicious bombs to Britain, but the news from the Continent was encouraging. It was only a matter of time before Peace.

"I do hope someone in the camp will share their Christmas box with him," continued Wallace. "Do you think they might? Tom would his. It's too late to get presents to him in time now. He'll love

the chocolate, when he gets it. It's a pound and a half, isn't it? I hope
he isn't cold. I've been knitting so I can send things straight away. I'm
so pleased, Emmy. So very pleased."

I listened as she chattered on, thrilled with the news and now able
to be a young wife excited about spoiling her boy. What a strange life
it was when sending Red Cross–issued chocolate and a knitted vest
in a cardboard box now counted as *spoiling*. I shook myself out of
that line of thought. It helped no one.

"Toothbrushes," I said, matter of fact. "Charles says they always
go missing."

"What sort of food do you think they get for Christmas dinner?"
said Mrs. Mahoney. "The men will have been saving supplies, won't
they?"

"Tins of things," I said. "We sent pears in syrup, and I bet they've
made their own decorations. They'll probably have carols and do
games or something, just like we will."

The idea of the men creating something that might mirror what
we always did at home was a comforting thought. I had read old
copies of *The Prisoner of War* magazine, and it did at least sound
as if the men in the German camps managed quite well. I kept my
slight feelings of cynicism about the probable use of propaganda to
myself. It was better all round if you chose to believe that things
would be well.

The phone rang and Miss Peters answered it, calling to Hester
that it was for her. Moments later, there was a loud gasp.

"Really? He's definitely sure? No, that's wonderful. We don't need
any more than that. I'll arrange everything. I've done a list. Oh, Clarence. Won't it? I will. Bye-bye."

Then she put the phone down. It did not take a genius to guess
what the call had been about.

"We're getting married," said Hester, as if it had just dawned
on her. "Clarence has got twenty-four hours' leave in January." She
looked up at me as if in a trance. "I'm going to be Mrs. Boone."

"That's smashing news," I said. "Well done. What's the actual date?"

"The fourth. It's a Thursday," said Hest. "Would it be all right if I have the day off?"

Guy had come into the room holding some copy to be typed up.

"Day off?" he said, teasing her, which was one of his favourite things to do. "What's this, one of those holiday camp places?"

"Clarence has got his leave," I said. "The fourth of January."

"Then we'd better get cracking," replied Guy. "That's not long to go at all." He gave Hest a big smile. "Of course you can have the day off," he said. "You're planning on Swindon, aren't you?"

"Yes," said Hester. "Thank you, Mr. Collins. I'll make up all the hours."

Guy waved his hand at her as if swatting a fly. "Nonsense, we probably owe you at least a month as it is. I assume everything has been ticked off and is meticulously planned?"

"Well, we don't want a fuss," said Hester. "But we thought we might go to the pub after the registry office and it would have been lovely if everyone could come, but it's a long way away and on a Thursday, so not to worry. I don't think Mum will, and it's quite far for Nan, but Clarence has his family and some of them might be able to come."

"Hmm," said Guy. "I don't want to push in, but are you saying we would be invited if it wasn't on a workday?"

"Oh yes," said Hest, shyly. "Clarence wanted to buy the first round."

"Clarence buying a round," said Guy, thoughtfully. "Hold on the slack."

Now he marched out to the hall.

"Mrs. Edwards," he shouted, up the stairs. "Managerial decision required if we could, please?"

There was a call of, "Right you are," and a minute later Monica appeared.

"Yes, Mr. Collins," she said.

"Mrs. Edwards," said Guy. "In your role as Publisher might I ask your permission to give the day off to anyone who can get to a wedding in Swindon on the fourth of January?"

"Mr. Collins, you're the Editor in Chief," replied Monica.

"Then I say, 'aye,'" said Mr. Collins.

"Me too," said Monica. "Emmy?"

"Aye."

"Everyone else?"

There was a unanimous call of agreement.

"Carried," said Monica. "I shall buy a new hat."

Hester, who had been speechless since Guy dashed off and shouted upstairs, managed to say "Thank you" several times.

"Are you all right, Hest?" I asked. "I know you'd hoped it would be a festive wedding, but it will be a lovely boost to the new year, and now it's set in stone, we can all look forward to it. It's less than two weeks."

A huge smile spread across Hester's face.

It would be the best possible start to nineteen forty-five.

Before then there was an enormous amount of work to do. Even though we would only have Christmas Day and Boxing Day off, it always felt as if we had to battle like fury to get ahead of ourselves. As over half of us planned to join Hester and Clarence in January, it was an additional day to make up. Mrs. Mahoney was busy with production schedules, which included my finished piece on Charles being a prisoner of war, and Wallace and I were keen to send out a newsletter that might bring some yuletide cheer to the other wives. As ever it was a balancing act. It was nice to share any good news that had come in letters from the men overseas, but at the same time not rub it in for those who were struggling without updates.

None of us were particularly looking forward to Christmas itself. It had been fun to have the jolliness of the fayre, and the office looked cheerful decked out, but Christmas Day was something of a non-starter for most of us. My mother and father planned to visit my grandmother over the festive period, and I would be spending it at Dower Cottage, helping to make it as jolly as possible for the children in the absence of their mum, and for now at least, their dad. It would be noisy and full of games and as much food as we could find, but secretly my heart wasn't particularly in it. The only present I wanted was having Charles back.

A couple of days before Christmas, I waited until the quiet of the evening to phone Mrs. Bagley and see how she was. She was stoic as ever, and tireless in her quest to find out where Johnny might be. As the call neared its end though, she mentioned something new.

"Emmy, you're always in the know, so may I ask, have you heard any rumours about the prisoners being moved?"

"Not at all," I said, frowning. "Moved where?"

"I'm not sure. I went to a meeting this week at a local branch of the Prisoner of War Relatives' Association, and two of the ladies there were talking about it. They think, or have heard, that with the Russian advance from the east, the Germans are going to have to let the men go."

"Let them . . . go?" I said, slowly. With the news full of the Red Army's rapid advances I felt foolish for not having thought about it before. "Gosh, Juliet, I feel rather dim for not thinking of that. I mean I've thought about what will happen at the end of the war, but I hadn't thought about it while the fighting's still going on. Where will they move them to?"

"That's exactly what we were wondering," answered Juliet.

"They'll hand them over to the Russians, surely?" I said, getting my brain into gear. "If the Germans surrender, they'd have to." There was a silence at the end of the phone. "Or at least they should," I added. "Geneva Convention rules and all that."

"Quite," said Juliet. "But my friend Mrs. Douglas, who I'm afraid does call a spade a spade, made the very good point that why would they? It would mean they're letting huge numbers of experienced troops bolster the Allied ranks. They might as well leave the Red Army tanks with the engines running."

"Have your friends contacted anyone to try to find out if it's true?" I asked her.

"They've written to the central POWRA office, which I shall too. I've written to my Member of Parliament, although I imagine he hardly bothers to read my letters any more. And I shall of course write to all the other organisations." She paused for a moment. "If the Germans empty the prison camps it will make it even harder to find John, of course."

"Of course," I said. "I shall see who I might ask as well. Someone will know. They just may not want to tell us."

"My thoughts exactly," said Mrs. Bagley. "However, if enough of us ask . . ."

Now I was thinking as fast as I could. "Do you think we should put it in the newsletter? It would mean more of us asking questions, but especially with Christmas coming, I don't want to make things worse for everyone. It's worrying enough as it is. My apologies, Juliet. I'm thinking out loud. How about if we put it in the one after Christmas? You and I may have heard more by then and can galvanise support."

Juliet agreed. It was less than two weeks until the new year.

"My very best wishes to you and your family," she said as we finished the call. I searched for the right words to say in return. What did one say to a woman who had no idea if her son was alive or dead?

"And my warmest wishes, to you, Juliet," I replied. "Here's to nineteen forty-five and far better times."

"They will be," she answered. "I am sure of that."

After we had said goodbye, I sat quietly by the telephone in the hallway for some time. The rumour made sense. If the Germans needed to retreat, surely they wouldn't just leave the men to be liberated?

This was where the questions began. How would they move thousands of men? Where would they go? And more to the point, how would they protect them in the middle of a war? Would they even bother to try?

Guy was downstairs in the kitchen, listening to a concert by the BBC Symphony Orchestra. I was keen to know his thoughts. Hester was writing a letter to Clarence in her room, so biting my lip, I stood up and made my way down the hall.

Later, Guy and I agreed we would keep the rumour to ourselves until the new year. We discussed it well into the night, skirting around our fears at first and then, after Guy had said, "Bugger it, do you want a drink?" sharing them over glasses of whisky.

"Cards on the table," I said, narrowing my eyes as the alcohol had made me feel fuzzy. "How will the Russians get the men back to us? They'll be unarmed and behind enemy lines. They could even get killed by our own bombers." The more I thought about it, the worse it seemed.

"Emmy, you do realise the Allied Governments have a plan for this, don't you?" said Guy. "They're not making it up as they go along."

"All right then," I said, crossly. "How will you feel if Charles is moved? It's the middle of winter for a start. We won't have a clue where he is or if he's safe."

"I think we take this one day at a time," said Guy, firmly.

It wasn't the answer I wanted, but falling out was the last thing we needed.

"Guy," I said, in a softer voice. "I don't think this is good."

Guy didn't say anything. He didn't have to.

———

When Christmas arrived, I headed off to the country on the train and did my best to hurl myself into the festive spirit at Dower Cottage.

"It's an order," said Bunty. "Your mother came down in the week to deliver sweets for the children before she and your father went to your granny's, but she's worried about you so I promised that you'd have a lovely time. You know that she'll check, and I can't possibly tell her a lie."

I replied with my hand on my heart that I would, and knew that despite everything, everyone would make it a special day.

The cottage had been beautifully decorated, as if only the very best branches of holly, trails of ivy, and bunches of mistletoe had volunteered to be chopped down and taken indoors to do their bit. Somehow, we had cobbled together presents for the children, despite the shops having almost nothing to buy, and as ever there was an enormous amount of food. Meat was limited of course, but a decent-size bird did appear on Christmas Day, and vegetables were in huge supply. There was even a Christmas pudding with custard. We all ate until we could burst.

As I had agreed with Guy, I didn't say anything about the rumours we'd heard, not even to Bunty, whom usually I told everything. This was her first Christmas with Harold, and despite the war and the worries, it was clear they were blissfully happy. I didn't want to spoil it for a moment. The children did well, too. It was the second Christmas without their mum, and it was never going to be easy. The three of them dealt with it in their different ways, George more grown-up than ever, not wanting to talk about it, Marg quiet at times but then enjoying remembering all the things they had done with Thelma, the traditions and anecdotes, particular presents and games. Stan, as he always did, turned to his animals. He had a dog now, a stray called Sparky, who Bunty had said could come in for a night as it was raining, in the full knowledge that Sparky was never going to leave. It was a dream come true for Stan, and everyone enjoyed having a dog around. Monty the rat wasn't as keen, but he kept himself to himself and things had worked out.

On Christmas Day we proposed toasts, one by one. Bunty said to the end of the war, Mrs. Tavistock raised her glass to everyone serving overseas, I, of course, raised mine to Charles, and the children as one, cried out, "To our dad!," at which I didn't dare look at Bunts. When Harold quietly called for a toast to absent friends, it was jolly hard to keep a stiff upper lip.

All any of us wanted was to get everyone home in one piece.

While Bunty was not entirely herself and had some sort of a tummy bug, she manfully soldiered on. I thought little of it until Boxing Day when the others had gone out for a walk and Bunts and I stayed to play cards in the warm.

Mrs. Tavistock was having an afternoon nap, and it was nice to sit by the fire, listening to carols on the gramophone and having my friend all to myself. I told Bunty about Hester and the wedding plans and how Guy had managed to cajole Hest's mum into doing the decent thing, and then how Hest and Wallace had become nice chums, and Wallace was going to lend Hester the loveliest dress for the day. Bunty listened, smiling in the right places, although saying very little. When I paused for a moment, she put down her cards.

"Em," she said, twisting her wedding ring around her finger rather awkwardly. "I've got some news."

Her expression did not reveal if this was good or bad.

"Is everything all right?" I asked, carefully.

"Oh yes. Absolutely." Now she smiled. "I'm going to have a baby."

"Oh, Bunts," I said, jumping out of my seat and giving her an enormous hug. "That's the best thing ever. Well done, you!"

"Really?" she said as I sat down next to her on the sofa.

"What do you mean, 'really'?" I laughed. "Of course it is. It's utterly lovely. I'm so pleased. Is Harold excited? I can't believe you haven't said anything."

"It's happened sooner than we'd planned," said Bunty. "I rather hoped everything would be settled first. You know, Arthur back for the children, Charles back with you."

I sighed. Then I took hold of her hand.

"Bunts, I really am *so* thrilled for you both," I said. "And I want you to be as happy as you possibly can be. You deserve this so much. You and Harold. You don't have to worry about the rest of us. We'll have our good news. You enjoy every second of yours. And let us join in and be happy for you."

It was so typically Bunty. Not wanting to wave her good fortune in the faces of people still waiting for theirs.

"Are you sure?" she said, wrinkling her face up. "I've not done this very well, have I?"

"What—this announcement?" I laughed. "No. Hopeless. Do you want to start again?"

"All right," said Bunts. "Em. Guess what?"

"What?"

"I'm having a baby."

"Bunty Thomas! CONGRATULATIONS! Why didn't you say the moment I arrived?" Now I threw my arms around her again. "You clever, clever thing. Tell me everything! When is the baby due? How is Harold? Oh, my goodness, the baby could be enormous. How are you feeling?"

"Rather sick," she replied. "Apparently, it goes after a few months. I jolly well hope so. Harold's thrilled to bits but is now treating me like a piece of rare Venetian glass and keeps threatening to buy liver on the black market. He says he read somewhere that it is good for the baby."

"There's bound to be a leaflet in the office," I said. "There's always a leaflet by Nurse McClay on this sort of thing."

"Well, I'm rather hoping *you'll* bone up on this sort of thing, pretty sharpish," said Bunty, regaining her usual direct approach. "Em, I might be rubbish at it. I've only changed a nappy once and it fell straight off again once the baby sat up."

"I don't know anything, either," I said, grinning at her. "What about Harold? He could always pitch in."

It took a while for both of us to stop laughing at that. But when we did, Bunty looked me straight in the eye.

"Will you be the baby's godmother?" she asked. "Please?"

Now I nodded.

"I would love to," I said.

CHAPTER 23

Woman's Friend Makes the News

For the next hour, Bunty and I had a lovely time thinking of baby names and coming up with awful ones with which she could horrify Harold. I was so pleased I hadn't spoiled things with rumours and worries. I stayed the night, enjoying a slight feeling of escape for just a few hours more.

The next morning, I got up very early to catch the first train back to London. It was freezing cold, but nevertheless, George, Marg, and Stan wrapped themselves up and walked with me to the station, Sparky trotting along by our sides. It was still dark with a freezing wind, and I was very glad of their company. We skidded and slid our way down to the village, one dimmed torch showing us the way, although we all knew it well. The children didn't yet know about the baby as it was early days, but there was much happy chatter and holiday spirit. Arthur, their dad, had made sure they had Christmas letters sent months in advance, and he had arranged postal orders with Bunty for their presents. Now we discussed what they would buy with their Christmas riches. Stan's money, predictably, was going on a wicker dog basket if he could find one, Marg was saving for her own bicycle, and George wanted a tool kit, only he didn't think there would be any for some time. We also deliberated on new year resolutions, and all decided that having a summer holiday at the seaside was the best one.

"They'll have to clear all the mines and barbed wire first, though," said Stan, making a good point.

"Dad'll be home then," said Marg. "He'll buy us ice creams."

"He always used to do that," said George.

"Did he?" said Stan. "I can't remember."

Arthur had been away for three years. I was quite sure Stan did remember, but he had a tendency to be selective about his father. Almost as if by being vague it would mean he didn't miss him so much.

"If I remember rightly, your dad also buys you sweets every Saturday," I said. "I hope you haven't forgotten that. And he'll teach you how to go fishing in rock pools. That's what your mum told me he used to do."

"My mum was good at rock pools," said Stan.

"Your mum was good at everything," I replied. "She was the very best." I stopped in the middle of the lane and opened my arms wide as if I were a ringmaster. "What was she?"

The kids knew exactly what I was expecting.

"THE BEST. OUR MUM WAS THE BEST."

The four of us shouted it at the top of our voices into the dark. Bunty had said, "Your mum was the best," a few months after Thel died, and we'd got them to shout it back so that everyone would know. Since then, we'd done it a hundred times, all of us joining in. I used to fancy that Thel would hear us and smile. As we walked on, I thought how much she was missed.

The children insisted on waiting until the train arrived, and by then it was beginning to get light. Once we had said our goodbyes and I'd climbed onto the train, I pushed the window down and hung out of it, waving to them as I left. A businessman harumphed at me for letting in the cold, but he was awfully British about it and didn't actually complain, so I ignored him and waved long after the platform was out of sight.

Leaving them was always bittersweet. I loved London, and as I had lived in Braybon Street for over six years, it had become home. Recently though, I had begun to think that home wasn't about where you were, but who you were with. I wasn't sure where home was now.

As I opened the front door to the house, I pushed those sort of thoughts to the back of my mind. I was days away from the new year, with a full schedule of work and deadlines, and a wedding to attend. Now that Christmas was over, I was also keen to see if I could find out if there was anything in Juliet Bagley's theory about the prisoners being moved.

Most of the *Woman's Friend* team had already arrived and were sharing their Christmas stories and showing off a variety of new woollies. Everyone had a new cardigan, or scarf, or in Miss Peter's case a jaunty beret. Mrs. Shaw had brought in a chunk of cake, and Mr. Newton had an orange, which he generously insisted on sharing. It was a jolly start and was then helped no end when Guy arrived, waving a newspaper.

"Morning, Emmy. Good Christmas?" he said, sounding chipper. "I nipped out to the newsagent, and these have just come in. I think it's the issue with the fayre. I thought you might want to see. Hester, would you like to do the honours?"

He passed the newspaper to Hest, who laid it on the table and began to turn the pages, past the advertisements and news and then on to the entertainment section.

"It's in!" she cried when she found it. Everyone waited with bated breath. Even though we all worked on a magazine, it was exciting to think we might have been mentioned in the paper. "Oh, doesn't Mrs. Edwards look lovely," said Hester. "And Buzz. They've even got her trombone in."

I peered over her shoulder. "They've given us half a page. That's nice. What have they said?"

"Read it out, Hester," encouraged Miss Peters from her desk.

"It says, *National Magazine Raises Funds in Pimlico*. That's the headline."

"Very nice," said Mrs. Shaw.

"Woman's Friend, *the popular ladies' magazine, recently held a successful Christmas Fayre in St. Gabriel's church hall. The publication, which last year opened an office in Braybon Street, held the event in aid of the Red Cross Prisoners of War Fund.*"

Hester paused to take a breath.

"*Opened an office,*" I repeated. "Makes it sound as if we have them all over the place. Very swish. Go on Hest."

"Right-ho. *'It's the least we can do,' said Publisher, Miss Hester Wilson.*" Hest gave a small gasp as she spotted the mistake. "Oh, no," she said, in alarm.

"Don't worry," I said, seeing the look of horror on her face. "Misprints happen all the time. Keep going."

But Hester was reading on in silence, now with her hands covering her cheeks, which had gone puce. I leaned forward to get a clearer view.

"It's the least we can do," said Publisher, Miss Hester Wilson. "Everyone has mucked in."

The magazine, Miss Wilson said, had invited the wives and families of British POWs to the well-attended event, which also included a tombola stall and talented dog show.

"We wanted to show them that we care," said the magazine's Publisher, "because lots of people think the Government doesn't and it makes things very hard for them."

Housewife Mrs. Enid Harris, who had travelled all the way from Barnet to be at the event, later echoed Miss Wilson, adding: "We're never told anything, other than by the Red Cross who always do their best, so it's very nice that at least the people at Woman's Friend *care."*

It wasn't all woe though as the crowd enjoyed numerous entertainments including a kiddies' Lucky Dip and a well-run tea shoppe.

Hester looked as if she was going to pass out. The blood had now drained from her face, and she was trembling like a leaf.

"I didn't mean it to sound like that," she whispered, looking at me with the biggest eyes. "It looks awful written down."

"Of course you didn't," I said fiercely, putting my arm around her. I shot a look at Guy, who frowned and picked up the newspaper. He winced almost imperceptibly for a second as he read it, and then dropped the paper back on the desk.

"It's just poor journalism," he said.

"The man's misquoted you," I added. "It's horrid but it doesn't matter."

Hester went even more pale. "I'm so sorry, Emmy," she said. "I think that *was* what I said." She looked down at the paper again. "I'd been listening to some of the ladies." Her eyes were now brimming with tears. "I've let you all down."

"Hest," I said. "It's all right. Honestly. These things happen. I made far worse blunders when I first joined. Dreadful. I nearly got the sack. Guy saved me. Actually, Clarence did really."

"But what will Mr. Langley say?" asked Hester.

"He won't even see it," I said.

"And if he does," added Guy, "Mr. Langley was a journalist himself for long enough. He'll know that by tomorrow this will be wrapped around a portion of chips and forgotten. Now then, everyone." He raised his voice. "Please ignore this, and if anyone from *The West London News* should telephone again, you can put them straight through to me. Thank you." He turned to Hester and softened his voice. "Come on, chin up, and don't you dare cry, or you'll look like an ugly bug for your wedding, and then what will Clarence think?"

Hester took a deep, slightly shuddery breath.

"I'm sorry," she said again. "I've really let you down."

"Now stop that," I said, firmly. "You're the last person who would ever let us down. If anyone should be sorry, it's me for not talking to him myself."

"Don't *you* start," said Guy to me. "It's no one's fault. Now, back to work. Hester, two words: chip paper."

"Just chip paper," I repeated to her. "Nothing more."

"Hester may have said it," said Monica, later. "But that rotten hack saw a cheap opportunity to write something vaguely controversial. Sloping around chatting to women at a party, doubtless buying them drinks. Poor Mrs. Harris. Poor Hest. I still remember my first work howler." She shuddered. "I sat up all night thinking I'd lose my job. They were very nice about it. But the first time's definitely the worst."

"I won't share it with the other wives," I said. I was perched against a chair, with my arms folded. "Hopefully it will blow over."

"Well," said Monica, "at least Hester's got the wedding to look forward to. We'll all give it our full attention and brush this under the carpet. I managed to get hold of Clarence's aunt's number—don't ask me how; I'm a proper journalist, unlike some. I asked her what she thought we could do for a wedding gift. She'll have a think, but it could be an IOU for when they're setting up home."

"She does have a Post Office Savings book," I said. "I wonder if we could put something into that. I know the staff want to have a whip-round."

"Count me in, of course," said Guy. "Now, let's get on. As it's just us three, can I change the subject? Monica, Emmy's friend Juliet Bagley has come up with something I think our readers are going to want to know about."

———

Everyone was disappointed by the shabby newspaper article, but other than the fact it was irritating and unfair, there were far bigger fish to fry. I needed to get to grips with an increasingly full list of war work interviews, and increasingly full bags of letters from readers, some of whom were unhappy, not with their own lives, but with us.

Dear Miss Lake
I read your article on becoming a cleaner and wondered, have you ever done it? Mopping up after people all day and none of them thanking you? You made it sound like we'd be winning the war all on our own. Please don't try to make it sound fancy. There's no shame in cleaning for a living, and I've done it very well for the last fifteen years, but it's not flying a bomber over Hamburg, is it?
Yours
Annoyed, Trowbridge

I had perhaps tried too hard on that one. Richard Langley had liked it, but then he would.

To the Editor
I have taken your magazine for over twenty years, but I have never read so much filth in all my life as the "Yours Cheerfully" page. These days it's all encouraging girls to marry foreigners and telling them they can keep babies born out of wedlock. I don't know who this Emmy Lake is, but she lacks any moral standards whatsoever. She looks very young in her picture, and I fear is not even married. How can she give out advice?
I have cancelled my subscription at the newsagent.
Yours
Disgusted, Monmouthshire

Sometimes I couldn't win either way.

Dear Miss Lake
I am seventeen and was going to write in with a question, but you always take the side of readers' parents. My friends say it's a waste of

*time to ask you anything as you'll only say to tell my mum, so what's
the point? I don't mean to be rude but thought you should know how
we younger people feel.*

 Yours sincerely
 Marjorie French, aged 17

PS: we like the fashion and beauty these days.

At least Monica had a fan.

I took it all on the chin. Guy had once said that writing an advice page was not a popularity contest and he was right. One had to develop a thick skin, especially as Disgusted from Monmouthshire was far from alone.

On New Year's Eve morning I was at my desk, looking through the most urgent problems and, as it was a Sunday, taking advantage of the quiet of an empty office. It was always easier to tackle the grittiest problems or the grumpiest people without distraction. I was chewing my thumbnail as I thought through a particularly diplomatic answer when the phone in the hall rang. It was bound to be someone with good wishes for the new year, so I hopped up and went out to answer it.

"Hello Miss Lake, um, Emmy," said a voice that I recognised as Clarence. He still struggled with first name terms.

I said, "Hello," as he fed money into the phone. "An early Happy New Year to you, Clarence. I'll get Hest for you."

"Happy New Year," he answered without an enormous amount of enthusiasm. I shouted down to the kitchen for Hest and returned to my desk, shutting the door so the couple could have their privacy, and I could grapple with the difficult query.

I vaguely heard Hester answering the phone, as ever her high-pitched voice full of excitement to be hearing from her beau. Now fairly confident I had found the right words for my letter, I fed a piece of *Woman's Friend* notepaper into my typewriter and began to type my reply.

A moment later, there was a cry from the hall.

"No, Clarence, no." It was more of a wail.

I stopped typing and listened. I could hear Hester still on the phone, but she was now sobbing. Any concerns about eavesdropping forgotten, I tried to hear at least her side of the conversation, although from her distress it was easy to guess what had happened. I went to the door, but didn't open it for a moment, not wanting to interfere.

But listening to Hester trying to speak between huge, racking sobs was too awful.

I slipped into the hall where she was sitting, almost doubled over, cradling the phone receiver to her ear. Quietly I went over and crouched down by her, putting my hand on her leg. She looked at me in absolute despair.

"Yes," she said down the phone. "I will. Emmy's here. Yes. Yes."

Hester reached for my hand, gripping it tightly.

"I love you too," she said to Clarence. "I'll write. Don't forget. Bye-bye. Bye-bye. I love you, Clarence."

I could hear the dial tone, so knowing that Clarence had gone, I gently took the receiver from Hester and put it back on the phone.

"It's all right," I whispered, although we both knew that it wasn't.

"They're going tomorrow," she managed. Then she just cried and cried.

CHAPTER 24

The Woman Who Knows

All leave had been cancelled, the regiment was being deployed to Europe, and Clarence would be departing the next day, three days before he and Hester were to get married. Hest was inconsolable, even after the shock had worn off. Scalding hot tea with two sugars was little help. Her disappointment was all-consuming. They had been so close to the wedding. I sat with her in the kitchen while Guy pottered in and out, checking up on progress and trying to find the right thing to say. He was, to his eternal credit, the rare kind of man who did not head for the door at the first sign of tears.

"Come on, old sport," he would say occasionally, at one point mouthing, "Whisky?," at me, bafflement at what else to suggest etched across his face.

Poor Hester was too wretched to help. It made me think of the times when Charles had left to go back to the war. It was always horrible. But I had been twenty-three when I met him, and Hester was still only eighteen. The five years made a big difference.

"I'm going to make you another cup of tea," I said. "It's a rotten business all round and horrid luck. But we will make sure you have the biggest, fanciest wedding we can manage the minute Clarence gets back. And he *will* be back," I added, firmly.

It had occurred to me that Hester's distress was not helped by the fact she had spent so much time in the company of women whose husbands, boyfriends, and sons had been at the rough end of things in recent months. Captured, wounded, missing. It was a hard list. It wasn't just Wallace and the others; it was the problem page too. Although Hester didn't read the letters so did not see the very worst, ever since she was a fifteen-year-old office junior she had seen the sacks full of problems, and of course, the ones printed in *Woman's Friend*.

Hester was young, scared, and too well-read.

"We thought we would be married," she said, "before he went away."

"It's horribly disappointing," I said. "But it doesn't mean he loves you any less, or you him, does it?"

I didn't mention that Clarence leaving before they were married also meant that as far as the army was concerned, Hester didn't exist. If anything happened to him, she would be the last to know.

"You don't understand," she said in a sad little voice.

"Oh Hest," I said. "I really do. The first time Charles was posted, we weren't married. And the second time we'd only been married two days. It's ghastly, but there's nothing you can do. You just have to muddle along. That's what I do. We can do it together if you like. We'll sit here writing letters like two old ladies. Every night."

Hester nodded, trying hard. "I'm sorry for crying," she said. "I've let you down." Her face began to crumple again.

"Those words are off the menu," I said. "Hester, we're so very proud of Clarence and we're *always* terribly proud of you. Aren't we, Guy?"

"I'll say," said Guy, in a hearty manner.

"It's ever so hard being brave about things," I said. "But I know you can do it. And anyway. I always cry buckets. I'm very good at a brave face, and then I go to my room and blub. I pretended I had hay fever when we were at Rose House. Utter lie."

"Hester, you should try being a chap," said Guy. "We're not allowed to do anything other than shake hands and blink a bit. If I cried, you'd have me locked up. It doesn't mean I don't want to, though."

"You'd never cry," said Hester, aghast.

I looked at Guy, who I knew could have told Hester a hundred stories about his experiences in the Great War that you would never read about in books. He had once told me that it was where he first realised grown men could cry. Just not in front of anyone. Now he gave Hest an encouraging smile.

"You weren't there when Emmy made me go to see that film about the sheepdog last year," he said. "What was it called? Far too sad. I had to go and stand in the foyer with all the other men and talk about rugger."

Hester managed a small smile.

"*Lassie Come Home*," I said. "Guy, Lassie didn't even die." I turned to Hester. "I had to tell the children Guy had eaten something that had gone off."

"I cried at *Lassie* too," she said, bravely trying to rally.

"Then we're doomed," said Guy. "Now then, it's been a shock for you, Hester, and postponements are always a shame, but it's very nearly the new year and I think we need to take our minds off things. Who fancies afternoon tea? My treat. Or even a brisk walk around Hyde Park and over to the palace. Either way, I think we should go out."

"That's a super idea," I said. "Do you think Wallace might come? She can bring Daphne." I knew Hester would enjoy that. "Hest, we won't force you, if you'd rather not."

"That would be lovely," said Hester, after a deep breath. "Thank you, very much."

Hester Wilson, eighteen-year-old, tear-stained fiancée of Gunner Clarence Boone, much-loved friend, and all round plucky young woman, was going to do her best.

———

A brisk walk, a teatime dainty, and Guy's version of a cup of tea, which happened to be a cocktail in a hotel, and the new year would at least start with an attempt at jollity.

The fact was, however, that none of us were really jolly at heart. Christmas had seen no let-up in the bombing raids, and as nineteen forty-five dawned and I began to ask around among the other wives and contacts in POW organisations, it was clear that Juliet Bagley was not alone in hearing rumours. The Government said nothing, but civilians weren't stupid, especially where their families were concerned. When the newspapers ran reports of the Red Army pushing through parts of occupied Poland where people knew their boys were being held, they wanted to know what would happen when their men were released.

By the second week in January, I hadn't heard from Charles for a month, and while I knew there were strict limitations on how often prisoners were allowed to write, it was too easy to start counting the days and reading alarming things into the lack of a letter or card. Guy hid his concerns well, getting on with his job as editor, but with bursts of bonhomie, and sometimes keeping himself to himself when I knew he preferred his own company to ours.

Hester was trying very hard to push on, but I could see it was a huge effort. She worked diligently, read and listened to the news obsessively, and joined in everything as she always had. But like the rest of us, she was scared, and her joy and optimism had been wiped away overnight. The rest of the *Woman's Friend* team became more robust than ever, embracing every piece of good news and downplaying anything they thought would cause concern. Anyone listening through a window would think the British Army was currently battling against a group of children with a pop gun, not the full might of the Wehrmacht.

I allowed myself a moment of professional pride when the issue came out with my article about being the wife of a prisoner of war.

Guy and Monica had approved the piece, and Guy said it was the most honest thing we had published in the whole of the war. Funnily enough my name wasn't on it. We had decided I should remain anonymous, not because we wanted to disassociate *Woman's Friend* from what I had said, in fact the whole point was that it would be about us. The anonymity was for Charles. There would be no mention of course of his name or which service he was in, and there were no references to any of us. It was signed by "The Woman Who Knows," a common enough sort of pen name and so no form of identification.

The article was put into the part of the magazine where we printed readers' own views and ideas. It felt the right place to share something personal from us. All I did was write about how I felt, and how I hoped the readers might understand.

WOMAN'S FRIEND TO FRIEND
A Message from Us to You

You may find this an odd kind of article, and I do hope you will forgive me for not giving my real name. You see, I am writing on behalf of all the team at Woman's Friend, *so I shall say "we."*

We know we ask a lot. We ask you to sign up for jobs that will help win the war, and you do. We write recipes that we hope will encourage you to grow your own food, and cook and keep to the rations, and you do. We try to come up with ideas to jazz up those clothes we know you're sick of, and you do. We ask you to keep your chins up, to look nice for your husbands when they come home, to fight the loneliness when they are away, to say a prayer and keep smiling when you don't hear from your sons. And you do.

We ask you to keep going. And you do.

Sometimes letters come from readers asking if we really understand how much is asked of you. If we understand what it is like to live with a mother-in-law who doesn't like us, or cope with distressed children, or keep going when great loss comes our way. The pages of this magazine are almost always hopeful, looking to the future and to when there is Peace. Of course, sometimes we get tetchy—you may have seen how we grumble at the Government for equal pay or nurseries or help for new mothers! But we try to make sure things are mostly cheerful.

Because of that, it may be easy to wonder whether we understand. Perhaps we don't know what it is to be worried, or frightened, or sad, or wishing we could just throw it all in.

Well, we decided to print this piece in our magazine because we very much want you to know that we do understand. We remain cheerful and hopeful because we hope it helps you, and also, if we're honest, because sometimes we too are worried, or frightened, or sad, or wishing like anything we could just throw it all in.

The person writing this is the wife of a British prisoner of war. She watches when the post arrives and hopes every time for a letter, even though she knows they are infrequent. If one doesn't come, she breathes less easily, sleeps less well. She is new to this situation and knows there are thousands of women who have lived with this for years. She wishes she could speak with them all and admit how scared she is.

Some of us here have lost loved ones, just as you have. Some of us remember the last war and cannot believe it has happened again. We all have friends and families who have been split up, bombed out, bereaved. Isn't it foul? There, we've said it. War is foul.

But we're still going and doing our best. Many of us have been very lucky and we know many of you have faced challenges far beyond what we have had to bear. Sometimes we know we can't possibly imagine how you get through. But you do. And we want you to know that we'll keep trying to do everything we can to help out. Please keep writing to us, keep telling us how we can help. We never feel we're doing enough, but we want to try.

The next few months are going to be a challenge. We'll keep our spirits up, and we'll try to help you do the same! Victory is coming. When things get ropey, and we feel our stomachs tremble and our hearts miss a beat, we're going to try to remember that too. There will be Peace!

Together, we'll get there. We are with you. We know you're with us too, and boy, that keeps us going! We hope it does you, too.

Your friend,
The Woman Who Knows

In the spirit of anonymity, Guy, Monica, and I had not told the team who had written it, even though they would all know. I waited in some trepidation to hear what they thought. The house copies of the issue came in as usual the next morning.

"I've no idea who wrote this," said Mrs. Mahoney, looking directly at me. "But they know us inside out and I'm jolly proud of them for saying it."

We all pressed on. I was expecting a phone call from my contact at the British Red Cross when Hester asked if I would speak to Richard Langley, who was on the telephone. I knew Guy had asked him to keep an ear to the ground about the prison camps, so I keenly agreed.

"Hello, Mr. Langley," I said. "Guy is out, but how might I help? Is it about the POWs? Guy said he had been speaking with you."

"Good morning, Miss Lake," said Richard. "Yes, it is, in part. Perhaps I should wait to speak with him. Would you mind asking if he would return my call, please?"

"Of course," I replied. "He'll be back soon. In the meantime, may I ask if there are any further briefs coming up on the careers side? I hope you would have seen my piece on the domestics in Woolwich last week, and we have another in this week's issue about the landlady for war workers in Wrexham. I just have the ATS girls working with the Dutch refugees to go and then I have several available slots. I wondered if we might meet or speak further?"

I tucked the phone under my chin and reached inside a drawer to get my desk diary.

"Mmm, right," said Richard. "Probably best to put that in with my secretary. I don't have the schedule to hand."

"Oh, right-oh," I replied. "Do you have much coming up?"

"Not as much as we did," said Langley, sounding very noncommittal. "End of the war coming and all that."

Every single briefing and conversation we had had for months had been about the Big Push. We all knew there would be no end to the war without it. This was odd. I repeated that I would tell Guy he had called. An exchange of polite goodbyes and he was gone.

Something was up.

"I'm sure it's nothing," said Guy, unconcerned when I told him. "You know they're always like that. Enigmatic, hush-hush, slightly more important and in the know than everyone else. I'll give him a shout."

"Well?" I ventured when Guy re-emerged from his office. His unconcerned look had been replaced by a thoughtful, almost suspicious glower.

"They want us to go in for a meeting at the Ministry on Friday. Best suits on all round I feel." He narrowed his eyes. "You were right. Something is definitely up."

Dearest C

How are you, darling? It's been a month since I heard from you, but hopefully something will arrive very soon. I am dying to hear your news as ever. Not much to report since yesterday's letter. Guy, Monica, and I are off to see Richard Langley for work—he's gone a bit odd. Bound to be a rap on the knuckles as I wrote rather an emotional piece for the Friend. *Wallace and I went to a Laurel and Hardy tonight. Very silly but fun. Hester is still low but soldiers on. I'll take her down to Bunty's at the weekend for some larks. Bunts says she's eating for eight and is big as a whale. It's only been about three months, so I think she's overreacting slightly. Harold is aching to start building cots etc. with George, but B is making him wait just a bit. Mother says hello—she and Father are bedding in as it's so jolly cold. All his patients have the flu and chilblains. Oh, darling, are you warm enough? I hope they give you some sort of heat. I hear the weather is fearsome there so hope all the woollies got through. Mrs. Bagley is still waiting. Wallace is knitting a jumper for Tom. I hope he's put on at least 5 stone since I met him as it's vast!*

Well, I'd better go as I'm asleep on my feet. More of this prattling tomorrow.

Take care my love. Know I think of you always.

Yours ever,

E.xxxxx

PS: a new parcel is also on its way!

———

Mr. D. F. Stanwick-Hughes

The Prisoner of War Department of the War Office

Whitehall

London

Dear Mr. Stanwick-Hughes

With reference to my letter of last week, I am writing to enquire once again as to the availability of information regarding British prisoners of war currently being held in German camps.

As you know, I have written to all relevant departments of the Ministries, together with the various organisations with remits covering POWs and their families. To date I have not received any information, and indeed, minimal responses.

I write as the wife of a POW (Major Charles Mayhew, RA), in my capacity as the Readers and Advice Editor of the national magazine Woman's Friend, and as a member of the Wives and Families Group, an informal voluntary group of women with family members and friends under my husband's command. You will be aware that many of the women mentioned have also written to you, as well as to the other relevant organisations, Members of Parliament, and national newspapers and magazines. We are not affiliated to any specific organisation (although some are members of and in contact with POWRA) but write on an entirely personal basis.

I respectfully ask you to acknowledge and respond to our concerns and questions. What will happen to the prisoners when the Russian Army or other Allies liberate the camps? Are the prisoners being moved by the Germans in advance? If so, what provisions for their safety are being made? Is the International Red Cross aware of this and how will they police any transportation and the conditions therewith? How will we be able to track our men and ensure their safety if moved?

As you will appreciate, this situation is most distressing for the fam-

ilies, many of whom have borne the incarceration of their loved ones without complaint for years.

I would be most interested in meeting with you and will telephone your office once again tomorrow.

It is extremely tempting to publish the diary of my attempts to receive an answer from you in the magazine referred to above. I will not, of course, but I hope you understand my frustration.

Yours sincerely

Mrs. C. H. Mayhew

CHAPTER 25

No Friend of Mine

"So, we just sit and nod and apologise," I clarified, as Guy, Monica, and I walked along Malet Street to the meeting.

"I should think so," said Guy. "Langley wasn't forthcoming, but he wasn't raging. He's quite hard to read. But I think we're in their fairly good books. We'll see."

"It's just Dickie and us, isn't it?" said Monica. "We'll be fine."

I hoped so.

"Do you think he knows Stanwick-Hughes at the War Office?" I asked. "That man's office is impenetrable."

"Still no luck?" said Guy.

"None. I'm tempted to phone my grandmother and ask for tips on how to storm Government buildings."

"You take along a brick and throw it," said Monica, amiably. "Although if you get caught, Holloway is vile. My mother did three months. Here we are."

Long used to the drill, we had our identification papers ready and passed through the security procedures at Senate House without incident. A young woman I didn't recognise came to meet us and took us up to the seventh floor. Guy raised an eyebrow but said nothing. Richard's office wasn't on the seventh.

We were shown to a meeting room, large enough to seat at least twelve around the table but with the usual lack of any wall coverings to give any clue as to which department we were in, or who we would be meeting. The three of us hovered by the table in the awkward moments before our host arrived. By this point we were assuming Richard would not be alone.

He was not.

Richard introduced Mr. Brewer, who had a very long job title and, by implication, a very important job. He was a man who would not stand out in a crowd, pale-featured and with the expression of someone trying to work out some recent, rather confusing news. He carried a large box folder, holding it tightly under his arm.

"Mr. Brewer has recently transferred to the department," finished Richard, who appeared to be his normal, if slightly quieter than usual, dignified self.

Mr. Brewer thanked everyone very sincerely.

"I'm sure you realise why I have called this meeting," he opened, as the two factions sat down on opposite sides of the table. He placed the folder in front of him and rested his hands on the top of it for a moment as if to tell it to stay put.

"Actually, Mr. Brewer, we would be grateful if you could elucidate," said Guy.

"Yes. Most unfortunate," said Brewer, in his high-pitched, rather reedy voice. He opened the folder just slightly and brought out the current issue of *Woman's Friend*, placing it on the table and rotating it until it faced us. It had been folded open on the piece by "The Woman Who Knows."

Then, he did the same with *The West London News*, the paper that had reviewed our Christmas Fayre. And following that, what appeared to be every mention of POWs we had ever printed in our magazine.

Then, and one by one, he produced a photostat of every letter I had written to official departments about prisoners of war, whether about Charles, or enquiring about the rumours we had been following up for the past weeks. There were some by Guy as well, but the majority were from me. As Mr. Brewer took each one out of the box, he looked at it briefly, made a little "Mm" noise and added it to the display.

"Dear me," he said. "Dear me." Then he pointed to the newspaper piece with his pen. "It won't do," he said, looking at Guy. "It just won't do."

"Mr. Brewer, that, I believe," said Guy, politely, "is a rather badly written piece in a very small local newspaper about an event we held to raise money for the Red Cross." He looked Mr. Brewer in the eye, a courteous smile on his lips.

"Mm." Mr. Brewer began to read from the article. He sounded like a very diligent prosecution barrister, confidently about to surprise a witness with a box of irrefutable evidence of guilt.

"'We wanted to show them that we care,' said the Publisher, 'because the Government doesn't and it makes things very hard for them.' This from your Publisher, Miss . . . Hester Wilson?"

"I'm very glad you chose that part," said Guy. "It illustrates the worthlessness of the rag. Miss Wilson, who I might add, has just given up her wedding arrangements so that her fiancé can join our servicemen overseas, is not our publisher."

"That would be me," said Monica, in the silkiest of tones.

Mr. Brewer frowned and carried on.

"'Housewife Mrs. Enid Harris, who had travelled et cetera, et cetera . . . echoed Miss Wilson, adding, 'We're never told anything, other than by the Red Cross who always do their best, so it's very nice that at least the people at *Woman's Friend* care.'"

Then he shook his head, did another little hum and moved on, this time reading out extracts from my article.

"Miss Lake," he said, once he had finished. "You seem to think that you can use your magazine to access classified information not available to the public, while mounting what appears to be an increasingly aggressive campaign against the Government's handling of the situation with prisoners of war. It simply will not do. Will it?"

Mr. Brewer was most disarming. He didn't shout or show off, but displayed the self-belief of a school swot who knew that one day he would get a knighthood while everyone else would end up as a dud.

His argument was nonsense, but he seemed to very much believe it. Guy patiently explained each document. Yes, they showed a frustration with the way in which families were treated, but there was not a shred of evidence to suggest any form of campaign. My—and Guy's—letters were clearly from a personal position. The newspaper review was unfortunate, but no more than that.

"The ladies attending the public event had every right to say what they like," Guy finished. "It's the democracy we're fighting for."

"Hmm," said Mr. Brewer, his face showing no emotion at all.

Guy turned to Richard, who had said nothing, almost managing to merge into the background.

"Mr. Langley," he said, briskly. "You've spent enough time with my team. Surely you don't think we are running some sort of a campaign. You know these letters are about my brother, Miss Lake's husband. They've nothing to do with the other items."

Richard said nothing.

"Mr. Langley?" prompted Monica.

"You were at the Christmas Fayre," I said, leaning forward. "It was a family event. Won't you assure Mr. Brewer that it was far from a revolt?"

At this Mr. Brewer turned his head towards Richard, displaying the slow steel of a tortoise spotting a lettuce being poked into its cage.

"I did indeed accept a request to open the charity event," Langley said, archly. "But I really can't comment further."

Then he was quiet.

Mr. Brewer wrote something down, carefully applied blotting paper, and then moved his attention to me.

"Miss Lake, or is it Mrs. Mayhew? You don't use your married name?" he said, appearing perturbed at the concept.

"Miss Lake is my professional name," I replied. "I am Mrs. Mayhew as far as my personal life is concerned."

"Mm," he said. "Well, I'm afraid, Miss Lake, you cannot use a magazine that on occasion works in the interests of the Ministry of Information as your own personal soap box." He paused in order to look especially grave. "I understand this is not the first time you have 'rocked the boat' as I believe the saying goes, and I am afraid I must tell you that while I appreciate that you have worked with us for some time, it just won't do."

"Mr. Brewer, what exactly are you saying?" asked Monica, fixing him with a very direct stare.

"I am saying, Mrs. Edwards, that we will no longer require the journalistic services of Miss Lake, and in terms of attending the Ministry's briefings we are placing your magazine under review."

It could not have been clearer. I was getting the sack, and so it seemed might *Woman's Friend*. For years, every single member of our team had worked their hearts out to help the Ministry's propaganda activity. From Mrs. Croft finding a new carrot recipe for the hundredth time, to Mr. Newton moving all the other advertisers so that the Ministry could run its campaigns, to Nurse McClay writing about inoculations over and over again. And now Mr. Brewer, this power-mad little man whom none of us had ever met in all our dealings with the Ministry, had just got a promotion and wanted to show that he was in charge.

"Whose decision is this?" asked Guy.

"Mine," said Brewer.

Guy turned to Richard, shrugging his shoulders as if to ask, what on earth is going on? Richard just shook his head.

"I believe that is all," said Brewer.

"Mr. Brewer," I said, now aware there was very little to lose. "As long as the wives and families of British prisoners are kept in the dark and treated like an irritation, we have very little choice but to keep writing letters and making telephone calls until someone replies. I appreciate the Government can't share sensitive information, but currently there are rumours circulating that are causing enormous concern." I was quiet and measured, and as polite as I could manage, but my blood was boiling. "Do you know how often our readers write to us asking for help? If you ever want to find out, please come to our office to see for yourself. I promise it puts the volume of documents in your file *very* much in the shade."

Mr. Brewer was packing away his many press cuttings. Guy moved in while he still could.

"Mr. Brewer," he said. "Our publication has been working with the Ministry throughout the war. Miss Lake's contribution in particular has been commended by your colleagues on many occasions. She has been all over the country reporting on war workers and was sent to report from Brussels with Ministry accreditation within weeks of its liberation. The rest of our staff are entirely dedicated to the war effort, and quite clearly, we are wholly within our rights to enquire as to the safety of a family member being held as a prisoner of war. This decision makes no sense. I know people like to make changes when they take over, but really."

Mr. Brewer had gone an odd salmon pink.

"My decision has been made," he said, his voice even reedier. "Mr. Langley, would you show your friends out?"

The emphasis was on "friends."

"Business colleagues really, sir," said Langley. "But of course."

"Mm," replied Brewer. "Good day."

Then he left the room.

There was a moment's silence.

Guy was staring at Richard in disbelief. I didn't know what to say. Monica was the first to find her voice.

"Richard. How could you?"

Richard Langley did not meet her eye.

"Sorry, everyone," he said, sounding uncomfortable. "Brewer's known to be a stickler. I didn't think he would go that far. I'll see if I can have a word. One has to watch one's step here of course."

What a turncoat.

"Don't bother," said Guy, coldly. "We wouldn't want you to jeopardise your career just for some business colleagues." He was looking at Langley in disgust.

"Guy," said Langley. "You know that's not what I meant."

"I know exactly what you meant," said Guy, and the three of us began to walk towards the door. Then Guy paused for a moment and turned to Langley, the slightest sneer on his lips. "You couldn't find one word. Not one. After everything Emmy has done. All her work."

"Look, I'll see what I can do," said Langley again. "Let me show you out. You can't go wandering around here on your own."

Guy gave him a glare of pure contempt. "It's a two-minute walk to the lift," he said, with no emotion whatsoever. "Even we can't bring down the bloody Government in that amount of time."

"I'll call you," said Richard.

"I shouldn't," said Monica.

Then we were gone.

The three of us remained in silence until we were out of Senate House, and even then, as we walked towards Goodge Street to get the tube, no one said a word. Guy brought out a packet of cigarettes and offered one to Monica, who took it, slowing down for a moment so that Guy could light it for her.

My head was spinning with everything Mr. Brewer had said, and everything Richard Langley had not. What a spineless creep he had turned out to be. Monica's face was like stone. I didn't dare look at Guy's.

Finally, he stopped.

"Well," he said. "Bugger the bloody lot of them." He took a long drag on his cigarette.

"I can't believe Langley didn't even try," said Monica. "I thought he was a good friend."

Guy exhaled, shaking his head dismissively. "He was right about one thing. Just a business colleague. No friend of mine. Come on, let's go home."

As the three of us walked on, I slipped my arm into Guy's.

"Thank you for being on my side," I said, quietly.

Guy looked at me. Then, his face softened. "Always," he said.

THE WAR OFFICE

PRESS RELEASE

Issued by the Chief Press Censor

So far the War Office has received no information of the release of any British and Commonwealth prisoners of war by the advancing Red Army. An announcement will be made as soon as any reliable information is available.

It is known that the German authorities have been moving to the west prisoners of war and civilians from camps which are likely to be overrun. It should be appreciated that in the present conditions in Germany it must be some time before details of these transfers reach London.

ENDS.

CHAPTER 26

Why Does Nobody Listen?

The War Office press release was hardly more than a public version of the Wait and See responses that as the wives of prisoners of war we were used to getting in letters. But it was something.

"At least they've acknowledged the rumours," I said to Wallace, as we re-read the nine-line release.

"We could have told them that for nothing," she replied.

"They are busy trying to win the war," I said, gamely. "We don't really count."

"Just the men's flesh and blood, keeping their families and homes going and trying to do our bit," said Wallace. She was usually awfully good at keeping up a chipper front, but today her shoulders slumped, and her chin was down. "Sorry, Emmy," she said. "I'm tired. Daphne is teething so it's been a long night. I agree it's better than nothing. Do you think Mr. Langley had anything to do with the announcement?"

I gave a very hollow laugh. "Not remotely," I said. "He doesn't have any influence."

I hated the feeling of being useless. I was good at sorting problems, looking for an answer, or at least giving something a go, but now I couldn't do anything. Along with every other family I just had to wait.

Without anything to do, my mind turned to conjecture. Was the silence from Charles just a postal delay, or was he ill, or no longer at the same camp? I continued to write to him every night, becoming an expert in cheerful pretence and in the blind faith that my letters were reaching him. All was well here, how was it there? How was the weather? Over here it's started to rain. Wallace and I had secret conversations in the kitchen where we admitted that not knowing anything was driving us barmy. We both felt awfully guilty about that, more than aware that some women had not heard a thing about husbands who had been held captive in the Far East for years. We shared the news without comment in our newsletter to the other women, aware that while some like us would be frustrated, it was far worse for others like Juliet who were having to hold on to dwindling hope.

Everyone had someone they wanted back. Mrs. Mahoney's son-in-law was with the RAF in Egypt, Miss Peters' brother was in the navy out in the Far East, Mr. and Mrs. Brand's granddaughter was in the Wrens down in Gibraltar, and her brother was in the infantry somewhere in the Ardennes. The finishing line, for the war in Europe at least, was in sight, but getting there was excruciating.

I continued to talk with people I thought might be in the know. I had become friendly with a kind woman at the Red Cross office in West London. She told me to brace myself, that off the record, even when Peace came, Europe was going to be chaos.

Our newsletter became busier as everyone shared any snippet of information, such that it was. Edna Harris knew someone who spoke good German and was permanently glued to the radio listening for clues. We tuned ours into the European Service channel, which was based in Berlin but broadcast in English. It was probably German propaganda, but we didn't care. When they reported that Allied prisoners had actually requested to be relocated *away* from the Russians, we took it as another reason to believe the boys were on the move.

It became all-consuming.

January seemed to last forever, the weather utterly bitter through-out. Cheer was in short supply. Mrs. Shaw heard from a friend who had lost everything when the north of England was bombed over Christmas. Mr. Newton's cousin told him about the local theatre that was hit during a children's pantomime. More than ever, we all just wanted the war to be over. In an attempt to boost morale in the house, I managed to persuade Hester to come with me to visit Bunty and the children, but snow made the trains even worse than ever, and we were only able to escape the gloom of London for one weekend. The icing on the dispiriting cake was of course the meeting with Mr. Brewer, and if anyone wanted a cherry to go on top of that, Richard Langley had certainly delivered.

None of us expected him to put his job in danger, but Langley hadn't even tried to give us an idea of what was coming. He was only an acquaintance to me, but Monica had known him for years, and he and Guy had been close. I didn't much care about losing out on further work, but I did care that he had hurt my friends. His name was not mentioned again. *Woman's Friend* was kept on the press briefings list, and Monica attended purely to avoid specula-tion or gossip about our magazine, but I knew I wasn't welcome, and for that alone Guy said he would not set foot in the place from now on.

I decided to look forward. The readers would not see a difference, which was all that really mattered, and as Guy put it, we could now write what we damn well pleased.

When my piece by "The Woman Who Knows" was published, the readers' responses were almost all positive. A handful wrote to complain that they didn't care how we felt, but there were always a few of those. I wrote more articles, admitting to the frustration of not knowing what was going on, but tempering it by saying it was a comfort to know Victory was on its way. I wrote again about the wounded men I had met in Brussels. How I hoped they would now be home. I interviewed a psychologist, and we came up with advice on how to help the men cope when they did return. It was a modern approach, and it went down well.

I was still concerned about Hester. After the initial disappointment about the wedding, she had become stoic about Clarence being away and thrown herself into her work, more diligent than ever, and almost anxious, which I put down to the feature in the local paper. Her confidence had taken a wallop. I had a word with Guy and Monica, and we called Hest into Guy's office with some good news.

She arrived looking terrified, so I got straight to the point.

"Hester," I said. "You are being promoted. You've been doing sterling work. You are now Office Co-ordinator and there will be a salary rise, too."

Hester was astonished.

"But . . ." she began.

"Not a word!" said Guy. "There is never a 'but' when someone gives you more money."

"But . . ." said Hest.

"NO," roared Guy. Then put his hands over his ears.

"You'd better accept it, or he'll stay like that," I grinned. "Hest, from moving the entire office to the country and back again, to keeping us all going day in and day out, you deserve this. There is no 'but' and you can use the pay rise to save for when Clarence is back, and you set up home."

At this poor Hester was even more overwhelmed. Her eyes began to fill up.

"NO CRYING," thundered Guy.

"Hester Wilson," I said, mock sternly, "you've been promoted and I'm afraid there's nothing you can do to stop us being pleased with you."

Hester didn't seem to believe it. "Thank you," she managed. "I'll do my best."

"You already do," I said.

But something was still not right. In the evenings Hester was increasingly quiet and by the time the vicious January weather gave way to a mild and drizzly February, she was spending most of her time in her room, writing to Clarence and keeping a diary, she said.

When Valentine's Day came into the equation, I hatched a plan for an evening out that I hoped would help avoid a dip in morale. Guy said the entire day was not his thing at all, but I rallied Wallace and Hester and forced them to go to the films with me.

"We're not sitting around feeling sorry for ourselves," I declared, jamming a hat over my hair. "We have three fit and healthy men doing their bit in Europe, and moping around here is playing straight into Hitler's hands. Come on, Hest, get your skates on. Miss Peters is coming and so is Mrs. Shaw. Wallace is meeting us there."

"What are we seeing?" said Hester, giving in, which was just as well as I was feeling firm.

"*Frenchman's Creek*," I replied, shoving her into her coat as if I were her mum. "*Picturegoer* says it's an escapist romance, which is just what we all need, and best of all, it's got nothing to do with the war. Are you ready, Mrs. Shaw? Arturo de Cordova's a pirate with smashing hair which I am sure will be a tonic for us all."

It was a gloomy early evening outside, but the four of us set off at a pace. I was grateful to the other ladies for making it into something of a party. We all needed a boost. I took Hester's arm and started grilling her about her favourite film actors.

"You can't have Jimmy Stewart," I said. "He's too old for you, and anyway Miss Peters has bagsied him. What about Mickey Rooney? He's more your age."

Hester shrieked and said that he was too young and too short. For the first time in weeks, she sounded more like her old self.

As we walked along, she suddenly changed tack and said, "Emmy, thank you for being so nice. I'm sorry I've been a bit low."

"Good Lord, don't worry about that," I said. "It's a tricky time. I think you're doing awfully well. Honestly." I gave her a big smile, pleased to have the opportunity to try to bolster her up. "I know it's really hard, but everyone says how well you've been doing getting on with things. Guy says you're the best person at organising him he's ever worked with."

"He's been ever so kind," she replied. "Sorting out Mum about the wedding and everything. If I had a dad, I'd want him to be like Guy." She looked sad for a moment, which wasn't what I wanted at all.

"Oh, Hest," I said. "That's the loveliest thing anyone could ever say."

"Don't tell him, will you?" she said, quickly.

"Gosh no." Then I added jokily, "It's a good job Guy isn't your dad. He wouldn't have let you go out with a boy until you're at least thirty. He'd have put Clarence through the mill and probably made him fill out a questionnaire about his intentions." I laughed, knowing I was spot on.

"Would he?" Hest said, wide-eyed.

"Oh yes. Don't tell him I said so, but he's very fond of you. He agrees with me that you're a shining star. It's all right though, he thinks the same of Clarence, so he'd have passed with flying colours. Oh look, there's Wallace. Come on."

I dragged Hester into the cinema and into the world of piratical romance. It was no bad place to be, and for the next hours we all gratefully escaped into the film.

"We need to do this a lot more often," I said as we left.

Not a woman among us disagreed.

———

The next day, if a pirate ship had sailed smartly up the Thames and offered me a berth, I would have bitten off their hands at the chance. Nothing was going well.

I had stayed up late after the pictures, first writing a letter to Charles and then trying to think of what to put in the latest Wives and Families newsletter. The evening out had taken my mind off it, but in the quiet of the night, it was easy to become glum. Two days previously, Wallace had heard from one of the ladies whose husband had been wounded at Arnhem.

It was the worst possible news. Gunner Dawson had died. Mrs. Dawson had asked if we would include it in the next letter. Of course we'd said yes, and I had asked if she would like us to put in Gunner Dawson's picture as well. She had sent a lovely photograph of a handsome and very young man, and I had asked Herbie, our printer, if he wouldn't mind doing something nice. I was extremely touched that Mrs. Dawson had entrusted me with such a precious belonging and I had put it in my bedroom rather than risk losing it in the bustle of the office.

It was on my bedside table, next to the photograph of Charles and me, and the one of us with Hester and Clarence at Bunty's wedding. Three young men, all very different, but enormously precious and loved. Even at this point in the war, I found it hard to imagine that Mrs. Dawson and so very many other women would not see their boys again. I wished them all goodnight before I went to bed, but I didn't sleep until the small hours.

I was tired and out of sorts when I woke up, and my mood was not improved by my first meeting of the day, which was an interview with a regional director of one of the railway companies.

"I don't mind talking to you, Miss Lake," he said. "But won't your readers want to stay at home once the men are demobbed so they can look after them properly? After all, they're the ones winning us the war."

It was a disheartening chat.

It was raining hard as I trudged back into the office, but I was keen to get on, so, slightly damp, sat down at my desk next to the Letters Ladies to tackle some readers' concerns. As the rest of the team continued with their typing, Mrs. Shaw joined me to take dictation, and we set off at a lick to get through the hefty stack of concerns.

The first was a sad letter from a nice girl whose boy had been imprisoned by the Japanese for three years. She was determined to stay the course, even though her friends were all courting, and she was feeling terribly alone.

"I thought you might want to help that one, especially," said Mrs. Shaw, dropping her voice.

"I certainly do," I replied. "We can find a space in the next issue available." I gave a helpful reply, telling the reader she was doing very well and suggesting she might have a chat with one or two of her pals as well as listing options on how she might find some friends who were in a similar position to her.

The next problem was from a girl who had, as she put it, "*let passion overcome us*" with a chap who at the first sign of trouble had disappeared without trace. She had been left to face her very strict mother who was insisting she give her baby away. I felt extremely sorry for the girl and wanted to help more, but she hadn't given her address.

"Let's find room for this one as well," I said.

"Actually, we've had quite a few like that this week," said Mrs. Shaw. "Do you want to see them first? I think it might have something to do with Christmas."

"Good idea," I said. "Perhaps we can amalgamate them. Gosh, yes that is a lot. I think people have been carried away with the festivities." I began to skim through the other letters. ". . . *my parents are very Victorian . . . it will kill my mother to know . . . Very much in love, but now I find I need to go away for some months . . . I wasn't in love with him, but he swept me off my feet and now I am having a baby.* Oh dear. Are they all from this week?"

Mrs. Shaw nodded. "These are on the same theme, but from a different point of view," she said, almost apologetically. I began to read them out loud.

"*Dear Miss Lake, I have read your advice telling the girl she does not have to get married, and I am horrified. What will the baby do when it grows up with the shame of being 'nameless'? Do you not believe in marriage?* That sounds like the Victorian parent of the other reader. *Dear Miss Lake, why do you encourage young girls to sleep around?* Oh, I say. That's very direct. *It's women like you who make girls think it is acceptable to . . .*" I put the letters down. "Oh, Mrs. Shaw," I said. "You would think there's enough sadness in the world currently, without needing this sort of judgement. These are just horrible. May I see any of the others please?"

I really should have stopped, gone upstairs to change my wet clothes, and had a nice cup of tea before continuing. I had answered problems about pregnancies so many times. Some were extraordinarily sad; some, it had to be said, could have been avoided. More than anything, whatever I wrote in reply, someone would write in to tell me I had said the wrong thing.

Mrs. Shaw passed across a different folder, also stuffed full.

"Right. *Unfaithful husband.* No, we did that last week. *In love with an American. Cross with my mum. My mum won't let me . . .*"

Several in a row were all complaints about mothers who as far as I could see were doing their best. I looked at Mrs. Shaw and shook my head.

"Do you know," I said, sighing heavily. "Sometimes I wonder if anyone ever actually reads this page. Look at this: *I'm sixteen and my mum won't let me and my boy be alone together . . . I reckon I'm old enough to make up my own mind.* Yes, I dare say she probably is, but how many times have we tried to say that if things go wrong, life can become terribly hard?"

Mrs. Shaw nodded in agreement as I looked into mid-air for inspiration. "I know we get parents who are rotten," she said, "but I did think these particular mothers are just trying to help."

"Perhaps we should run a whole page with letters like these," I said, picking up the ones accusing me of being lax or immoral. "Remind everyone of the real world, which clearly isn't sympathetic and modern and hoping to help. It's judgemental and nasty and these poor girls are going to be facing it whichever way they turn. If they keep their babies they'll be given a wretched go of things. If they give them away for adoption, they'll never see their child again. And then if they choose the course of direction that we can't even talk about in the magazine then they'll be put in simply awful, awful danger."

I dropped the letters on the desk where they landed in a messy heap.

What was I supposed to advise?

Whatever I said, in the end, couldn't make things better. I couldn't change the way people viewed girls who had babies out of wedlock. I couldn't change the minds of people who grew up in a time when "nice" girls didn't even speak to a man unless they were introduced by their fathers.

Normally, I would have pushed on. But today it was one more thing I was powerless to fix. Just like I couldn't get anywhere with ministries and Government departments, and I couldn't stop men declaring war on each other, and I couldn't do a damn thing to help someone like young Mrs. Dawson who did not deserve to lose her husband.

"I'm sorry, Mrs. Shaw," I said. "It's just it feels as if I've spent half this bloody war begging these girls to wait until they're married or to keep away from horrible men who only want one thing. Just wait. It's all I can suggest. Waiting is what we all have to do, isn't it? We're waiting for our husbands. George, Margaret, and Stanley are waiting for their dad. Juliet Bagley is waiting for her son. Waiting to show your boyfriend how much you love him is a walk in the park compared to all of those. My God, I'd give my right arm to have Charles here. I wouldn't even need to touch him, as much as I would love to. A game of Ludo would do if it meant he was safe, and I knew where he was." Now I ran out of steam. "I can't change the way of this world," I said quietly. "Why doesn't anyone listen?"

It wasn't really about the letters. It was about *everything*. But I couldn't say that. I was the positive one, the person who dragged people out to the cinema and insisted they forget their troubles for an hour or two.

I took a deep breath and put my hand to my forehead, aware that swearing, and not to mention talking about my husband in such a way, was appalling behaviour in an office, particularly in front of a junior member of the team. I realised that while no one had said anything, all my colleagues were watching me. Wallace and Hester looked horrified, and even Monica, who was standing in the doorway with a concerned expression, stayed silent.

"I'm sorry," I said, pulling myself together. "Hester, Wallace, everyone, I do apologise. That was entirely uncalled for. I really shouldn't stay up late and get overtired, but that's no excuse for this sort of talk. It won't happen again. Mrs. Shaw, please take down this reply. *'Dear Up a Gum Tree. I am sure your mum has your best interests at heart. You have years and years to become closer to your boy, and while I can tell you like him very much, do take your time as sadly, consequences can be harsh.'* That should be short enough to go in," I finished. "Thank you. Now then, perhaps Hester could find another more positive stack of letters for us to work on. Hest, would you mind . . ."

But when I looked up, Hester had gone.

CHAPTER 27

Where's Hester?

As Monica said later, when she insisted on taking me out to dinner, sometimes something had to give.

"I have been a little worried about you, recently," she said. "But I hadn't realised it was so bad you'd rather play Ludo with Charles than sleep with him."

She raised an immaculate eyebrow at me as two Canadian officers at the table next to us nearly choked on their soup.

I laughed for the first time that day, before going pink with embarrassment.

"Of course, it could be Strip Ludo," said Monica, thoughtfully. "Which I've never tried, before you ask." She looked in her handbag. "Blast, I've forgotten my cigarettes."

One of the Canadians was over with a brand-new packet before you could say "knife."

"It's not funny," I said, in hardly more than a whisper, after Monica had thanked him. "You can't say things like that in front of people. I might in private with Bunty or you, but not at work. Mrs. Shaw has hardly looked me in the eye since. And Hester was appalled. I don't blame her, either."

"We're all just doing our best," said Monica. "Everyone knows that. It's about time Hester saw a crack in your armour anyway. Wobble the pedestal for a second or two. She'll be fine. Have a chat with her in the morning and say you were having a brainstorm and said some regrettable things, but you're perfectly normal again now. And don't mention Ludo."

"You're never going to let me forget that, are you?" I said, blushing all over again.

"God, no." Monica reached forward and took hold of my hand. "Don't worry, I promise you, it will be fine."

I slept a little better for Monica saying that, but I was still wincing the next morning when I replayed the whole episode in my head, and I was very keen to speak with Hester and clear the air before work. When I went down for breakfast though, she wasn't there, and by half past eight still hadn't appeared. It wasn't entirely unusual, one of the perks of living above the shop was that occasionally you could oversleep and still be at work before nine o'clock, but nevertheless, I went upstairs and knocked gently on her bedroom door.

There was no answer, even when I knocked again and called her name. Neither was she in the office, or the bathroom, or the kitchen, which I checked again just in case. This *was* unusual. I returned to her bedroom and finally, having knocked on her door one last time, I opened it just slightly.

"Hest? Are you there?"

I peered through the gap so that I could see the end of her bed. It was already made, hospital corners and all. I leaned in further. The whole room was pristine. The top of the chest of drawers had been cleared of the framed photograph of Hester and Clarence, and the one of Hest as a little girl with her nan. The crocheted doily had gone from the dressing table as had the blue glass vanity set we had managed to find for her sixteenth birthday.

I raced around the room, checking drawers, the wardrobe, even the back of the door where a pale pink candlewick dressing gown still hung. It was the one remaining sign that Hester had ever been there.

Within seconds I was up the stairs and hammering on the door to the flat. Guy, dressed for work but with a half-eaten piece of toast in his hand, came to the door immediately.

"Hest's gone," I blurted.

"What? Where?"

"I don't know. She's not here and everything's gone from her room."

"Good God," said Guy. "Let me see."

He abandoned the piece of toast and followed me down at a pace.

"Bloody hell," he said, as we stood in Hester's room. "Why on earth would she do this?" He scratched the back of his head, looking around the room as if a clue would appear out of thin air. "Perhaps her grandmother has been taken ill."

I shook my head. "She would have told us or left us a note." That was an idea. "A note. We need to check. Maybe I've missed something."

Downstairs, the front doorbell rang. I had not yet unlocked the door for the staff.

"Don't say anything yet," said Guy. "Let's wait until Monica gets in." He grimaced. "Where on earth has she gone?"

Trying to think of possible places Hester might be and not to mention why, I went down to the hall and let in Miss Peters and Mrs. Shaw.

"Good morning," I said, overly brightly. I was still embarrassed about the previous day. "Sorry, I forgot to unlock the door."

Leaving them to take off their hats and coats and hang them up in the hall, I went into the office, checking Hester's desk and then looking in and around mine to see if she had left a note where I'd see it before anyone else.

There was nothing. I headed to the kitchen, where Guy was doing the same thing.

"Not a sign," he said. "Let's go and wait for Monica in my office."

When Monica arrived ten minutes later, I was already drawing conclusions.

"Do we know when she would have gone?" asked Monica. "When did you last speak?"

"I saw her in the afternoon in the office, but I was out in the evening," said Guy. "I'm ashamed to say I didn't notice anything untoward. I returned here around nine and assumed she was in her room, so went straight up to the flat."

"Monica, you and I were out late, chatting for ages," I said. "I didn't get in until after half-past ten and then I did exactly as Guy did."

"What about during the day?" asked Monica. "Emmy?"

I was beginning to have a slightly sick feeling in my throat.

"It was when I was ranting about the letters," I said. "Hest looked so shocked, and then she disappeared." My heart was heading towards my boots. "I should have gone after her, but I was rather mortified at my performance. I continued working on the letters with Mrs. Shaw, and then we went into town for dinner." I started to chew my fingernail. "It has to have something to do with all my swearing and ranting, hasn't it? Crikey, I'm such an idiot."

"Let's not panic," said Guy. "Hester's a young girl and it's been a very emotional few weeks for her. I don't want to put this on your shoulders, but she does look up to you. Perhaps she found it upsetting, went off on an impulse and is already wondering how she can come back without a fuss. She could be back before we know it."

It was a good effort, but it didn't help.

"That's exactly my worry," I said. "She's very young, quite possibly on her own and we don't know where she is."

"Let's think," said Monica. "Her grandmother's is the obvious place. I don't think she would have gone to her mother's."

We began to compile ideas. I used the telephone in Guy's office to call Bunty, who said she would stand by and call back immediately if Hester appeared there.

"I think we should speak to Wallace," I said. "She and Hester are close. And it wasn't just the swearing. I was very grumpy about the readers, especially the girls not listening to their mothers. Perhaps that hit a nerve?"

Guy was drawing squares on his blotter as he often did when he was thinking. Monica, though, had a strange expression on her face.

"I don't think it was that, Emmy," she said, slowly. "I think it might have been about the girls themselves. All the letters about them being in trouble."

Monica and I looked at each other as the pennies began to rain down.

"Oh no," I said, putting my head in my hand. "Not Hest."

"What are you thinking?" asked Guy, looking up. He hadn't been there for my outburst and probably more to the point, he was a man.

Monica was the one to answer.

"I think Hester could be pregnant," she said.

———

It was all guesswork, but it added up.

"Hest was so very distressed when Clarence phoned her," I said. "Panicky, almost."

"She was extremely upset," said Guy. "At the time I thought it was a fair reaction as it was so close to the wedding. I do remember her saying that she was sorry, and that she'd let us down, and I thought it was an odd turn of phrase to use for crying under the circumstances. But perhaps that's not what she meant at all."

I was finding it hard to think sensibly. If Monica was right, poor, poor Hester must have been having a wretched time. No wonder she had been so quiet.

"I've been trying to cheer her up, jolly her along," I said. "I should have sat down with her and asked if anything was wrong. I just assumed she was upset about Clarence going off to fight and that I needed to help her crack on until he gets home." I could hardly sit still, I was so furious with myself. "I'm supposed to be good with people and their problems, and it was right there under my nose . . ." I stopped. "Hest's like a little sister," I said, almost to myself.

The thought was awful. If Hester was going to have a baby, but hadn't thought she could talk to me about it, what kind of a big sister was I? One who lectured people on how judgemental the world was and how every option for an unmarried mother was dire.

Sometimes when we were at Rose House we had joked that *Woman's Friend* had become a commune. Everyone had laughed, but to an extent it was true. Within our small, broad-minded world we would rally round, and we certainly did not judge, but we weren't the norm. Guy and Monica were from a bohemian, writers' world. Like Monica, I had been brought up by a mother who had fought in the women's suffrage movement, and even the more conservative members of our team were tolerant by most standards. People who weren't didn't stay very long.

We may not have been avant-garde, but most of us were of a liberal disposition. I knew I would not have to walk five yards outside the front door to hear a very different view of the world.

"We have to find her," I said. "We don't even know if she's told Clarence. I'll go to her nan's. I have the address."

"Emmy, I'm not sure that's for the best," said Guy, gently. "If Hester isn't there it will scare her grandmother, and she may contact Hester's mother. Do we want her to know Hester's gone missing? I don't wish to be disrespectful, but Mrs. Wilson is not the easiest person. She'd far rather Hester had stayed with her and got a job in a local shop. This would be the proof she's waiting for that Hester has been led astray. She could drag Hester home and when it comes, make her give the baby away."

I couldn't disagree with any of that, but I wished Guy wasn't such a prophet of doom.

"What about the police?" I asked. "We could report Hest as missing." As I said it, I knew that was pointless. Hester was just another girl who might have left home in a flap. London was full of waifs and strays. The police wouldn't do anything.

"I think we sit tight," said Monica. "Just for a day or so. Hester could come back, or phone, or write. I think she may change her mind, or it could be a false alarm. And anyway, we could have jumped to the wrong conclusion. I know it's horrid not knowing where she is, but I think we hold our nerve. Guy, do you have a cigarette?"

I'd never seen Monica smoke at nine o'clock in the morning. I didn't think she was half as calm as she was managing to appear.

I began to look at dates in my diary. "Excuse my indelicacy," I said, "but I would bet my hat that if Hest is pregnant, it's early days. Sorry, Guy, you might not want to listen to this." I turned to Monica, speaking under my breath. "I don't think they would have slept together unless they were certain they were getting married jolly soon. They didn't get engaged until just before Christmas. That's when she went to visit his aunt."

And just after she and I had sat together in the kitchen, talking about when she would be married.

Hest, just make the most of every minute, I'd said. *Enjoy every second you get. That's all that matters . . . he might have to go to war, so just make the most of having him here.*

Hester said that Wallace and Mrs. Bagley had said the same thing. I had a feeling that the utterly in love Hester and Clarence had thrown caution to the wind.

I would sit tight for now as Monica had suggested. But there wasn't a chance I was going to let Hester go through this on her own.

Wherever she was, I was going to find her.

———

It was the longest, most interminable wait. Twenty-four hours went by with no word. Monica, Guy, and I closed ranks, telling the team that Hester had been called away due to a family illness. None of us slept. Bunty phoned later that first day, waiting until the evening so that we could speak without fear of being overheard, most specifically by the children.

"I'm sorry, Em, she's not been in touch with us," she said. "How are you?"

My best friend's concern destroyed my brave front. "It's my fault, Bunts," I said, my voice wobbling. "It really is all my fault." I wiped my eyes, glad that she couldn't see me.

"You can stop that, right now," Bunty snapped. "It's rotten and worrying, but you mustn't do that. Honestly, Em, you've got so much on your plate. Boadicea, remember? It can't be done."

Now a big tear ran down my cheeks. I never thought I would let Hester, of all people, down. Not Hest.

"I told her to make the most of every second with him," I said. "I told her we were so proud of her, that she could never let us down. And then I lectured everyone about women needing to wait, because that's what we have to do. Because otherwise people judge and even though it's not fair, that's just how things are." My head pounded from thinking about it. "No wonder she couldn't tell me."

"Oh, Em," said Bunty. "She'll come back. It's all a shock at the moment. And if she's anything like me, being pregnant will be sending her brain right up the spout. I'm happy, I'm sad, I'm laughing, I'm crying. Last week Stanley marched into the kitchen asking if I knew when Arthur would be coming home and I took one look at his hopeful little face and started to sob. I had to tell him I'd just burnt my hand on the cooker."

"I don't suppose you have heard anything from Arthur?"

"Nothing. You?"

"No."

"Look," said Bunts. "Everything's such a worry, No one has any room left in them for more upset. When things simmer down, I'm sure Hester will call."

Bunty didn't sound very convinced.

We talked on, trying to put ourselves in Hest's position. It was impossible. When we were eighteen, we had just done our Higher School Certs. There was no war. There was no sense of urgency about anything very much, though the rules had been the same.

"Can I ask you something?" Bunts said. "I wouldn't say it to anyone else and you don't have to answer."

"Of course."

"Hester won't do anything dangerous, will she?"

"No," I said, straight away. "Categorically not. I've thought about it all day and I think it's the exact opposite. Clarence is the love of her life. If we've guessed right and she's going to have their baby, but for the wedding being called off she would be thrilled to bits. Hester and Clarence are victims of timing, that's all." As I spoke, I felt more and more certain of what I was saying. "Bunts, I will lay everything I have on the line that Hester will fight. She's not going to throw herself in the Thames or turn to some awful person in a back street. She's going to do everything she can to take care of her and Clarence's baby. Hest's brave. When things get rough, she has more backbone than anyone. Remember when we thought we would lose *Woman's Friend*? She was the one who never gave up."

It was easy to think of Hester Wilson as the baby of the group, but I was becoming more and more sure that she would be trying to work out what to do. Perhaps Hest was thinking she couldn't rely on help from her friends or her family, but when it got down to it, she would come through.

It didn't make me any less worried about where she was, but I knew she was strong, and that was something to hold on to.

And then a letter arrived.

Dear Emmy

I am very sorry to have left without saying goodbye. Thank you for everything, especially letting me stay at Rose House and Braybon Street as they have been the happiest time of my life.

Please could you apologise to Mr. Collins and Mrs. Edwards as I am not able to work my two weeks' notice. I have done my best to work more hours to make up for this although I know I am not yet up to the right amount, and I am very sorry to leave you in the lurch without an assistant. I know Mrs. Carter is keen to do more hours and I have been trying to tell her about what I do so that she will be able to take on some of my work until you find a new Office Co-ordinator.

My filing is up to date and if you look in the bottom drawer on the left by the fireplace I have written a list of notes so it is easy for the next person to be able to get on with the job. I hope that is all right with you. I am sorry to let you down like this.

I am afraid I have to go away because I have been very weak and foolish and made a mess of things. Please do not blame Clarence. He does not know I am leaving and I don't want to worry him. I will write to him when I can and see what he says then, but I know he will be very busy, and the main thing is he doesn't take his mind off of keeping safe. When the war is over I am hoping we might be able to be together, but I don't know what he will say. Please do not tell my mum or Nan. I have written to Mum telling her I have a very good new job somewhere. She won't mind where as she isn't much of a letter writer.

I am sorry I have let you all down. I know you said ~~Mr. Col~~ Guy and you think I am a shining star, but I'm not, not at all, and I couldn't tell you after everything you've said, and done for me. I should have known better.

Thank you for everything. I hope you hear from Charles very soon. I am sure he will be back as soon as he can.

I shall miss you all very much indeed.

Yours sincerely

Hester

PS I hope this is all right as my formal notice.

PPS I have taken my ration book from the dresser in the kitchen, but please share my part of the cheese in the cold room. There are also 3 Weetabixes and some cocoa, so please do have them too.

PPPS I really am so sorry.

CHAPTER 28

I've Let You All Down

The postmark was local so gave no clue as to where she had gone, but for now all that mattered was the letter inside. Now we knew that our assumption was correct.

"Almost everything in it is sorting out everyone else," I said, as once again Guy and I hid with Monica in his office. "That is so typical of Hest." I felt sad and flat, and angry with myself. I hadn't thought about what she was going through nearly enough.

"Hester must have been planning this," said Monica. "But I don't understand why she didn't stay longer." She was standing by the window, looking down onto the little garden outside. "No one would have guessed for some time."

"Hester is the most organised person in the world," I said. "But I'm sure she's embarrassed and feeling ashamed. How many times have we read someone refer to themselves as 'weak and foolish' in a letter?" I rolled my shoulders back as they were stiff and aching. "If Hest and Clarence had been able to get married, what is seen as weak and foolish now wouldn't matter. There would have just been a lovely thing to look forward to."

"I wonder where she's gone," said Guy, to himself. He was leaning against his desk, drumming his fingers on it, frustrated.

"I've been thinking about that," I answered. "We need a plan. Hester has one, and we need one as well. Otherwise, we'll have given up, and I'm not doing that." I opened my notebook. It wasn't a work one, so no one would see it by accident, but I had still written in a sort of code. Now I started reading my notes, as if I was part of an investigation. "Here's what we know. First, and this is I suppose, good news: Hest has all the information she needs for mother and baby homes and places to go to when it's time for her confinement. Second: it's obviously far too early for that yet, therefore she will be looking for a job. We need to consider what that might be. Third: she took her Post Office Savings book with her, and I know she has money, because she's been saving for months, even before they got engaged. So I think we can try to rest easy that at least she can afford a place to stay, for now anyway. This is all good."

I paused, half expecting Guy to make some sort of quip about Miss Marple, or say, "Good work, detective," because even I knew that's how I sounded. In any other situation he would have.

"I know," I prompted. "I sound like Miss Marple."

There were half-hearted attempts at smiles.

I pushed on. "I'm sure the baby can't be due until September so she'll work for as long as she can. I have a list of all the maternity homes we know of that accept unmarried mothers, and I'll contact them nearer that time. I just hope Hester picks one of the nicer ones. But I do think she's heard me talking about those."

"Will they tell you if she's there?" asked Monica.

"Some might," I said. "Not the ones that push the girls into having the baby adopted. I'll go on a charm mission until then."

"So, we do have some time," said Guy.

"We do, but Hester's still having to cope with all of this on her own."

"Family?"

"I don't know of any beyond her mum and her nan. I think Hest is going to try to do this alone. I just know that if she thinks she's

let us down, she'll think the same about her family and Clarence's."
I paused for a moment. "I think that's almost the worst part of this
because I am sure his family would come to terms with it and want
to help. They adore Hest. And every family has someone who's been
through something like this. Mother says my granny knows all sorts
of rumours she won't talk about."

"Really?" said Guy. "And I let you marry my brother?"

I knew he was attempting to sound like his usual self. "Don't tell
Charles," I said. "He'll want a divorce."

"I wouldn't advise it," said Monica, wryly. "It's nearly as bad as a
baby. To be serious, Hester's main challenge is going to be trying to
avoid people finding out that she's not married. If they do, she'll be
asked to leave boarding houses or lodgings, and employers will give
her the sack like a shot. Look, I'm sorry to go into the negatives, but
don't forget that once the war's over, jobs are going to go to the men.
And no one wants to see a young girl with child about the place, do
they? Hester's a slip of a lass and can easily pass as far younger than
her age. If she's unlucky, the baby will show quite quickly, too."

"Clarence will be home well before September," I said, firmly.
"The war can't go on until then."

Monica and Guy looked at me.

"Maybe not in Europe," said Guy. "But he could get sent straight
out to the Far East." He saw my face fall. "I'm sorry, but that's being
in the army."

I didn't have to be told that.

"Right then," I said, assertively. "We go back to my plan. We have
to find her."

"Em," said Guy, in the voice he used when he was about to say
something I didn't want to hear. "Hester could be anywhere."

"We'll find her."

"It's a needle in a haystack."

"Then *I'll* find her."

"Emmy . . ." began Guy.

"No, Guy," I said, fiercely. "Don't 'Emmy' me. I've let Hester down, very badly. I'm not going to sit around here doing nothing for the next seven months. I'm doing enough of that as it is."

Guy said nothing, but it wasn't hard to guess what he was thinking.

"And don't go making this about Charles," I added. "Because it's not. Neither you nor I have made any headway at all in finding out if he may have been moved. Does that mean we've stopped trying? No. Of course not."

"True," said Guy.

"Well then. I'm not giving up on Hest, either. You can either help me, or not. It's up to you."

"Of course we will," said Monica. "Don't be silly. We'll find a way."

She put her hand on my arm and smiled. I knew she meant it and I managed one in response.

Guy nodded. "Of course we will," he said. "You know I'm worried about her too. I'm worried about them both. I'm worried about bloody everyone. Now let's start again. What's number four on your list?"

Dearest C

It's been over three months since I've heard from you, so this will be yet more chitter chatter rather than answering you, but you'll have to put up with it for now! All is well here. March has been just as dreary weatherwise as February, but Easter is quite early this year and that's always a boost, isn't it? I'll be with Bunty and the chaps for it, I think. Stanley has loved lambing season although it has called for some interesting conversations for poor Harold. He says he'd rather defuse a 100 kg bomb than go through that again. Bunty is awfully well apart from wanting to eat mud. Wallace is well—if you get this, please give her love to Tom. She says to tell him Baby Daphne is enormous, with about 60 teeth, and can now say Dada. We went to Battersea Park to look at the allotments and it turned out Daphne is keen on scoffing mud, too. Ah, the joys!

Well, darling, I hope the weather is cheering up for you. We've heard it's been grim for months. I know we can't say anything, but I will just say, not long now. I live for seeing you and have become quite fixated on planning lovely things for us to do. Or we can do nothing, if that's what you'll prefer after all this war lark.

The daffodils are out now—do you remember them last year? I am looking out of the window at them now and remembering it too.

Take great care of yourself, won't you? All my love, forever, as you know.

Your own

Exxxxx

CHAPTER 29

I Don't Think I Do

Life became a never-ending circle of work and trying to find people who either couldn't or wouldn't be found. By the end of February, we knew that Germany was in collapse and that prisoners of war were being marched for hundreds of miles in thick snow and arctic conditions to get them away from the Russians. The Secretary of State for War admitted that conditions were "harsh" but that the Government was going to do everything possible to ensure that things improved. It did not fill anyone with confidence.

Wallace and I carried on with the newsletter, which wasn't so much news as a succession of hopeful platitudes and heartfelt condolences. We all knew that with the final push to the end of the war, it was highly unlikely that anyone missing would be found before the fighting was over. No one admitted that out loud, but with no word from Charles for months, even I knew that my letters to him were little more than a diary I wrote each night.

In comparison, trying to find Hester at least involved activity rather than being told that there was no news and nothing to be done. I phoned every mother-and-baby establishment I knew, trying to butter them up by thanking them for their terrific work, saying how much they helped our readers, and asking for their invaluable advice on finding my friend. Some were sympathetic, others less so. On several occasions the response to my cheery, "She's a smashing young woman," was a dour, "Aren't they all?"

The big problem was what Hester might be doing now. Finding someone who had gone missing was never easy, but currently it was an impossible task. Everyone was looking for someone. The whole of Europe was full of displaced people. Sections in the newspapers ran every day where families took out an advertisement with a picture of their boy, almost always in uniform, asking if anyone knew where he might be.

Lt. John Bagley last seen Holland, 20 September 1944 officially reported missing presumed taken captive. His mother is anxious for information. Her home is 71 Chester Road, London, W5.

I had lost count how many times Juliet had placed the advert. In the face of missing boys like Johnny who would care about a young girl who had "got herself into trouble"?

My aim was to find Hester long before the homes might be needed. I knew that once Clarence was back he would move heaven and earth to find her and get married as soon as they could. But Guy was right. We didn't know when he would come home. Worst of all, and none of us said it, we were all too aware there was no guarantee that he would come home at all. That thought went squarely in the no-go area of our minds. The fact remained that life for an eighteen-year-old girl who was pregnant and unmarried was not going to be easy. It broke my heart knowing that if only Hester would get in touch, there was a queue of us who desperately wanted to help.

I quite understood how she might not wish to return to Pimlico where she was known, but Bunty would welcome her with open arms in Hampshire, as would my parents.

"That poor, dear girl," said Mother the moment I told her about the situation. "We would love to have her stay with us if she would like and for as long as she needs. We can tell people that she's already married if she would prefer, and if not, should anyone get funny about things, I shall personally tell them to go and boil their head."

I wished Hest could have heard her. It almost made it worse that I couldn't tell her how many people she had on her side. Monica had volunteered a list of decent, if occasionally eccentric friends who also lived in the countryside with tons of spare room, and if all these failed, I had faith that Clarence's family would not let Hester down.

She just needed to know this.

With that in mind, Guy, Monica, and I began our plan, sitting together in the kitchen as if we were launching a new magazine.

"It's an advertising campaign," said Monica, straight-backed and focused as if she were in a boardroom in Fleet Street. "Simple as that. It has to be national as we don't know where she is. Must reach young women with Hester's interests. Must be immediately apparent to her. And entirely secret to everyone else."

"Challenging brief," said Guy. "I like it."

"It's all down to the creative approach," I said. I hadn't been to countless advertising agency meetings without picking up the jargon, even if half of them had been on how to sell Bile Beans. "That's the clever bit."

"And the message," said Monica.

"*Come home,*" I said, immediately. "Please just come home. But we can be cleverer than that. We can come up with an editorial and advertising campaign that no one will recognise except Hest." I leaned forward, keenly. "We know what she enjoys, the magazines she reads. We have to hope she may even still look at *Woman's Friend*. For a start, I'm going to put problems in 'Yours Cheerfully' that look exactly like normal ones, but if she sees them, she'll know the message is for her." I pushed some examples I'd drafted across the table.

Dear Miss Lake
I love my boyfriend very much, but I have been very weak and foolish
and made a mess of things. Please can you advise me what to do.
 Yours,
 Jimmy Stewart fan

Guy nodded as he read it out.

Dear Miss Lake
I have upset my mum, and I think she won't want me home. What
should I do? I miss everyone very much indeed.
 Keen on Crochet, Hampshire

"They're just drafts," I said. "I'll do better. But they use parts of
her letter. I think I can run various versions over several issues."

"I like it," said Monica. "Let's go through every section of the
magazine."

In the next hour we had found a way to secretly include Hester's favourite things in dozens of ways. A new series called "Meals
for Friends" in the cookery section meant we could run one of her
favourite recipes each week, with the suggestion to "*Call your loved
ones to come home for tea.*" Guy's film review section would focus on
Hest's favourite actors. The "Post-War Careers" section was a gift for
"How to Become an Office Co-ordinator," a job that needed the best
expertise and would guarantee that your colleagues adored you. Guy
said he would write some romance stories that Hester would love,
and he would commission Nurse McClay to begin a new series called
"You're Having a Baby!," which would give weekly tips for mothers-
to-be. Even if Hest didn't see it, if she made friends with other girls
in her condition, perhaps one of them would. It was a straw worth
grasping.

It looked howlingly obvious when written as a list, but we knew we
could manage it so no one would guess. Using *Woman's Friend* was an

easy start. Other ways to try to get Hester's attention in a newsagent's were needed. We worked on adverts for the Personal columns, putting in names she would recognise and a PO Box number. We guessed at the kind of jobs she might apply for and ran "Wanted! Office Co-ordinator" adverts in all the national newspapers that took them.

Only the best should apply . . . female should be aged 17 to 19 with experience in weekly women's magazines, with a boss who can be regrettably difficult.

Wanted! Guardians need help with 2 boys and 1 girl aged 14, 12, and 9. Exact experience required to include ducks, chickens, guinea pigs, and pet rat. The children miss their very dear friend and want her back.

The more ideas we had, the more determined I was. Monica came up with the best one yet.

"Do you remember when the ghastly Mrs. Porter owned *Woman's Friend*?" she asked. "And Mr. Brand had the quite brilliant idea to keep her happy by making all our cover illustrations look like a more beautiful version of her?"

Guy and I pulled faces at the very mention of the Honourable Mrs. P, but we nodded.

"Let's get him to do it with Hest," said Monica. "It worked a treat with Cressida. Totally recognisable. He won't need to beautify it of course, but can you imagine if Hester sees different versions of herself every week? That's a jolly strong signal she's missed."

It was another jolly strong idea all round.

Finally, I was beginning to feel less useless. I just wished I could do the same for Charles. His silence was painful. I had no idea where he was or how he was. His chirpy letters from the prison camp had never given much information because the censor wouldn't allow it, but I could at least enjoy his studied bonhomie. I could run my fingers along his handwriting, feeling as if I had something of him near me. Now there was nothing. Every night I sat in bed, looking at our photograph and willing him, wherever he might be, to know that I was thinking of him.

"Let's face it, darling," I said one night. "You're probably safely playing cards in a bunk room or learning to grow herbs, and I'm worrying like a silly fool." I shut my eyes, longing for something to give me a sign. "I don't even mind if you tell Mr. Trevin to spot something in his rotten old stars." I put my head in my hands. "Oh, Charles, there is a possibility I might be going mad."

I thought about him all the time. I had always felt that when people said they thought about someone every day, they really should detail how many times or for how long. After all, you could think of thousands of things every day. These days my capacity to worry about Charles seemed endless.

"When's the last time you left this building?" asked Guy one morning in late March. "Other than to go to the shops or post letters? Don't bother to answer. We both know it's ages. How do you fancy coming out this evening? I'm meeting some of the press chaps for a drink on the Strand at half-past eight. It may be horribly dull, but please come with me. They sometimes have good gen on what's going on if that might tempt you?"

Guy didn't go out much these days, either, but that evening we made our way to one of the bars in the centre of town where the international journalists liked to meet up. I had been there with Guy before and enjoyed myself. It was oddly glamorous, a sort of touring circus of worldly, confident types, many from the United States, who lived out of suitcases and travelled around the globe looking for trouble and aiming to be the first to find it and file their copy. Most of them were men, but occasionally there might be an American woman or two, and they were the sort I admired. Intelligent, independent, and with nerves of steel. I always hoped it might rub off on me.

Tonight it was busy, the room a fog of cigarette smoke, and in the low rumble of conversation it was hard to make oneself heard. Men propped up the bar airing their views on how the war would be won, while others shouted over their shoulders to order drinks. Everyone gave the impression of at least vaguely knowing all the others, and as I had done in the past, I adopted a confident expression and tried to pretend I felt entirely at home.

Guy spotted his friends quickly and we made our way over to where they had commandeered a decent position huddled around a table near to the bar. I recognised a couple of them, one an attractive American called Mac McCormack, who always looked as if he'd just fallen out of bed, and another shorter, rounder British man who liked to talk rather than listen. The others were new to me, but they welcomed us both and budged up to give me a seat.

"Let me get a round in," said Guy, after making the introductions. "Emmy? Gentlemen?"

I asked for a gin and tonic if they had one and said hello to Mr. McCormack.

"Nice to see you, Miss Lake," he said. "I hear you got over to Brussels last year. Will you be joining us back in Europe any time soon?"

"I think that was a one off, sadly," I replied, keeping the fact that I'd been sacked by the Ministry to myself. "If you know anyone who would give me a job, I'd be glad to go." I gave him a grin. I had learned that the Americans were very upfront and asking for a job was not at all bold.

"I'll see what I can do," he laughed. "Actually, no. I need the work myself."

"You're not missing much," said his friend. "It's pretty rough over there."

"And some," said Mac. "Doug's been down near the Rhine."

I hadn't met Doug before but hoped he would be happy to talk.

"When did you get back to London?" I asked.

"Last week. My ears are still ringing from the shelling," he said. "It's pretty fierce over there. But we're causing lots of damage, which is the idea." He took a large sip of beer. "I don't know how long it's going to take them to clear everything up once it's over," he said. "The whole of Europe's a wreck."

"Well, get our boys home, that's the first thing," I said, edging him in the direction where I might gather some information.

"I hope someone's got a decent plan," said Doug. "It's bedlam. People everywhere. Civilians, refugees, prisoners. It's all very well liberating people but what do you do with them next?" He shrugged.

"Did you come across any of our men from the POW camps?" I asked. I didn't tell him why. I'd learned you found out more if people didn't know you had a vested interest.

But he shook his head. "No. Not my remit. Geoff here knows more. Geoff, tell this young lady what you were just telling me." He nudged the man next to him.

"Emmy Lake," I said, as I shook hands with a wiry, bespectacled man.

"Geoff Lewis. What do you want to know?"

I took the direct approach. "How are the British prisoners getting on?" I asked. "The Government are being somewhat cautious with their information."

Mr. Lewis snorted. "The Government don't know what they're talking about. Or if they do, they're not saying." He took off his glasses and rubbed his eyes. "If you really want to know it's bloody carnage. It's probably why they're not saying anything. Thousands of our men have been dropping dead from frostbite and Churchill's lot want to send them bars of chocolate. Poor buggers. No help in winning the war so leave them to it. I suppose at least the weather's warming up a bit now, so they've got a fighting chance."

I swallowed, trying as hard as I could not to give away how horrified I was.

"We only get rumours," I managed.

"Which ones? There are enough." He took out a packet of cigarettes from his jacket and offered me one. I didn't enjoy smoking,
but I accepted one now. I already felt sick, so it wouldn't make much
difference. After he'd lit one for us both, he carried on.

"The American Red Cross boys say it's been a disaster. No one
has a hope in hell of finding anyone. There are a hundred thousand
POWs up by the Baltic coast. So, chuck a dart at a map on that one.
And then down in the south there's a million of them being marched
to Christ knows where. At least they've got a chance I suppose." He
paused to smoke for a moment. "But don't believe everything you
hear. You know, all the stuff about the Germans holding them as hostages if we win, or the Russians massacring them. That's propaganda,
I reckon. The Reds will be too busy massacring the Germans, given
half a chance. So, what's your interest?"

"I'm mostly Home Front."

My new friend nodded with the polite but faint disinterest I was
used to from the international chaps.

"Do you ever think about the families who are waiting back
here?" I asked.

Geoff frowned and pursed his lips.

"No," he said, considering it for a moment. "Now you come to
mention it, I don't think I do."

CHAPTER 30

As Mr. Collinsy as You Want

I kept my end up for a little while longer, but Guy could see some-thing was wrong and I made no attempt to discourage him when he suggested we leave. We managed to find a taxi and drove back to Pimlico in silence, but as soon as we got into the house, I repeated everything Geoff Lewis had said. Guy and I sat side by side on the stairs in the hall. He listened and didn't appear shocked.

"Have you heard rumours like these before?" I asked.

"Yes," he said. "More or less. I didn't think it would be helpful to share them. I'm sorry you heard them like that. I'm an idiot. I'd thought we'd go along, have a drink or two, Mac would be charming and call you 'Ma'am' in his accent, and it might be fun. But it was a terrible idea. I'm sorry."

I sighed heavily and leant my shoulder against his.

"It's all right," I said, patting him on the knee in a conciliatory way. I stared at the floor. I didn't know what to think.

"They are only rumours," said Guy.

"Do you mean the massacres or the hostages? The marches are real."

"I don't think it's wise to believe anything Hitler is putting out. He knows they've lost. He'll say anything. Doesn't mean it will happen."

"It doesn't mean it won't," I replied. "We all know what he's capable of." We sat in silence for a moment, with just the soft ticking of the grandfather clock, usually such a comforting sound. "Guy, I'm scared."

He nodded.

"So am I," he said. He put his arm around my shoulders. The clock chimed the half hour.

"Half-past ten," I whispered. "This is when I talk to Charles. Every night." I bit my lip and wiped away a tear that had arrived, uninvited. "We agreed, so he'll always know." I was trying to smile because I didn't want Charles to be somewhere, thinking of me if I was upset. Brave face and all that. It was silly really. "I know I sound as if Charles has married someone quite insane."

"No, you don't," said Guy, gently. "I used to do the same thing in the first war. If you both think of each other, you can be in the same place."

"That's it. It must be a family trait."

"Perhaps," said Guy. He paused. "Emmy, he will come back."

I shut my eyes for a moment. I wished Charles knew how much the two of us needed him.

"He has to come back," I said, slightly more briskly. "Otherwise, you're stuck with me and that's a nightmare for you."

"Yes, it is," said Guy, in his most serious voice. "Lunatic."

I laughed. "I'm really quite normal," I protested.

"Hmm."

"You are stuck with me, though. Even when Charles comes home. You're stuck with me and Bunty and Harold, and the children and Arthur when he's back. And Jack, and Monica, and even if it kills me, Hest. And Clarence. And . . ."

"Emmy," said Guy, still in his gentle voice. "This is very kind of you, but are you going to go through everyone we know? Because we do know quite a lot of people."

He was the master of deflection. This time he would not get away with it.

"Guy, you are so hopeless at taking a compliment." Now I sat up straight. "Actually, it's not a compliment. It's the truth." I turned round to face him. "You may not like this, but I am going to say it anyway. We all love you and you're lumbered with us. You can be as grumpy and Mr. Collinsy as you want, but it won't change anything. And it doesn't matter that most of us aren't related. It's still a family."

Guy looked at me properly, seriously, but didn't reply.

"Do you know what Hester told me?" I said, softly. "She said, if she had a dad, she'd want him to be like you."

Now Guy looked down at the floor. Then he took off his spectacles and blinked several times. I thought I could see tears in his eyes.

"That's . . . that's . . . very kind of her," he said. "Goodness. It's rather taken me aback."

"She'll kill me if she finds out I've told you," I said. "She made me promise not to."

"Of course," said Guy. "It's just a very nice thing to hear." He had taken his handkerchief out and was rubbing his glasses with it. Then he put them back on and looked at me. "We'll get her back, Emmy. Somehow. And Charles. And Arthur. They will all be back. And I am sorry about this evening. Please ignore Geoff Lewis and his rumours and his old hack cynicism. We don't know the truth, so let's just think about when everyone comes home."

"Yes," I said. "I want to do that. Very much."

Guy took a deep breath. "Thank you," he said. "For saying this. About Hester, and Bunty, and everyone on your enormous list. For what it's worth, I'm very glad to be lumbered with you all."

I smiled a tiny bit.

"Always," I said.

The clock chimed the quarter hour. I felt sure Charles had heard every word.

———

I tried to keep Geoff Lewis out of my mind. I had fished for details and now I needed to swallow them. There was nothing I could do, and I would not share the information with anyone else. Wallace was coping with the weight of not knowing where her husband was. She didn't need me to make that worse.

Our campaign to try to reach Hester was still going strong, but if she had seen anything, she had not replied. We had heard nothing more.

When Easter arrived, heralding April and what everyone hoped would be a spring end to the war, I grasped the break from work with both hands. The office would be shut for four days, and I was going to Hampshire. I admitted to Guy that I was worried I might miss a telegram should one arrive, and as he felt the same, we agreed to split the weekend. I would stay in Pimlico the first two days while he visited Bunty and Harold, and then we would switch. I was pleased he went on his own. It made me think that what I had said in our late-night chat might have sunk in. That he didn't need me around to be part of Bunty and Harold's life, or the children's. It was a rare and welcome comfort.

Easter Sunday was another. The train took an age, but the sun had come out and as we drew into the little Hampshire village station, Harold was on the platform to meet me, all big smiles and a welcoming hug.

"I'm the advance party. The children are waiting for you at the cottage," he said. "It's mayhem, but they've planned a surprise and are very excited. Bunts is in on it, but don't ask me."

He took my overnight case and chatted away as we walked along the country lanes, the early white blossom of the blackthorn rising up out of the hedgerows to show everyone that spring was definitely on the way. Harold was happier than ever, the same person I saw up at the office of course, but in the country he had a different contentment about him, exuding a calm that was almost infectious. He had fitted in so well with Mrs. Tavistock and had taken on all sorts of jobs for her. I had a feeling that Bunty's granny was secretly preparing

Bunty and Harold to inherit the estate. They would make excellent chatelaines of Rose House.

As we arrived at Dower Cottage, Harold stopped, gave me a huge grin and said, "Ready?"

I braced myself for whatever the children had cooked up this time, and Harold hammered on the front door, before opening it and booming, "Emmy's here!" into the hall.

Cries of "Ssshhh" and "She's here" came from the living room, and then Margaret raced out and opened her arms as if about to introduce an act on a music hall stage.

"Look who we've got," she cried.

I walked into the room to see George standing to attention and Stanley hopping from foot to foot with excitement.

Behind him stood a slimly built man in his thirties, with slightly sticking out ears and a huge smile. He was wearing the unmistakable uniform of the Royal Navy.

"IT'S DAD," shouted Stan, unable to contain himself any longer.

"Hello, Emmy," said Arthur, sounding a little self-conscious. "It's lovely to see you."

Relief hit me like a wave that could capsize a battleship.

"Arthur," I gasped and threw my arms around him before he had a chance to be all formal and British about things. "You're back. You're really back! Oh, my goodness. Oh, Arthur. Children, it's your dad!"

"WE KNOW!" yelled Stan.

I hardly knew what to say. After such a long time of constant worry about everyone, to have Arthur back, to know he was safe and that the children had their dad back, was almost too much.

"Don't worry, I've been crying all over him since he arrived," said Bunty, who had been standing to one side by the fireplace. She put her arm around George. "It's smashing news, isn't it?"

It was the very best news in years.

"When did you get in?" I asked, looking at Arthur Jenkins as if he was a marvel being exhibited in the British Museum.

"Yesterday," he said. "Docked at Southampton and they've given us forty-eight hours leave, so I came straight here." He looked over at Bunty. "I didn't even phone. I didn't think."

"Dad's been everywhere," said Stan. "And he says we've grown."

"You've all turned into giants," said Arthur. "You'll be taller than me, next."

Stan giggled and Marg looked a little shy. George stood even taller. They were all doing very well. It had been such a long time since they had seen their dad, and I knew that reunions were often not as easy as everyone thought. It would take a little time for everyone to get to know each other again, for Arthur to get to know these three young people who were considerably more grown-up since he last saw them, and for them all to get used to life without Thel.

The thought of her, now they were all together, was like another unexpected wave. It was so wonderful to see Arthur, but painfully bittersweet. I couldn't help but imagine Thelma's face if she'd been here. I almost expected her to walk in from the kitchen, put her arm through his, and give him a kiss.

She'd say something like, "He took his time Emmy, but we've forgiven him now that he's here, haven't we, kids?"

"Arthur, I can't believe it's you," I said. "We've been so looking forward to this. All of us."

Arthur studied his shoes for a moment and his forehead wrinkled a little. Then he looked at me, the enormity of his loss written right across his face.

"Thank you," he said, his voice low. "Thank you for keeping them safe."

CHAPTER 31

A Thin Hope

It was the most enormous weight off our shoulders. Bunty and I really didn't know what to do with ourselves. Arthur had to go back to his ship but was hoping to be demobbed within weeks. The plan was for the children to stay where they were, continue with school, and then their dad would join them as soon as he could. Mrs. Tavistock, who had become terrifically fond of the children, had offered Arthur the use of a cottage on the estate until he decided what he and the children would do next. Arthur was bowled over, although Mrs. T told him it was because she was selfishly trying to keep the children as long as she could.

It was said jokingly, but Bunty and I understood. She and I talked long into the night. As far as the children were concerned, we could finally breathe properly now that on paper our mission was accomplished. Arthur was home and the children had their dad back. After they had lost their mum, it had become our most important job by far.

But I had not thought how I would feel when Arthur returned and we would give the children back. Putting it like that made it sound as if we had looked after a goldfish for someone while they were on holiday. It didn't even remotely begin to describe how we felt. They were so very much loved. When Thelma and the children had moved in with us in Pimlico, we had grown into a family. There was already a gaping hole in our lives since Thel died. It would be a little bigger now.

I returned to London, elated that finally we'd had some wonderful news. It was something to hold on to, a tangible sign that the light at the end of the tunnel was a little brighter. It was helped by the fact that reports of bombing raids at home had gone very quiet in recent days, while the news from Europe was that Hitler and his henchmen were in disarray. The Allies were moving closer to Berlin by the day and Peace was definitely coming. The week after Easter, two men from Charles' battery were evacuated back to Britain. They had been wounded and they were not in good shape, but they were home. Surely there would be news about Charles, soon?

It was lovely to be able to put some truly good news into the newsletter. I very much meant that. I also realised, that to my great shame, I was jealous. It was not something I was proud of.

These men had had the toughest of times. They were injured and ill, and we all thanked God that they had got home. I hated that I envied their families. It seemed the most ungenerous, selfish response. I didn't say anything to Wallace, but I did question myself. It wasn't that I didn't wish them the joy they deserved. I just desperately hoped that Charles would be one of the next ones to come home.

When we planned future issues of *Woman's Friend*, we were all aware that although victory in Europe was on its way, many of our readers would still be living with great loss. Guy, Monica, and I discussed for hours how we would balance celebration with respect. Every man, woman, and child in Britain deserved to hang out the flags. But not everyone would feel that they could. We decided to remain calm. We would continue to write about the future, to look forward to the summer, and run our seasonal features as we always did.

"We don't know when Victory will be anyway," said Guy, "so we'll look very silly if we go bananas a week after everyone else. Let's leave that problem to the news magazines. We'll just carry on."

We had been just carrying on for years.

At the same time, in a full about-turn, Wallace and I began to avoid the news. In the papers, rumours were turning into reports, with British prisoners telling of the dreadful conditions through the winter. We didn't want to know. Not until our boys were home. I wrote to Alice and Winifred often. They always looked out for anyone from Charles' battery, and when Win moved on to a field hospital one of the first things she did was check the list of men there.

But with millions of people now displaced throughout the Continent, what chance did we have to get news? It was better not to think about it. We just had to remain strong.

For once I was happy that we were short-staffed, throwing myself into as much work as possible. Mother and Father begged me to go and stay with them for even a few days' break, but I said no.

"I need help in the garden," said Mother, who had taken to finding reasons to phone almost every evening. "Or I could come up and help you with yours."

"I'm fine, Mother," I said. "And your garden is always perfect."

"Not at all," she lied. "Darling, I know you're a grown-up, but are you sure you're all right? We would like to help."

"I *am* a grown-up," I replied. "And honestly, I promise, I'm fine."

"You're as stubborn as your mother," said my father calmly, from his position of listening over her shoulder. "Elizabeth, you need to let Emmy cope with all this as she sees fit. Em, eat your greens. Doctor's orders. Or your mother will come up and put the world to rights."

"I will," I promised. "Thank you, both. I promise that I am all right."

I knew they were far from convinced.

Trying to come up with more ways to send messages to Hester became a fixation. I wanted to write to Clarence, but Hester had been adamant in her letter that he wasn't to know. I kept the faith that she might have told him and that they had their own plans.

Then, to my absolute joy, Clarence wrote to me. I could almost hear him as I read it, partly very formal, partly a sweet and kind young man desperately worried about the girl that he loved.

Dear Miss Lake (Emmy),

I hope you are well, and that Major Mayhew will soon be on his way back once Victory has been won.

I am writing to you although it is breaking a promise to do so, but I have been going over and over this in my head for a long time and as it looks as if it will be a while before I can get leave or return to England, I am worried about Hester and how she is getting on.

I hope you will understand. Please do not think badly of her as it is my fault. I will never forgive myself for leaving her on her own. We thought we would be married but that is not the point.

I have told her that we WILL get married as soon as I get back. I don't care what people think and everything will be all right. The thing is, if I don't come back, I know it will be very hard on her own. I've said this in letters, but she won't have it. You know what she's like.

I wondered if it might be possible for you to go and talk to her please? I know my family won't let her down, but she says she doesn't want to bring shame on them and will be able to look after herself.

She is living just outside Birmingham and has a job at the labour exchange. I have enclosed the name and address and tele-phone number of her landlady with this letter. I would be very, very grateful if you might speak to her. I know my mum will take her in. She and Dad really will. They love children, Hest needn't worry. I haven't told them yet as she will be angry enough that I have written to you.

I am sure I will come back. Please could you tell her I just want to make sure she and our baby are all right.

Just in case I do not come back, I would like to thank you, Emmy, for everything you have done for me and Hester over the years. It has been my honour that you have called me a friend.

Yours,

Clarence

(Gr. C. Boone)

Guy, Monica, and I punched the air in celebration now that we knew where Hest was, but at the same time, my heart ached. It was one of the most beautiful letters I had ever received.

"He's such a lovely boy," said Monica, when she had finished reading it. "Dear me, I have quite a lump in my throat."

"Good chap," said Guy. "He always has been, that one."

"It's so very like him to try to do the right thing," I said. "He must have been tussling over this. Thank goodness he was able to get a letter to us." I scanned his words again. "He hasn't said if she is using her real name or not. I assume so as it will be on her identification papers. Mrs. Harewood says that she holds all her lodgers' ration books."

In the many weeks we had had to discuss it, we had agreed that if we could find Hester, I would go on my own to see her. Going mob-handed would not work one bit.

"Should you call her, Emmy, or just go?" asked Monica. "If you turn up on her doorstep it could look a little odd."

"But if you call her first, she then might bolt," said Guy.

"She won't just walk out on a good job," I said. "I can track down the labour exchange. I'm going to phone her. She may be secretly hoping we will. And then I'll go up there and see what she wants to do. Go to Clarence's mum, or come back here, or to Bunty, or carry on as she is." I pulled a face. "I do hope it's not that."

"There's only one way to find out," said Monica. She sighed and looked up at the ceiling. "Well done, Clarence," she said. "You clever, clever boy."

Waiting until the evening when Hester would be home from work felt like the longest day, but it gave me time to plan. I decided that as soon as she came to the phone, I would say that Clarence had asked me to call and that I was so pleased for her, and I was just calling for a chat as she was very much missed. It was a bit of a sprint as opening greetings went, but that way, I hoped she wouldn't put the phone down or run a mile.

"Come on, Hest," I said as I waited for someone to answer the call. Guy and Monica hovered by me in the hall, both as expectant and anxious as me.

"Good evening," I said in my best telephone voice when a woman did. "This is Mrs. Mayhew. I believe you have a young lady with you who is a friend of mine." It always helped to use "Mrs." in situations like this. "Would it be possible to speak to dearest Hester, please?" I took a chance, bluffing through without a surname, just in case.

"There's no Hester here," replied a disinterested, monotone voice. "Unless you mean Miss Wilson."

"Of course," I chimed. "Might I speak with her, please?"

"She's gone."

"I'm sorry?"

"I won't have girls like her in my house. I've got my reputation to think of."

I fought off the worst of sinking feelings, and ignoring the jibe, carried on. "Oh dear, did she leave a forwarding address?" It was a thin hope.

"No. I'm sorry, I can't help you. Goodbye."

And that was it. I put the receiver down.

"Damn it," I swore. "The wretched woman has kicked her out."

"Clarence's letter was written a couple of weeks ago," said Monica.

"Bugger," said Guy, with feeling. "She could still be in the area, assuming she still has a job."

"If the landlady noticed, it means it's getting harder for Hest to disguise things," said Monica.

"We were so close," I groaned.

It was a rotten knock back. After the surge of hope that morning, now I felt utterly crushed. It wasn't just the unpleasant landlady. I was tired, exhausted by the constant disappointments, of letters being returned, of "sorry we can't help you" phone calls, of rumours that turned into nothing other than horrible stories and nothing solid to go on.

"What do we try next?" asked Monica.

"I don't know," I said, realising I sounded dejected. "I need to think."

"You need fuel," said Guy. "We all do. Come on. I'll whip up a fish savoury and then we can drown our sorrows in stewed rhubarb while we come up with a new plan."

I nodded, grateful that someone else had the energy to take charge. Sometimes things were rather like being in a relay and you needed another runner to handle the next lap.

We started again.

In the coming days I tracked down all the labour exchanges in the Birmingham area and rang them all. None had a Miss Hester Wilson on their staff. We had to assume Hest had moved on.

The waiting continued for the rest of the month. I went down to Bunty's almost every weekend, in part because it was always cheery, and if I was honest, I was also making the most of seeing George, Margaret, and Stan. One weekend we had a picnic up by the canal where Harold had proposed to Bunts. Arthur was able to come and the children were bouncing with happiness. It was lovely to see.

Then at the start of May we had the greatest news about someone we hated. Hitler was dead. It would mean he would avoid the punishment he so richly deserved, but as Guy said, burning in hell for eternity would just have to do. It still wasn't long enough.

Britain was exhausted, but now with Victory close enough to touch, people were beginning to prepare for the biggest party in years. Mrs. Shaw reported that she had been going through her cupboards looking for anything worth bringing out for a tea, Mr. Newton had found bunting from the last coronation, and Miss Peters was considering a new hat. But our friends were thoughtful. No one suggested a Victory Fayre. That could wait until Charles and Tom came home. Wallace made Baby Daphne a Victory outfit, and I made her a little crown.

Guy and I now stayed put in London. We never left the house empty so there was always someone there to answer the phone or, if I even dared to dream it, the front door. The troops were coming back. Trains were full of returning servicemen, and we lived in hope.

But there was no news.

Then, one evening during dinner, the telephone rang. I raced up to the hall and answered it.

"Emmy," said a familiar voice. "It's Juliet Bagley."

I had seen Juliet only the previous week. We had had tea. As ever, she had been stoic, patient, and determined not to give up on her son. She had still been making calls, still, as she put it, being a pest.

"Hello, Juliet, how lovely to hear you," I said.

"Yes," she replied, and then hesitated for just a moment. "Emmy, I'm afraid I'm ringing with some rather sad news. Johnny's body has been identified. I just wanted you to know." I heard her take a breath before she continued, the slightest tremble in her voice. "My boy. My dearest boy."

She had never given up hope for his return. She had never, ever given up on her son.

"Oh, Juliet," I said. "I am so very, very sorry."

When our phone call ended, I sat down on the stairs. Then I wept for a young man I had never known, and for the brave, gracious woman who loved him.

CHAPTER 32

We're Looking for a Farm

Early May was one of my favourite times of the year. There was always the whole of summer to look forward to, the light mornings, and this year, possibly even getting away for a break. But now the days became interminable.

Bunty insisted I needed some company. I insisted I was fine.

"I'm coming up," she said. "Tomorrow."

When Bunts arrived, she had a suitcase, two bunches of radishes, and a cabbage. She also had Harold, George, Margaret, Stanley, and their dad.

"We've just come to say hello," said Arthur. "I hope that's all right."

Stanley marched into the hall and put his arms around my waist.

"We've missed you," he said, as I hugged him back. It had only been the usual few days since I had last visited. "And we're worried."

"Sshhh," said Marg, taking his place. "We're not worried, we just want to see how you are."

"That's right," said George, tall and grown-up next to his dad. "It's a courtesy visit."

"Well, whatever the reason, it's lovely to see you all," I said. "Let's go in the garden, although it's very boring as you took all the animals."

"Good Lord," said Guy, coming downstairs. "Who sent the cavalry? Hello troops."

"This is our dad," said Stan. "Dad, this is our Uncle Guy. He's really clever and Sparky likes him. Guy, this is our dad and he's been all over the world and has an anchor on his arm."

"It's very nice to meet you," said Guy, as the two men warmly shook hands. "I can't tell you how glad I am that you're home safe and well."

"I can't thank you enough for everything you've done," Arthur said. "I really can't. The children have told me how very kind you've been, especially over the last year." A look of pain crossed his face. "Thel always spoke very fondly of you."

"It's been a pleasure," said Guy. "I am very sorry for the circumstances, though. I greatly admired Mrs. Jenkins."

Arthur nodded. None of this was easy for him.

"Let's get some tea," I said.

It was lovely to have the house full again. While there was always a hive of activity when the staff were in the office, none of them made Spitfire noises or attempted to launch toy soldiers off the landing.

Bunty produced homemade biscuits from her bag, and George got the deckchairs out of the shed, which was the first time we had bothered with them this year. The sun shone and it was very nearly like old times.

"Emmy," said Marg, who was doing some much-needed weeding. "When is Hester coming back from her aunt's?"

It was out of the blue, but Bunty was quick-witted.

"I don't think she's going to, now, Marg," she said. "I think she has a new job."

Hester's fictional aunt had worked very well for some time.

"Do you think she will come and visit us?" joined in Stan. "It's just at the Christmas Fayre she promised she would come down at Easter, but she didn't."

"You've got a very good memory, Stan," I said. "Christmas was ages ago. We'll probably need to start planning the next fayre soon."

My attempt to change the subject fell on deaf ears.

"She promised though," said Stan.

"Maybe another time," said Bunty, vaguely.

"Will she come next Easter then, do you think?" asked Stan.

"I don't know. I think she's probably very busy," I said.

"Will she still come when she's married?" asked Stan. "At Easter."

I glanced at Arthur who gave a small shake of his head. Bunty shrugged.

"What is it about Easter, old man?" asked Arthur.

"Nothing, Dad," said Stan.

"Stanley," said Marg. "Tell the truth."

Stan looked pained. "I promised Hester I wouldn't say," he said.

I wondered what it was. It must have been significant as Stan was scrupulous about telling the truth. But anything about Hester caught my attention.

"That is tricky," I said. "I'm sure Hest would understand if it's important though. Perhaps we could help as she's not around." I gave him an encouraging smile. "It's all right, you don't have to say if you don't want."

Stanley gave a large sigh, as if the weight of the world were on his shoulders.

"We were going to get a puppy," he said.

"Oh love," said Bunty. "You've got Sparky, now."

"He wanted a friend," replied Stan.

"Maybe we could still get one," said Arthur.

"But Hest said it's a really hard place to find," said Stan, a trace of dejection in his voice.

Every adult in the group sat up.

"Where's really hard, Stan?" I said, trying to sound casual.

"Hest's friend. She lives on a farm and Hest said that their girl sheepdog almost always has puppies in the spring, and she knows that because the farmer gets cross because of the lambs. And Hest says they always have to try to find people to take them otherwise the puppies might get drowned. So, that's why it's very important we get one. But we missed out this Easter so it means waiting until next year."

"Which friend is it?" asked Bunty. "Is it one of the village girls Hest met last summer?"

Stan shook his head. "It's a girl from her year at school. She got a job on the farm because she wanted to be a Land Girl, only then she married the farmer. I think he's quite old. Thirty or something."

"Eeww," said Marg.

I glanced over at Bunts.

"And Hester is in touch with her?" I asked.

"Oh, yes. When we talked about it at the Christmas Fayre, Hester promised we could go on the train and get a puppy, but she said I had to ask you or wait until Dad came home. I said we could go secretly, but she said no. But now if she doesn't come back, I won't be able to find the farm because it's a long walk from the station and I might get lost. Hest's friend says no one can ever find it especially as they took all the signs down because of the Germans and they haven't put them back up."

"Stan," I said, "did Hester ever tell you her friend's name, or the name of the farm?"

"Oh yes," said Stan. "It's Maeve. She's married to Mr. Webb, and they have a baby called Cyril. But we'll never find it." He looked up from where he had been absentmindedly drawing pictures of dogs. "Harold, why has Bunty started to cry?"

———

Bunty would not take no for an answer.

"You're seven months pregnant," I said. "You can't go tramping around looking for farms in the middle of nowhere. I'll go on my own."

"That's very narrow-minded," said Bunty. "This is the modern world. Women have helped win the war."

"This is going to be a two-mile hike," I answered. "Each way."

"I could come," said Harold.

"That's very kind," I said, "but we have to tread very carefully."

"That's why I need to be there," said Bunty. "Look at me. I'm an advert for what's coming up. Hopefully, Hester will think it a good idea to come home before she turns into a barrage balloon too. A barrage balloon who is perfectly capable of walking a long way," she added.

I knew when Bunty had made up her mind.

"All right," I said. "We'll go together. Guy, will you stay here by the phone? Just in case there's any news from Europe."

Guy nodded. "Of course."

"Do you fancy some company?" asked Harold.

"Actually, yes," admitted Guy. "That would be nice."

With the men holding the fort back in London, the next day, Bunty and I headed to Dorset and the address that Stan with his usual attention to detail knew off by heart. Victory was expected any day now and as we made our way to Waterloo some people had already put the bunting out. When we got to the station, it was packed with people.

"Hold my hand," I ordered Bunty. "Don't let go, or we'll never find each other."

We pushed our way to the ticket office and purchased our return tickets, hoping that we would have to add one on the way back. When we finally made it onto the train, we quickly bagged two seats—a lucky move as the journey took twice as long as it should have.

We planned to arrive unannounced. The farm did not have a phone, but writing was too much of a risk and anyway, now that we had a firm lead, none of us wanted to waste a minute by waiting. Bunty and I were convinced that Hester would be with her friend.

We had grilled poor Stan for more information, trying to stop our-selves becoming too optimistic. But when Stan said Bunty's friend had a baby boy, we couldn't help but think that everything fitted into place. Now we just needed to get there and if we found Hest, persuade her to come back, or if she refused, try to convince her that we desperately wanted to help.

It was warm and sunny when Bunty and I arrived at what would usually have been a quiet country railway station on a sleepy Mon-day afternoon. Instead, it was a hive of activity, servicemen crowd-ing the platform, a harassed porter putting up with all sorts of joshing, and civilians looking for their loved ones or just caught up with the excitement of homecoming men. I smiled and greeted strangers, telling people I had never met how good it was to have them back. We were here to find Hester, and yet I wanted to rush around asking if anyone knew a Major Mayhew, or if they had seen him on their way home.

At the station we showed Maeve's address to the ticket collector.

"We're looking for a farm," I said. "Mr. and Mrs. Webb. Could you possibly help, please?"

"Oh dear, that's a canter from here," he said, staring rudely at Bunty's tummy. "Are you sure? It's a good mile 'n' a bit, if not more."

"We have lovely weather for it," said Bunty, admirably calm.

"I'll give you directions, but you won't find it," said the man, with confidence.

"You're very kind," I said, narrowing my eyes.

The collector ran through a very complicated route in a very fast way. I smiled politely while easily taking it all down in shorthand.

"Funny old squiggles," he said, screwing up his nose.

"I'm a journalist," I replied. "The last time I had to find an ad-dress it required flying over the Channel. Thank you very much for your help."

"Well done," said Bunty under her breath as we left. "Mind you, we'll look proper nitwits if we don't find it now."

"We will," I said. "And you will tell me if Baby Thomas starts feeling tired, won't you? I can always leave you somewhere and get you on the way back."

"Baby Thomas will be fine," said Bunty, firmly. "We both will. You know, Em, whenever you or I have been up against things, it's always been so much better when we've faced it together. I know you've had Guy and Monica and the others the last few months, but I should have done more."

"You were looking after the children. That was more than enough," I replied. "And anyway, there hasn't been much anyone has been able to do." I took her arm. "But I am glad that you're here, now. Whatever happens."

Bunty knew I wasn't just talking about Hest.

"We've been on a train for hours and you still haven't told me how you are," she said. "Now we've got each other for two miles, with no one to interrupt us. Come on old thing, I'm worried about you. All this stiff-upper-lip business might work on everyone else, but it doesn't on me. I can't imagine how you're coping with everything."

There was something about walking through the countryside, not knowing where we were, with some questionable directions and a mission to find our friend, that for a moment reminded me of being a young girl. My best friend and me on one of our adventures, making up stories, looking for pirates as we hid in somebody's tree. Now, though, we were off to try to save a real person.

"Did you ever think," I said, "that being a grown-up would be anything like this?"

"I don't think so," said Bunty. "And it certainly wouldn't have involved a war."

I trailed my hand through some early cow parsley beginning to flower in the hedgerow.

"I miss him, Bunts," I said. "I miss him every second of the day. At work, seeing you, worrying about Hest. Even if something nice is happening like the children coming to visit. It's always there. The missing. Sometimes I sit and think of times we've been together, and I try to slow it down, so it's not just a quick memory of the day we had a picnic, or the nice trip to the zoo, but every moment. Even the dull bits. What did he say when we got on the bus? Where did we sit? Was his arm around me, or his hand on my leg? And then I try to remember *exactly* how that felt. What did we talk about? What might I have forgotten? What silly, mundane things? Does that make any sense?"

Bunty nodded. "When Bill died, I used to worry that one day I would forget the details—the small things that you don't usually care about. I hated that I hadn't paid enough attention. I remember looking through diaries and thinking why didn't I write more? What good is 'went for a walk with Bill'? I wanted it all back and it was too late. I couldn't remember." She put her arm through mine. "You've done so well these last months. I know it's been awful for you."

"Thank you," I said. "And thank you for not just saying, 'He'll be home soon.' That's what everyone says." Now I stopped walking. "I know they mean well, but what if . . ." I couldn't look at her. "Bunty, what if he doesn't come back? I don't know if I can be as brave as you. I don't know how I'll do it."

"I'm not sure," said Bunty, in barely a whisper. "Everyone's different." She took hold of my hands. "Look at me," she said. "I promise you, Em, I will be at your side. And when no one can make it better, I will be with you. If Charles doesn't come back, I won't be enough. No one will. But I will be here. And if you can't be half of Boadicea, I'll be her for us both, until you can. Just as you did for me."

Then she put her arms around me and hugged me as tightly as she possibly could.

"Now we've squashed the baby," she said, and with tear-stained faces, we laughed.

Bunty was the only person in the world to whom I could admit I was scared that Charles might not come back. With everyone else, even Guy, it was always "when." I really did believe that. But Juliet's news had shaken me. I had always thought that Johnny would somehow still be alive. Since then, I had found it harder to stop dark and frightening thoughts.

But I felt comforted now Bunty knew. With her help, I would manage.

We walked on. Both Stan and the ticket collector were right. Maeve's farm was in the back of beyond. We kept up a sensible pace and were able to check that we were going in the right direction when a young woman rode up on her horse.

"Ah yes, the Webbs' place. It *is* tricky to find. You're lucky it's not the winter as this is all a mud bath then. In about half a mile look for the three little oaks. Miss those and you're done for. But you won't, you'll be fine."

We thanked her. The ticket collector had not mentioned the trees.

It was a good hour's walk from the station, but we found it. Webbs' Farm was hidden in an odd little dip between two rolling hills upon which sheep were grazing. It could certainly be easily missed and go unnoticed. The landscape was very Thomas Hardy, with a stiff breeze even in May.

Bunty and I made our way down to the small cluster of buildings, which included a little higgledy-piggledy farmhouse. The farmyard was untidy and a little run down, but certainly not derelict.

"Look," whispered Bunty. "That must be Maeve."

A young woman was drawing water from a well in the corner of a field. A toddler sat on the ground next to her, playing with a Border Collie. Bunty mouthed, "Ready?" at me and after I had nodded, we walked over, calling out a polite, "Hello there."

Hester's friend looked around, taken by surprise. This wasn't the sort of place people might wander past on a whim, especially if one of them was in Bunty's condition. Maeve looked at us suspiciously. I wondered how much Hester had said.

"Sorry to bother you," I said. "I wonder if you could help. We're looking for our friend. We're very much hoping she might speak with us."

Maeve Webb finished filling a bucket and set it on the ground.

"Hello," she said, with a small smile. "You wouldn't be Emmy Lake by any chance, would you?"

I nodded. "I am. And this is Bunty Thomas. Is Hester all right? We've been trying to find her for months."

"She's fine," said Maeve. "I promise. Why don't you come inside and see?"

CHAPTER 33

Time to Come Home

Bunty and I stood in the kitchen as Maeve went to find Hest.

I felt quite cold with nerves, as if we were waiting to meet the King of England, not our own dear friend.

Finally, they appeared, Hester white as a sheet. She did look to be well—bonny even and very clearly pregnant. She looked at me in trepidation. It broke my heart.

"Hello," said Hest. Her eyes darted anxiously between Bunty and me.

"Hello, love," I said, gently. "It's lovely to see you. We've all been terribly worried." I took a small step forward, wanting desperately to give her a hug. "Hest, I'm so sorry. I said some very stupid things before you left."

But now Hester backed away, pulling her cardigan over her stomach.

"We thought we'd be married the next week," she said in a small, sad voice. "So if anything happened it would be all right."

"It doesn't matter," I said. "You've done nothing wrong."

"I'm sorry I've caused so much trouble. I know I let you down."

"You haven't, you daft thing," I said. "Not for a moment."

"Everyone's missed you like mad," said Bunty. "And I was hoping we could be mothers-to-be pals. It's all a bit different, isn't it?"

"Please let us help," I said. "Guy's half sick with worry."

Hester frowned. "I didn't want to worry you. I was trying to sort it all out. Like you would."

I took another step towards her. "Hest, I wouldn't have been half as brave as you. You're extraordinary. To go off and find a job and a place to live, and keep going, all on your own. That's quite something. I wish you hadn't, and we all want you to come back, but I'm awfully proud of you. You never give in."

"Shall we sit down?" suggested Bunty. "We'd love to hear where you've been."

The three of us sat and Hester began to explain. She was hesitant at first, but once she started, the details flooded out.

"It's why I was so upset when Clarence phoned," she said. "The moment the wedding was cancelled, we knew we had made a mistake. I knew for certain that we had when he'd been away about a month, but I didn't tell him at first. He was so proud to have finally gone off to war, and then I spoilt everything."

"I don't think you're the one spoiling anything," I said, softly. "I think we can blame Hitler." I smiled a little. "Hest, it's just awfully bad luck on the timing. Once Clarence is home you can get married, and no one will ever know."

"But we don't know when that will be," said Hester. "People don't like girls like me. I was all right until I started to show. Then my landlady was horrible. The people at the labour exchange were ever so cross. They called me all sorts."

I could have strangled the miserable old bat. And everyone at the labour exchange.

"There's no such thing as 'girls like you,'" I said. "There are just girls who for one reason or another are having a baby although they aren't married. It's not the girls who make the rules or decide what's morally right. And let's not forget that Clarence is part of this too. I know I'm very modern, but I've no time for double standards. You and Clarence love each other, and you're going to have a baby,"

I finished. "And that baby is going to be beautiful and very much loved."

At last Hester broke into a real smile.

"So, stop bashing yourself up," said Bunty. "I'm sure you've done more than enough of that already."

"If anyone should be kicking themselves, it should be me," I said. "When I was ranting in the office I put things very badly. What I was trying to say was that in fifty years' time, we may realise that unmarried mothers are not harbingers of the end of the world. Until then, I just try to help people avoid the situation. Not because I think they've done something dreadful, but because I know what a rotten time they get, especially if they're on their own." I leant forward. "But you're not, Hest. You might be in a bit of a pickle at the moment, but you're not on your own. We'll all help."

"Maeve says I can stay here," said Hester. "It's very kind, but I am a bit worried about when I have the baby. Maeve said Baby Cyril took ages."

"You can come and stay with us if you want," said Bunty. "Harold and I would love to have you. There's plenty of room. The children's dad is home, so they're moving into a cottage."

"Mr. Jenkins is back?" Hester's eyes lit up again. "Oh, I am glad." Then her face dropped. "Emmy, is Charles home yet?" she asked.

"Not yet."

"Have you heard from him?"

I shook my head. "Please come home, Hest. Let us help. You can come back to London if you prefer. Whatever you want."

It took a moment, but then she nodded.

"Yes please," she said. "I would really, really like to come home."

———

It did not take long for Hester to collect her things. Maeve was lovely about it all, saying what a hard worker Hester was and how nice it had been to have the company. They would stay in touch, and she would definitely let us know when Bella the dog had her next litter. It was the least we could do for Stan after he'd been the one to save the day. Then Mr. Webb came in and turned out to be about twenty-five and not ancient at all. He took one look at Bunty and said to give him five minutes and he'd get the horse out of the field and give us a lift to the station. Bunts thanked him very much.

"I admit it," she said. "It was further than I thought."

We left Maeve and Baby Cyril with a mass of thank-you's and a grateful hug from Hester, and then we headed off.

"If you prefer, we could go to Monica's," I told Hest. "You don't need to see everyone at work or bump into half of Pimlico if you'd rather not just yet."

Hester stuck her chin in the air. "I don't mind seeing everyone," she said. "I don't mind what they might think. The main thing is that you need to get straight back in case there's any news from Charles."

She sounded almost like her old self.

"Gosh, Hest," I said. "I've missed you."

As Mr. Webb took us to the village, Bunty and I did our best to keep up a non-stop chat about anything other than Hester's disappearance. She was still a ball of embarrassment, relief, and high emotion, and any further discussion could wait for another time. For my part, as Hester could tell, I wanted to get home and quite simply wait by the telephone.

Mr. Webb dropped us at the railway station, kindly saying we were all welcome back any time. Then he left us to reacquaint ourselves with our ticket collector friend.

"It's a right bunfight, madam," he said when Bunty enquired as to the time of the next departure. "The London trains are all over the shop and you'll be lucky if you get there by midnight. Are you sure it's wise to be travelling in your condition? You won't get a seat."

"Thank you," said Bunty. "I shall be fine. I'm not trying to go up the Khyber. It's hardly an hour and a half."

The ticket man laughed at her optimism.

Nothing arrived for the next hour. I kept trying to place a call to Guy in the phone box outside the station, but there was a long queue of people, so we had to keep taking our turn, and when we did get a go, it was a devil to try to get through.

Finally, I managed. Pushing a penny into the slot I heard Monica's voice.

"Monica, it's Emmy. Is Guy there? We've got Hester."

But as soon as I started to speak, Hest started hammering on the glass and Bunty heaved open the phone box door.

"Train!" she yelled. "Quick."

"That really is super news," said Monica. "Now then . . ."

"COME ON," yelled Bunty.

"Tell Guy we're coming home," I shouted, then I slammed the receiver down and ran after my friends.

The train was packed solid, and as the ticket collector had said, there wasn't a seat to be had. None of us minded, but a cheerful if exhausted group of soldiers who had already crammed twelve men into a carriage for eight insisted that Bunty and Hester should sit down on a proper seat, and when Hester and I refused, we had to give in and at least sit on their kit bags. As we joined in with their good-natured chat, I put my arm around Hester.

"One day this will all seem like the most enormous adventure," I whispered. "You'll be able to tell your grandchildren about it."

She gave me a tentative smile.

Bunty was quizzing the soldiers about where they had been in Europe.

"We're waiting to hear where my friend's husband may be," she said. "Major Charles Mayhew. You don't happen to recognise the name, do you? Emmy—do you have the photograph with you?"

Of course I did. I had carried his picture around for months.

With the familiar jolt of hope, I took it out of my handbag and gave it to the boys to pass around.

"Arnhem? Good man. Those boys did a hell of a job, pardon my French, miss."

"It's a mess over there, love, but they're getting them back as fast as they can."

"I heard the surrender will happen tomorrow or Wednesday."

"He'll be back soon enough, love. You'll open the front door and there he'll be, big and ugly and wanting his dinner."

The journey was filled with kindly comments, easy chat, and cigarettes being passed round.

But no one recognised either Charles' name or his picture.

I kept up my usual smile.

"I'm sure it won't be long," I said, as ever, as brightly as I could.

Hester took my hand and didn't let go.

Finally, the fields turned to suburbs and then into London itself, and by the time the train eased into Waterloo station it was as if we had been at a good-natured, if noisy, party. As we got off the train, we wished the men well, and Bunty and I even gave two of them a kiss on the cheek when they asked, which raised a loud cheer.

"Are you sure we can't help with your suitcase?" one asked Hester. "Or I can get you a porter?"

"We're fine thanks," I said. "You get going. Someone will be desperate to see you."

"I hope so," he grinned. "I've been away two years."

"Good luck finding your major," said the corporal in the group. "Don't you go worrying. He'll be doing his best to get back."

I thanked him for his kindness, for *all* their kindness. I said I hoped Charles would enjoy his dinner when he got home.

"Big and ugly," laughed the corporal, and then they were all gone.

Bunty, Hester, and I stood on the platform and waited for it to clear a little.

Thousands of men were on their way home and it seemed that

many of them had women and children there to meet them. The noise was enormous.

"Are you two all right to go on the bus, or shall we try to get a cab?" I asked the others. "Bunts, you must be on your last legs."

"I'm fine," said Bunty. "Strong as an ox."

"Me too," said Hester, and the three of us began to make our way slowly down to the platform gates.

Once we were past the ticket collector, the crowds on the station concourse were even bigger than earlier that morning. People were pushing all over the place, eager to get to somewhere or someone.

"Crikey," I said. "Everyone's going mad. Let's stick together and take it slowly."

It was a struggle to make much headway. Then, to my surprise, I saw Harold in the midst of the throng, towering over everyone as usual. I waved keenly, and when he saw us, he managed to swiftly make his way through.

"Hello, darling," said Bunty, as he gave her a big kiss. "This is terribly kind of you to meet us. We can manage, honestly." She sounded relieved as anything to see him.

Harold took Hester's suitcase anyway.

"Come on ladies," he said. "We need to get going."

"But we're getting the bus," I said, as he began to stride off in the opposite direction.

Bunty shrugged as we all followed him.

"I bet he's sorted out a cab," Bunty said, already beginning to pant. "Very kind, but I wish he'd slow down."

Harold had motored on, but now he looked over his shoulder and stopped.

"Ladies, we really do need to move," he called.

I trotted after him, Hest and Bunts trailing some way behind, until he stopped abruptly at Platform Three.

To my surprise, Guy was there, peering through the crowds of people who had been getting off a newly arrived train.

"Guy," I cried. "We found Hest."

Guy nodded and gave Hester a big smile, but it wasn't quite the response I had expected.

"Wonderful news," he said. "Great to see you, Hester." Hester looked tentative but began to say hello. Guy raised his forefinger. "I'm so sorry, Hest. One moment, please." He turned to me and grabbed me by the arm.

"Come with me," he said, urgently, and began to half drag me towards the platform gates. Then he stopped.

"Guy," I said. "What are you doing?"

Guy didn't appear to have heard me, but instead was craning his neck to look up the platform. Then he turned to me. His eyes were shining and his grip on my arm became almost uncomfortably tight.

"Look, Emmy," he said, as his voice almost cracked. "Just bloody look."

It was hard to see very much as the steam from the engine was obscuring the crowd, who in the main, as on all the other platforms, were servicemen, dozens of them. They were still pouring out of the train's doors, swinging their bags over their shoulders or pausing to light cigarettes before they headed for the exit.

But as the crowds and the steam cleared just a little, much further down the platform a lone figure in uniform appeared.

I stared, blinking.

He was tall and terribly, terribly thin, but of course, I recognised him at once.

Guy had let go of my arm.

Ignoring the collector asking for tickets, I started to run.

CHAPTER 34

Charles

I wanted to call out his name, but nothing would come. Instead, I pushed and dodged around the other people on the platform, somehow managing to do so without taking my eyes off him for a second.

And then we were together.

I was never going to let go of my husband ever again.

Charles was skinny as a rake, his cheekbones almost painfully prominent and his face etched with lines and wrinkles I had not seen before. But the blue eyes were the same. I couldn't stop looking into them.

"I'm afraid I look a bit of a wreck," he said, in between kisses.

I didn't care. He looked awful and he looked perfect.

He was alive.

"Did you miss me?" he asked.

"No," I said, not sure if I was laughing or sobbing. "Not a bit."

We held on to each other as if there was nothing else going on in the world. Now I couldn't even speak. I was shaking like a leaf.

"It's all right," he said into my hair. "It's over. It's going to be all right."

We gazed at each other again and then, tearing my eyes off him I saw Bunty, who was holding Guy's hand and leading him along the platform towards us.

I let go of Charles and stepped slightly back. If I hadn't already been in tears, the look on Guy's face would have been enough. Nothing in the world meant as much to him as his brother. He had lived through the months of worrying and hoping and trying everything we could to get news, just as I had.

Now, all that was gone in a second.

"Thank God. Thank God." It was all Guy could say to him at first.

I understood. The overwhelming feeling of relief.

The brothers hugged each other, then slapped each other on the back.

"You look well," said Guy, which wasn't true.

"I am well," lied Charles back.

"Well done. Bloody well done," said Guy and hugged him again.

Bunty and I stood together, the happiest we had been for so long.

"Hello, Mrs. Thomas," said Charles. Then his smile got even wider. "What's all this then?"

Bunty threw her arms around him. "I won't pop," she said, "and I'm not missing out. Don't worry, the baby's used to getting a squash."

"Many congratulations," said Charles. "What lovely news."

Guy and I looked at each other, not saying a word but understanding exactly what the other had been through. He shook his head as if he couldn't quite believe Charles was actually here.

"We made it," I whispered.

The level of noise in the station was such that Guy couldn't possibly have heard me, but I could see he understood as he nodded slowly and as if he was at peace with the world.

As the ticket collector finally lost patience and bellowed at us to get a move on, the four of us walked arm in arm back along the platform.

Harold and Hester had been stopped at the gate and we had just reached them when an almighty clamour erupted in the station.

People began cheering and shouting, kissing each other or throwing things into the air.

"What is it?" I shouted at a young officer who had just let out the biggest roar.

"They've surrendered," he yelled back. "It's on the wireless. Churchill's doing the Victory announcement tomorrow. We've done it. We've won."

I looked at Charles and my dearest friends, and we were hugging each other and crying all over again.

The war was over. It was time for us to go home.

EPILOGUE

December 1945

Harriet Hope Thomas was having the time of her life. She had just been christened in the church where her parents had married and was now being proudly watched by them as her godparents posed for photographs at Dower Cottage, her godfather being particularly careful not to drop her.

"I think it's your turn now, Emmy," said Guy, as he handed Baby Harriet to me. "I've done my bit without disaster and don't want to push my luck."

"Well done, old chap," said Harold. "Very impressed. Time for a drink?"

It certainly was. As ever Roy and Fred had come through on the supplies.

I carried Baby Harriet over to where my parents and Mrs. Tavistock were listening to Charles tell Stanley how he thought the pig shed could be extended. Charles was so much better these days, but it would take more time before he was entirely well. He wouldn't talk to me about the forced march from the prison camp in Germany as he said he was not one to dwell on the past. But the little I had picked up from him made me glad I had not been aware of the truth for most of the time he was away. Hundreds of miles in the snow, sub-zero temperatures, attempts to escape, beatings by the guards. Friends he did not see again.

We were looking forward. After a medical discharge from the army, which had been, Charles said, the worst day of the lot, he was about to start a new top-secret job, which he was not allowed to talk about. I didn't mind. It would not involve going to war.

Stan's face lit up when he saw me. "Major Charles reckons there's room for more stock," he said. "Dad and George and me are going to build it, aren't we, George."

"I'll say," said George in his new, deep voice.

"That sounds excellent," I agreed. "Marg, are you going to help out as well?"

"Oh yes. And I can look after people if the shed falls on them and they're squashed," replied Marg, sounding keen on a disaster so that she could administer first aid.

"That's the spirit," said my brother, making Marg beam. "Hopefully the whole thing will fall down, and then you can set up your own ward."

Stan frowned.

"Jack's just kidding," said his dad, reassuringly. "At least I think he is."

The Jenkins family were now firmly ensconced in the country. Arthur worked on the farm and the four of them lived in a cottage with Sparky and his friend, Stan's new sheepdog puppy, Spider.

Harold had taken on Mrs. Tavistock's estate and was learning the management under her watchful eye. He and Bunty were investigating how Rose House might be turned into a country hotel of all things. We were all queueing up to book in.

When Guy had returned to his own flat, Charles and I set up married life at the top of the house in Pimlico. Charles said going up and down the stairs had speeded up his rehabilitation no end. We were most likely to be found sitting in the kitchen, listening to the radio, or planning what we would do with the rest of our lives together.

The christening had been the first time everyone had been able to gather since the end of the war. After the absolute euphoria of Charles coming home and celebrating VE-Day, things had slowly gone back to normal, and on a practical level, normal meant not an enormous change from many of the things we had become used to over the previous years.

If anyone had been naive enough to think that the minute Peace was declared everything would be all hearts and flowers and loveliness, they were in for a shock. Britain had taken a hammering and was as poor as a church mouse. The queues were as long as ever, rationing seemed as if it would never end, and at *Woman's Friend* there were just as many readers writing in with problems as there had been before. There had been too much upheaval, too much sacrifice, and too much loss to expect anything else. Without a doubt, I counted my own blessings every day.

Mrs. Hester Boone sat on the sofa with her baby on her lap. Her husband was back in Europe following a dash home on leave for a quiet but very special wedding, and to meet his new son. The latest resident of Dower Cottage, Baby Colin Boone, happily slept as Sparky leapt onto the sofa and tried to join in.

"Would you like to hold him?" Hester asked Guy.

"Go on then," said Guy cheerfully, as he put down his drink. "Budge up, Sparks."

"Clarence says he's counting on you until he comes home again," said Hester as she handed the baby to Guy. Guy blew out his cheeks and made a noise at Baby Colin, who started to laugh.

"You're the perfect honorary grandad," I said. "Don't you agree, Hest?"

"Good Lord," replied Guy, as Hester said that she did. "That makes me sound ancient."

For all his blustering, Guy, it turned out, was excellent with babies. He had also finally started writing the novel he had been promising for years. Now Editor at Large for *Woman's Friend*, he spent as much of his time down here in Hampshire as possible. I had never seen him so happy.

As Guy told Hester that he was already confident that Colin was Cambridge material, I glanced around the room. Almost all of the people who were dearest to me were there. Chatting, laughing, enjoying a drink or some food. Nothing fancy, just a simple get together to celebrate Harriet's christening, but it was, nevertheless, something to be cherished. Twelve months ago, this was only a dream.

Absences, however, were very keenly felt. We were missing too many of our friends.

More than anyone, Thelma would have loved today. All the children together. The dads and brothers and sons and closest friends finally home. While it filled my heart to see Wallace chatting to her husband Lieutenant Tom Carter over by the fireplace, I couldn't help but think of his friend, young Lieutenant Johnny Bagley, who had not come home. I wished I could have met him. I still saw his mother as often as I could.

The day after Bunty came home from hospital with little Harriet, she and I had taken her to see Bill's grave. Bunty was very blissfully married to Harold, but Bill had been her fiancé and my dear friend, and he had been much loved. Fireman William Barnes would never be forgotten.

Now, I took Baby Harriet over to join Bunty who was chatting with Monica.

"Editor incoming," Monica announced, getting up to give me her seat. "No, no, it's quite all right, I'm going to give Fred a hard time about his dancing. He hates it when I tell him he's nothing on Roy. I may get them to put the gramophone on."

I thanked her and handed Harriet to Bunty as I sat in the old armchair. My baby goddaughter was quite happy being the main prize in a sort of Pass the Parcel that had been going on all day.

"So," said Bunts. "On the subject of editors. How does it feel to now be the official Editor in Chief of *Woman's Friend*? What with the old one turning to literature and only bothering to come into the office now and then?"

"I think I can get used to it," I said, leaning back into a plump cushion. "As long as the team doesn't desert me, and Monica promises to be Publisher for the rest of her life."

"They'll stick with you," said Bunty. "We'll all stick together."

We sat in happy silence for a moment.

"Isn't it nice to sit and do nothing?" said Bunty.

"Isn't it just," I agreed. "Although, I have been thinking that perhaps things have become just a Tiny Bit Quiet."

Bunty looked at me and raised an eyebrow.

"Go on," she said.

"Well," I replied. "It is an awfully long time since the Christmas Fayre. We haven't had anything to plan for ages."

"Are you saying we should organise something?" Bunty asked, smiling broadly. "Because if you are, I'm definitely in."

"Ooh, good, Bunts," I said as I reached into my pocket for my little silver notebook. "Funnily enough, I've been coming up with some ideas."

Woman's Friend to Friend
Our Best Wishes to You All

As we come to the end of 1945, we are sure that like us, you are very much looking forward to the new year and the first full year of Peace.

Finally, and very thankfully, most of our men are home and others are finding their ways back to us from far-flung corners. Still more are abroad, helping to rebuild a world for which we all have high hopes. Others will live in our hearts and shall be remembered, always. We join you in celebrating and remembering them all.

Now, in our small way on this page, we salute *you*, the women of Britain, whom we are very proud to call our friends. What women you are. What work you have done, what spirit you have shown, what bravery and strength you have found throughout the past years. You have written to us, supported us, told us when we have got things wrong! And you have laughed, cried, and got through it all with us. We cannot begin to tell you how much this has meant to us all. Whether you have spent thousands of hours working in a factory, learning how to plough heavy fields to ensure we have all been fed, looking after your and your fellow women's children, or wearing the uniforms of our services, we hope you will look back with pride. Because good gracious, you deserve to.

Here, in our little office, when we look back, we feel that above everything else, it is the friendships we have made and the people who have helped us that we shall never forget.

We are looking forward to best times ahead. We know it won't always be easy. There are many things we have to repair and restore, and many things that can never be replaced. But together, we will get there, and we hope you will allow us to continue along on the road with you.

Our fond and best wishes to you for a happy and very peaceful 1946!

Until next week,

Yours,

Emmy Lake (Editor in Chief) and all your friends at *Woman's Friend*

Author's Note and Acknowledgements

As with all the books in this series, inspiration for *Dear Miss Lake* came from a wide range of sources.

From the very beginning when I first started to write *Dear Mrs. Bird*, British wartime women's magazines have continued to provide a fantastic insight into everyday life on the Home Front, as well as inspiring much of Emmy's working life at the magazine. This final novel has been no different, from the type of readers' problems Emmy tackles through to her war work advice and journalistic assignments. (Although, I should say, of course, that Emmy's run ins and fall outs with the Ministry are entirely made up.)

If you're ever lucky enough to track down an original magazine from the period, do grab it (very gently) with both hands as they are always fascinating to read. Providing everything from advice and support to entertainment and escapism, these magazines didn't miss an issue throughout the war, no matter what was going on, including air raids and bombings. The publications and the journalists who worked for them really did do their bit.

My desk is always stacked high with reference books, and several were particularly helpful in writing this novel. Barbara Hately-Broad's *War and Welfare: British Prisoner of War Families, 1939–1945*

(2009) made me realise the enormity of the practical as well as emotional challenges that families faced. Brenda McBryde's excellent memoir *A Nurse's War* (1979) left me with renewed admiration for the extraordinary role played by our nurses during the war. John Nichol and Tony Rennell's *The Last Escape: The Untold Story of Allied Prisoners of War in Germany 1944–45* (2002) was hugely valuable in helping me set Emmy Lake her greatest personal challenge. (The War Office press release at the end of chapter twenty-five was taken from this book. For the original see TNA WO 32/9906.)

Dear Miss Lake is of course a work of fiction. If there are any errors in this book, they are mine.

Finally, the stoicism and spirit of the characters in all four novels in Emmy's series is without doubt down to the women whom I have been privileged to speak to over the last ten years about their wartime memories. For this book, the character Alice was inspired by a wonderful ex-nurse called Margaret who at one hundred years old, kindly let me interview her about her wartime experiences. In the recording you can hear me say how amazing I thought she had been. From Margaret's surprise you can tell that she didn't think she had been in the least. I think that sums it up.

I owe thanks to tons of people:

To my editors Sophie Jonathan at Picador and Kara Watson at Scribner, as well as my copy editor Nicholas Blake and assistant editor Daisy Dickeson, for their help on this book.

My hugest thanks to everyone across all the departments at Picador and Scribner, both past and present, for their support throughout Emmy's adventures.

To my agents Lizzy Kremer and Deborah Schneider who put up with me asking daft questions and worrying about things to an Olympic standard on a regular basis. I really am so grateful.

To everyone who has helped me during the research of both *Dear Miss Lake* and throughout this series.

And as this is the final book in Emmy Lake's wartime story, I really want to thank everyone who has been part of taking the characters I love to a point of being in actual books in actual shops. From my family and friends who now have an extended social group of imaginary people I talk about as if they are real, to the very, very many lovely people in publishing, agenting, bookselling, library lending, reviewing, and spreading-the-wording, without you it would just be me sitting in a room making stuff up. Thank you so much.

Most of all, thank you to the readers for coming with me on Emmy and Bunty's adventures! I do hope you enjoyed how it turned out. And if you are one of the many people who messaged me about the safety of the characters in the final novel when I was writing it, I'm sorry I dodged every question you asked—I couldn't say anything without giving the story away!

Now, I can almost hear Guy telling me to crack on and start writing about somebody else, and Emmy being slightly less forthright but gently reminding me it's time to move on. For now, I'll leave *Woman's Friend* in Emmy's very safe hands and see what other stories I can come up with. I very much hope I'll see you all there!